Wray Wrigley's

TAYEL TOWER

EDITED AND PUBLISHED BY

D.M. CHADWICK

www.dmchadwick.com

First published in 2019 by D.M. Chadwick
South Australia, Australia

Copyright © D.M. Chadwick 2019

ISBN 978-0-6485209-3-1

CONTENTS

Wray Wrigley's

TAYEL TOWER

Book 1

THROUGH THE
FRONT DOOR

CHAPTER ONE
STANLEY MOVES IN

Newspapers are a dying breed.

I, being a writer by trade, appreciate the work that goes into print journalism and the newspaper that will inevitably finish its life as a papier-mâché piñata or fly swatter. Tayel Tower receives exactly 10 newspapers a day, delivered to the lobby and placed on a small coffee table by the lobby couches. Given that Tayel Tower has over 100 residents, there is often a frenzy in the morning to guarantee a copy of the daily edition. I have discovered, after many years of living here in Tayel Tower, that the best time to secure a copy of the newspaper is to wait until late morning. At that time those that work 9-5 day jobs have disappeared, and those that are retired are busy getting ready for a walk or making a cheesecake. If you wish to find out more about newspapers, I suggest you read one or find a Spanish-themed birthday party.

A couple of weeks ago I was in the lobby picking up the daily edition newspaper when I spotted someone I had never seen before struggling his way through the front door. He was carrying a stack of large moving boxes. Once inside, the man looked unsure where to go or who to speak to.

"Excuse me," he asked the first person he saw. The person the stranger asked was Arnold the Artist. Arnold, holding a camera in his hands, looked the man up and down like he was a sundried squished-bug, unworthy of any attention.

"Yes?" Arnold the Artist snapped.

The stranger, clearly uncomfortable with the weight of the boxes, adjusted his grip. "I'm Stanley; I'm moving in today. Do you know who I need to talk to about getting the key for my apartment?"

"Do I look like the key keeper?" Arnold the Artist asked, bending over to take a close-up photo of a crack in the lobby floor. "I am an artist; not a key keeper. If I wanted to be key keeper, I would have gone to key-keeping school, not art school."

It should be noted that the photo of the crack in the lobby floor that Arnold the Artist captured was subsequently labelled 'The Misery of Concrete', and would go on to win many art awards. Stanley, a little taken aback by the rudeness of the artist, looked for someone else to ask. Another man was heading for the front door. This man, Samuel the Salesman, was dressed in a cheap looking suit with a cheap tie and shoes that even a penniless bird was say looked 'Cheap!'.

"Excuse me, sir," Stanley asked the suited man. "Do you know who the building manager is?"

Samuel the Salesman gave a cheap smile. "Why hello there!" He nodded towards the boxes. "You look like a man that could do with a hand or two! I would lend you one or two of my own hands, but I need to be at a client meeting. I'm a mice salesman."

"Animals or computer accessories?" Stanley asked to be polite.

Samuel the Salesman laughed but failed to answer the question. "You look like you could do with a mouse. They are very helpful, especially around the office. I have a black mouse, a white mouse, a little mouse you can add lights to. They really are good fun!"

"I'm not in the market for a mouse for the moment. I just need to find someone who can help me get my key."

Samuel the Salesman's smile vanished; disappointed his failed sales pitch. "Ask Damien the Doorman."

Damien the Doorman, hearing his name, put down his newspaper. He saw Stanley standing looking awfully lost and became very excited. "Oh, hello there! I do apologise, so rude of me. I was a little distracted by my crossword."

Damien the Doorman was a shorter gentleman in his late 60s, but he moved swiftly from behind the concierge desk. "You must be Stanley; I'm so glad to meet you. My name is Damien and I am the doorman, here for your every request."

Stanley, relieved to finally find an employee, put down his boxes, reached into his pocket, and pulled out the letter from the real estate office. "Thank you. Yes, I'm Stanley. I think I'm moving into room nine-oh-nine?"

Damien clapped his hands together. "Yes, room nine-oh-nine is ready to go. Let me help you with your things."

"Thank you, that's very kind," Stanley said.

A middle-aged man in a floral shirt, cargo shorts and sandals came over and gave Damien a pat on the shoulder.

"While you do that, Damien, let me show Stanley around. My name is Perry; a new neighbour of yours. How would you like a tour of Tayel Tower?"

Stanley looked through the window at his heavy boxes sitting on the outside sidewalk. "Thank you, but I think I should help the doorman take my things up to my apartment."

Perry shook his head and placed an arm around Stanley, talking quietly. "He'll be fine. Damien enjoys his job no matter how heavy the lifting. It's not every day a new occupant moves in, and it gives him something to do." Damien the Doorman was already moving in and out of the building like a snail on a mission. He waved Perry and Stanley on. "Go take a look around! I'll take your things straight up to your apartment."

Stanley felt uncomfortable; he didn't feel good about making an aging doorman do the heavy lifting and he didn't want a tour from someone he just met; he also didn't want to be rude.

Taking Stanley's silence as permission to start the tour, Perry began walking to the centre of the lobby, and Stanley reluctantly followed.

"Tayel Tower was built in 1943, but has been renovated many times since," Perry said.

Stanley looked around the vast lobby. It was a mix and match of décor and furniture from every decade since the early 1900s.

"The tower currently contains one hundred apartments over ten floors; ten apartments on each floor. There are one hundred and three permanent occupants at this time, however, this number will increase to one hundred and six in a couple of years."

"How do you know that?" Stanley asked.

Perry began walking to the elevator. "Because I'm a psychic."

'Oh great', Stanley thought. 'This building is full of crazy people'.

"A psychic? You can see into the future?" He asked.

Perry pressed the 'up' elevator button. "I have seen into the future. After you have seen it once, there is no reason to look again."

"Alright. If you have seen the future, who is going to be in the elevator when the door opens?"

"That's easy," Perry replied. "There will be Ernest the Elevator Operator and Clare the Cleaner."

The elevator doors opened and sure enough, there stood a man in the same waistcoat and jacket as the doorman with the name tag 'Ernest', and a lady with a cleaner's cart with the name tag 'Clare'.

Stanley was genuinely amazed. He stared with his mouth agape while the cleaner exited. His sceptical mind quickly took over. 'They probably come down at the same time every day'.

Perry and Stanley entered the elevator.

"Which floor gentlemen?" Ernest the Elevator Operator asked.

"10th floor please," Perry requested. The doors closed and they rode up the first few floors in silence.

"Ernest here knows everything about everyone in the building," Perry said, giving Ernest a pat on the shoulder. "Everyone talks in the elevator without realising that the elevator operator has ears. So, if you need to know what others think about you, just ask Ernest."

"Wouldn't everyone learn to stop telling secrets and gossiping in the elevator?" Stanley asked.

Ernest shook his head. "I don't tell every secret, Mr Stanley. I am just honest to the people worth being honest to."

The elevator slowed as they arrived at the tenth floor. Stanley and Perry stepped out and walked down the hallway. The hallway was quite a sight; the carpets were a deep red, and each apartment door was painted green with gold door handles. At the end of the hallway was a large window that gave a view across the city. Stanley had to admit the view was majestic.

"As you can see, the best views are up here, and that is why the tenth-floor apartments are the most expensive and prestigious," Perry explained.

"What kind of people live on the tenth floor?" Stanley asked.

"Rich people. Subjectively important people. Mooney the Millionaire for example…"

Stanley was surprised. "A millionaire lives here?" He had researched the real-estate in the city, and there were certainly much nicer dwellings than Tayel Tower for a millionaire to choose from.

Perry sat down on the lone hallway chair. "Although Mooney is a Millionaire, he only owns exactly one million dollars. If he was to move somewhere else more expensive, he would no longer be a millionaire. He would just be Mooney."

Stanley raised an eyebrow but didn't further the topic. He was quite familiar with the rich and eccentric. Having the occupation of a business consultant, he dealt with the rich and eccentric daily.

Perry the Psychic looked at his watch. "My goodness is that the time? I'm sorry, I didn't realise; I need to head off to work. You are in apartment nine-oh-nine, yes? I'll take you there on my way out."

Instead of the elevator, Stanley and Perry took the stairs down to the ninth floor; the very short tour ending in awkward silence. Perry continued on and left Stanley to find his apartment. Stanley was greeted in the hallway of the ninth floor by Damien, having delivered some of his belongings. When Damien saw Stanley, he opened 909's door for the new owner.

"There you go, sir. I'll be returning shortly with the rest of your boxes."

"Thank you, Damien. I'll come down and help." Stanley said. Damien held up his hand in protest. "I won't hear of it. You stay here and get familiar with your new apartment."

Stanley walked inside his new apartment and expected to hear the front door close. It didn't. He turned and looked at Damien the Doorman who stood in the doorway with a smile.

"Am I supposed to give you a tip?" Stanley asked, reaching for his wallet.

Damien waved his hands madly. "Oh no, sir. I was just holding the door open in case you wanted to run away. The last occupant hated it here so much, he ran out of his apartment without even opening the door."

Stanley took ten dollars out of his wallet and handed it to the doorman. "I don't really have a choice whether I like it here or not; my company is paying for the lodging."

Damien looked disappointed. "But everything I have seen looks decent enough," Stanley said, trying to be polite.

Damien gratefully accepted the money and tipped his hat. "Well, if you do find it unpleasant, let me know so I can hold the door open while you run away. Doors are expensive these days."

As the door closed, Stanley took in his new surroundings. The apartment was bright and modern with white painted walls and slate-grey furniture. He wondered what was so bad to cause someone to want to run away. He walked into the living room and sat on the couch, looking at the pile of boxes with disdain.

Moving to a new house, as anyone can tell you unless they're a flower pot, can be quite a chore. Stanley only had about a dozen boxes of things, but the thought of unpacking it all just reminded him that, one day, he would need to pack it all up again. His thoughts ended with a need for a cup of tea.

He was opening the box marked Kitchen to find a mug when there was a shrill scream from the hallway. Stanley ran to his front door and swung it open. He looked out and saw Rosemary the Retired and Leah the Librarian fighting over a bright red umbrella.

The fight looked heated; both older ladies had their hands on the red umbrella and were tugging with all their might. Stanley walked briskly between them. "Ladies, are you both okay?"

"I saw this umbrella first, and I intend to use it!" Rosemary the Retired snapped.

"She lies! I saw it first, and I need it to get to the library." Leah the Librarian snapped, equally as snappy.

Stanley didn't know how to handle the situation. The elevator doors opened at the end of the hallway and out stepped Perry the Psychic. He shook his head at the sight of the fuelling geriatrics.

"Don't bother yourself with these two," Perry said to Stanley. "They have been bickering since they first moved into Tayel Tower and will continue to squabble until the day they die. Respectively."

Leah rolled her eyes. "Be quiet, Perry. No one wants to hear about their future." And with that, she made another firm tug for the umbrella.

Stanley stepped in once more. "Ladies, I have a spare umbrella in my apartment that I can lend you. But, by the way, have you looked outside? It is not rainy or particularly sunny. I think you would be okay without an umbrella."

Leah and Rosemary simultaneously let go of the umbrella, letting it fall the floor. The ladies walked down the hallway to the window and looked up at the sky. They saw that Stanley was correct: It was just a regular day; neither particularly sunny nor chance of rainy.

"But what if it begins to rain?" Leah asked anxiously.

"Or what if the clouds clear and the sun begins to shine ferociously?" Rosemary asked.

Stanley moved towards his apartment. "I already said that I have a spare umbrella."

Leah shook her head. "No, don't worry about it. If it begins to rain I will move quickly undercover. You take the umbrella, Mrs Rosemary."

Rosemary pondered over the umbrella on the floor but eventually shook her head. "No, I will be okay. I will put on sunscreen. And anyway, some sun will be good for me."

Stanley gave a forced smile. "Well good. Crisis averted."

The two ladies, apparently satisfied with their decisions, left down the stairwell, chatting happily like nothing was ever amiss between them.

"May I please borrow your umbrella, lad?" Jarvis the Jobless asked holding the red umbrella that had been left behind. Jarvis was an older gentleman, dressed quite shabby and yet perfectly clean. From a distance, he looked hopelessly homeless, but up close he was just a regular older man; the weight of his many years beginning to bend his back like a contortionist tying his shoes.

"You have an umbrella," Stanley noted, pointing at the red umbrella.

"I need two umbrellas," Jarvis said sternly. "One for the rain, and one for the sun."

Stanley was flabbergasted. Jarvis the Jobless broke his stern look with a laugh. "I'm just joking, lad. I'm actually building an umbrella fort and need as many umbrellas as I can get my hands on."

The innocent expression on Jarvis' face told Stanley the umbrella fort was no joke. Stanley, in a daze, got his umbrella out of his apartment and handed it to the man. Jarvis looked thrilled and left quickly via the stairwell.

Stanley looked at Perry, puzzled. "How did a homeless man get up here to the ninth floor? Does this building have any security?"

Perry laughed. "Jarvis the Jobless isn't homeless. He lives here in Tayel Tower, on the first floor. He just likes to occupy his time by letting his imagination run wild. Very harmless fellow. A very smart fellow, in fact, as you'll discover one day."

Stanley felt a little bad calling the man homeless. He began back toward the door of his apartment. "I thought you said you were going to work?"

"I've been to work and I'm home again," Perry replied.

"Where do you work?"

Peery laughed aloud, almost obnoxious laugh. "You ask a lot of questions, and you are going to ask many more. I work at an investment firm and, being psychic, I tell the brokers what way the financial market is heading; up or down."

"Isn't that cheating?" Stanley asked.

"Oh, absolutely. That's why I only tell them the name of the company that is going up or down. They spend the rest of the day guessing whether they should buy or sell shares in that company. It's always good fun for me to watch."

Stanley thought about this for a second. "But aren't companies almost always going up or down? You could say the name of any company, and you would be right in saying the price of the shares would be going up or down."

Perry winked and pressed the down button on the elevator.

Stanley returned to his apartment. He really needed a cup of tea. He found the kettle, a mug, and a small box of teabags. As the kettle was finishing boiling, Damien the Doorman returned with the last couple of boxes.

"That's the lot of them," Damien said, rubbing non-existent dust from his jacket. "Just ring down if you need anything; the number for the concierge desk is on the phone."

Stanley thanked the old man and closed the door. He

poured himself a steaming hot cup of tea, and, while it cooled, rummaged through a box marked 'Clothes'. He was aware time was moving quickly; he needed to be in the office for his first day at half-past-one. His uniform was a pair of black pants, a shirt, and a tie. He pulled out his black dress pants, creased as they were, and a light blue collared shirt. Over the years he had amassed a good dozen neck-ties from various weddings and parties which required one to wear a piece of cloth around one's neck. On the move from his parent's home in the suburbs, he had placed the ties in a blue shoebox and written 'Ties' in black marker on top.

Stanley looked over at the pile of boxes in his living room but couldn't see it. "Where is it?" he asked aloud. He moved this and that box out the way, reading the labels as he went. He could not find what he was looking for. "I swear I brought it!" Stanley said, frustrated. He went to the phone and dialled the number for the 'concierge'. It was unnecessarily long and potentially hazardous in the case of an emergency.

After a couple of rings, the phone was answered. "Hello, this is Damien."

"Hi Damien, this is Stanley. I was – "

"Oh, Stanley! Good to hear from you. How are you getting on since we last spoke all those minutes ago?"

"I'm fine, thank you. I just seem to be missing one of my boxes. Are you very sure that you brought them all up?"

"Yes, Mr Stanley. All your boxes were brought to your apartment. There are no more here in the lobby or outside. What type of box was it?"

"It was a blue shoe box that had 'Ties' written on it."

There was silence as Damien apparently scanned the lobby like a myopic hawk.

"I'm sorry, I can't see it. Might I recommend the Asian supermarket the next road over? They might have Thais there?"

"No: 'Ties'. T-I-E," Stanley spelled out. "Not 'Thais' from Thailand."

There was another pause on the phone. "Oh, that does make more sense. I was looking for quite a large shoebox. Wait… what's this here… was your shoebox a blue shoe-box with 'Ties' written on top?"

"Yes, that's the one," Stanley sighed.

"Well, then I do have it here. I must have missed it. I do very much apologise."

Stanley looked at the time on his phone. It rudely read 1 pm, only half an hour until he needed to be at the office. Any clock can be rude when telling you the time, but it's always your own fault, not theirs'.

Stanley's heart skipped a beat. He did not want his first impression at the office to be of a late person. "It's okay. I need to leave for work now. Please leave the box on your desk and I'll grab it on the way out."

He hung up and quickly changed into his shirt, pants and black suede shoes. He hadn't even had time to eat lunch yet and his stomach was grumbling. He picked up his work bag out of a box labelled 'work bag' and ran out of the apartment.

He arrived at the elevator and furiously pressed the 'down' button. He looked at his phone once more. It read 1:15. He had to be at the office in 15 minutes: a fact he repeated in his head that gave no benefit or comfort to the situation. Finally, the elevator arrived. The doors slid open and Stanley jumped on-board.

"Lobby please," he said to Ernest the Elevator Operator.

"Lobby it is!" Ernest said, coursing the elevator down.

It stopped at the seventh floor and the doors slid open. In walked Rosemary the Retired. "Seventh floor, please."

"This is the seventh floor ma'am," Ernest said politely.

Rosemary looked around in awe. "Oh. So it is." And she exited.

Stanley shook his head in disbelief as the elevator doors reclosed. "Ernest, would it be possible to get an express pass to the lobby, please? I have a work meeting at 1:30 pm and really shouldn't be late."

"Oh sure, Mr Stanley, express pass it is. There's a handy little button here that makes it go straight down, but you need a key. I have the key, which is fortunate. There's quite a number of fun buttons… I'll explain them when you have more time."

Stanley looked at his watch and mumbled, "I haven't even had lunch yet."

"Oh, lunch is a very important meal, Mr Stanley. It fills the stomach for work and play for the rest of the day." Ernest said. "I haven't had lunch since this morning. But I call lunch in the morning 'breakfast'…"

Stanley reflected on his situation: Tayel Tower, although cheaper than other apartments in the city, was furnished nicely; it was certainly liveable. But the occupants? Stanley had only been in the building for less than half-an-hour and he already found his neighbours to be less than charming. He made a note to have a word with his boss to see if

there was the possibility of moving and ending this gaunt-
let of trials.

CHAPTER TWO
THE MEETING

Stanley ran to the concierge desk where he could see his blue box of ties sitting on the counter. He picked it up to find it was empty. He looked around in confusion. "Where are my ties?" he asked aloud to no one in particular.

He spotted a man walking away towards the stairwell holding an armful of colourful and shiny materials.

"Excuse me!" Stanley called out. The man entered the stairwell; unaware of Stanley in hot pursuit.

"Excuse me," Stanley said again firmly as he also entered the stairwell. He placed a hand on the man's shoulder. "Those are my ties!"

The man, Tanish the Taxi Driver, turned around. His arms were full of neckties of all colours; all Stanley's.

"No, no," Tanish protested. "You'll need to get your own. I was first."

"What are you talking about?"

"The box of free ties at the concierge desk; it's always first come, first served with free things."

"No. You see; they're not free ties. They are my ties, I left them there."

"You're trying to sell them?"

"No, I'm not selling them!"

"Who is then?"

"No one is…" Stanley took a deep breath. "I am moving in today, and that was one of my moving boxes that was left behind. I asked Damien to leave the box on his desk and I would collect it on my way out."

"Well, the box is still there…"

"With the ties! Look, I'm sorry if I appear rude or aggressive, but I will be late for work and I need a tie."

"Which one would you like? I have many nice ones here…"

"I would like all of them. Please. They are my ties."

Understanding seemed to wash over the tie thief.

"I am very sorry for misunderstanding you," Tanish said, handing the ties over. "Are you a tie collector?"

Stanley was not a tie collector; he was a business consultant. Describing what a business consultant does day-to-day is only useful if you wish to lull a baby to sleep or are asked in a relevant job interview. In concise terms, Stanley went to university and learned how to run a business and upon graduating with valiant dreams of starting a business of his own, he was offered a job telling other people that they were managing their businesses wrong. The attraction of a job where one gets paid for doing very little (being a business consultant) is stronger than the pull of doing a job where one gets paid very little for doing a lot (starting a business).

'It will help with experience,' Stanley told himself as he accepted the job at PLKO consulting, pretending not to know he was taking the easy road.

The adventure-seeking part of him that wanted to start his own business was the same part that made him accept the job in a city distant from his family and friends. The other part of him that liked comfort was the same one urging him to quickly fulfil his duty in the city-branch so that he could get a promotion and move back to his home-town. The adventure-seeking part of Stanley also encouraged him to go on a run for exercise at least once a week. It was this running that helped Stanley cover the distance between Tayel Tower and the offices of PLKO consulting in only 15 minutes.

Stanley arrived at the office building panting and sweating. It was 1:45 pm when Stanley entered the meeting room as directed by the secretary. He was red with embarrassment. Being 15 minutes late was not the best way to start your first day; just ask a marathon runner.

His new boss, Richard Richardson, was waiting; passing the time by typing an email on his laptop.

"Ah, welcome Stanley," he said warmly, rising from his chair and giving Stanley a firm handshake.

"I'm sorry I'm late. I was moving in and—" Stanley began, but Richardson held up his hand. "Don't worry about it. I know how stressful moving can be. You're here now, and that's what matters."

Stanley breathed a sigh of relief. He took a seat opposite Richardson at the long meeting room table.

"Have you had a chance to settle into Tayel Tower?" Richardson asked.

"No, not really. It's been a crazy morning."

"Is that so?"

Stanley gave an unconvincing laugh, aiming to appear

unphased. "Yes, I arrived and everyone was quite rude to me. One man claimed he was a psychic and offered me a tour, but left halfway through. Then, two women had a fight outside my apartment over an umbrella. Then, someone stole one of my moving boxes with all my shirt ties!"

Richardson, now again tapping on his laptop keyboard, seemed to be only half-listening. "That is quite a crazy morning! So Tayel Tower will do then?"

"Well, no Sir," Stanley replied timidly. "I was wondering if there might be a possibility of looking at other residences in the city? I wouldn't mind if I had to live outside the city. I could catch the bus."

Richardson looked up from the laptop screen. "Respectfully, Stanley: I thought you were just the man we needed here at the city branch."

"Well, I am," Stanley said defensively.

Richardson leaned back in his chair. "If I remember correctly, in your job interview, you said you were looking for an adventure. I don't feel that two ladies fighting over an umbrella and a man claiming to be psychic is beyond your capabilities to handle, especially for an adventure-seeking man. If you do feel this city is too much for you to handle, we can talk to human resources and find you a job at one of our branches out in the suburbs. But that job won't have the opportunity for you to grow."

Stanley was silenced; he didn't want to appear weak. And maybe Richardson was right; maybe he had made everything worse in his head. Stanley's stomach gave a hungry grumble. He spied a platter of sandwiches sitting in the middle of the table but wasn't sure whether he was allowed to take one.

Richardson used his laptop's mouse. "Okay, let's jump straight in. Today we will be discussing goals for this year."

The meeting room door opened and the secretary poked her head in. "Sorry to interrupt but; Stanley, there are two women here who wish to see you."

Stanley was puzzled. He wasn't expecting anyone.

Richard Richardson winked at Stanley. "Look at you! You've only been in the city half a day and you already have two women waiting for you at reception."

Stanley took this as permission to leave and followed the secretary. His puzzlement grew even more puzzled when he saw that the two women waiting were Rosemary the Retired and Leah the Librarian. Rosemary held a basket, Leah held a pile of books, and they both held a giant smile.

"Did you need something?" Stanley asked the two ladies, trying hard not to sound brisk.

"Oh no," Leah the Librarian said quite loudly. "But we do know that you need something." Rosemary held out the basket. "Lunch!"

Stanley accepted the basket and peeked inside. There was a red apple, a banana, a sandwich and a packet of chips. "Thank you kindly, ladies, but how did you know that I hadn't had lunch?"

Rosemary kept her smile. "Why, Ernest the Elevator Operator told us of course."

Stanley made a mental note not to tell Ernest any secrets.

"Once again, thank you very much. I need to get back to work now," He said to the women.

Leah waved her hand, "Of course. Go! We're not staying for a chat. We're going to the library now."

Rosemary's smile disappeared. "I thought you said we were going to the cemetery?!"

"The cemetery? Why would we need to take some books to the cemetery? You need your hearing checked, Mrs Rosemary."

"But I was hoping for a fresh bouquet of flowers for my kitchen table."

"You can't just take flowers from the cemetery, Mrs Rosemary. We can get some from the park on the way back."

"You definitely said cemetery, Leah…"

Stanley snuck away with the basket to avoid having to settle any more arguments. He returned to the meeting room and put the basket under his seat for later. "What's in the basket?" Richardson asked.

"Oh, well, it's a long story but in short; it's my lunch," Stanley said quickly.

Richardson accepted the answer without question and began reading off a document on his laptop. "Alright. Where were we? This first quarter, I'd like there to be a real focus on acquiring new clients…"

The meeting room door opened and the secretary stepped in. "Sorry to interrupt again, but, Stanley, there is a man who says he needs to see you right away."

Richardson's forgiveness seemed to be faltering, but he waved his hand dismissively to Stanley. Stanley quickly walked down to the reception area. He almost turned 180 degrees when he saw who was waiting for him: Jarvis the Jobless.

"Morning, Stanley," Jarvis called.

"Hello, Jarvis, what can I do for you?" Stanley asked through gritted teeth.

Jarvis revealed something from behind his back. "Oh, I'm just returning the umbrella you lent me. It turns out you need more than two umbrellas to make a good umbrella fort, and I couldn't find any more."

Through his forced smile, Stanley accepted the umbrella. "Thank you, Jarvis. Do you think you could do me a favour?"

"Absolutely, what do you need?"

"If it isn't inconvenient, can you please tell the people from Tayel Tower not to visit me at work?"

"Absolutely, I'll tell Damien the Doorman immediately."

Stanley thanked Jarvis once more and headed back to the meeting room, not before quietly telling the secretary not to alert him unless it was a real emergency. He returned to the meeting room and placed the umbrella under his chair.

"Are you ready now?" Richardson asked coldly.

"I told the secretary that I am unavailable to any more visitors," Stanley answered, avoiding eye contact.

****

It was five o'clock by the time Stanley managed to leave the office. It hadn't been a great first day at work, but he felt he could redeem himself in the eyes of his boss tomorrow.

On the way home, he stopped by the supermarket and picked up a steak for dinner, and milk and cereal for breakfast the next day. The basket turned out to be very useful for carrying the groceries home.

Stanley walked through the front door of Tayel Tower into the brightly lit lobby. "Good evening, Stanley," Damien the Doorman said from behind his desk. I will point out that although Damien is employed as a doorman, he doesn't actually open too many doors. Old age often renders him forgetful of his job duties.

Stanley gave a smile and nod in return on his way to the elevator. The sleek silver doors glided opened, Stanley stepped in, and the doors were halfway closed again when a voice echoed down the lobby; "Please hold the elevator!"

Ernest the Elevator Operator pressed the 'door open' button and in jumped a young woman wearing nursing scrubs. "Thank you. Fifth floor please, Ernest."

The girl noticed Stanley. "Hello there." She stuck out her hand. "I'm Mandy."

Stanley re-juggled the basket of groceries to shake her hand. "I'm Stanley. Nice to meet you. I've just moved in on the ninth floor."

Mandy's eyes lit up with excitement. "Oh, that's great! It's nice to have a new neighbour. If you need a hand with anything, don't be afraid to ask and I'll see if I can help." Mandy had a seemingly permanent smile that made any room feel warm and cosy.

The elevator stopped at the fifth floor. "Well I guess I'll see you around," Mandy said to Stanley.

"Sounds good," Stanley replied with a tired smile.

As the elevator resumed its course, Ernest looked at his passenger with raised eyebrows. "Do you think Mandy the Midwife is pretty, Mr Stanley?"

The question took Stanley by surprise. "Well sure, I guess."

Ernest the Elevator Operator smiled mischievously.

"Wait, you're going to tell people that I think Mandy the Midwife is pretty!" Stanley realised.

"Oh no, Mr Stanley. I don't just go spouting secrets to anyone who walks into this elevator. As I said this morning, I only tell people things that they need to know or know to ask."

"And who exactly would it concern that I think Mandy the Midwife is pretty?"

Ernest thought about this for a moment. "Well firstly; Mandy the Midwife of course. Perry the Psychic would already know. It might also concern Belinda the Beautician. Belinda is always very interested in other people's love affairs."

Stanley sighed. "Would it be possible to make a request that you don't tell people?"

"I promise to you, Mr Stanley, that I will not tell a soul unless they ask me a question like, 'Who does Mr Stanley think is pretty?' or 'Is there anyone who thinks Mandy is pretty?'."

Stanley shook his head. "Speaking of telling people things; why did it concern Rosemary the Retired and Leah the Librarian that I had no lunch today?"

For the first time, Ernest broke his smile. "Because Rosemary the Retired likes to help people in need. I knew that you had a need, and I knew it would bring her joy to bring you lunch. Was that wrong of me?"

Although they had arrived at the ninth floor long ago, it was only now that the elevator doors slid open. Stanley didn't know whether to say 'thank you' or 'good night' or 'sorry', so he left the elevator in silence.

Perry the Psychic was sitting on a little hallway chair, apparently waiting for Stanley to come home. "How do you think your first day in the city has been?" he asked.

Stanley wasn't in a talking mood. "Something tells me you know exactly how it went."

Perry laughed. "I know the events that have happened, but I cannot see into your mind. I don't know how you think your first day in the city has been."

Stanley walked to his apartment door. "But if you're psychic, you know what I am going to say about how I think today has been."

Perry nodded. "That is true. Sorry to hear it has been a crazy first day. On the bright side, you and Mandy will make a lovely couple one day."

The stairwell doors opened down the hall and outstepped Jarvis the Jobless. "There you are, Perry. Can you please give me the winning numbers for tomorrow's lottery please?"

"46, 29, 65, 3, 22 and 9," Perry replied nonchalantly.

"Thanks, Perry," Jarvis said. And with that, Jarvis returned into the stairwell and out of sight.

"So I'm guessing that's how Jarvis stays jobless but not homeless?" Stanley asked.

Perry shrugged his shoulders.

Stanley was about to go inside when he looked at his neighbour's door, nine-oh-seven. "Hey, Perry. Do you know who lives next door, in nine-oh-seven?"

"Nine-oh-seven belongs to Paxton the Pacifist. Nice bloke but don't try getting into an argument with him. He loves arguing."

"This definitely has been a crazy first day. Have a good

evening."

"You too, Stanley."

Stanley closed his door, Perry left the via the stairwell, and Jarvis the Jobless finally sold the building's doormat online.

CHAPTER THREE
A WELCOME PARTY

The next morning, at precisely 6 am, there was a loud series of knocks upon Stanley's front door. Wearily, Stanley rolled out of bed and lumbered towards the knocks. He opened the door and found a young lady in a suit. She held a clipboard to her chest and smiled as if she had just won first prize in a smiling contest.

"Hi, how are you? My name is Elaine."

"It's 6 am," Stanley stated.

Elaine almost frowned (almost) as she looked at her watch. "Dear me it is too; I'm so sorry. It's just that when I'm planning a party, I get so excited. I'm an event planner, you see."

Stanley stared at her blankly. "Is there something I can help you with?"

Elaine grabbed a piece of paper from her clipboard and held it out. "Tonight, we are having a welcoming party for you in the lobby, and you're invited, of course."

Stanley ran his hand through his hair as he looked at the floral embossed invitation. He didn't like parties all that much. The parties he attended back home were just excuses to gossip and compare incomes. This welcoming party was apparently all planned out and happening whether he like it or not. "Thanks. I'm sure I'll be able to stop by."

Elaine's smile somehow got bigger. "Oh brilliant. I was really hoping you would be able to make it to your party. It's going to be wonderful now. Plan 'B' was to have your party without you, but that would have made it more like a funeral."

"Do I need to bring anything?" Stanley asked.

"Oh no. You just need to bring yourself. Charlotte the Chef will be cooking a feast. Have a good day."

Without waiting for a response, Elaine left down the hall, to knock on the next door. Paxton the Pacifist clearly wasn't happy about being woken. He threw the door open, snatched the piece of paper from Elaine's hand and slammed the door shut.

Two hours later, Stanley was dressed and ready for work. His daily starting time was 8:30 am, and today he would be given an office with everything he needed to get settled into his new job, including a free stapler. With staples. According to Richard Richardson that was the staple welcoming gift for new employees.

Stanley called the elevator and stepped inside.

"Morning, Mr Stanley," Ernest the Elevator Operator said with a nod of his head.

"Morning, Ernest. Lobby please," Stanley said politely.

The elevator began its descent but came to a stop at the fifth floor. The doors opened and in stepped Mandy the Midwife. Stanley looked at Ernest. The elevator operator was again smiling in a mischievous way. Stanley's muscles tensed up, wondering what Ernest would say.

"Good morning, Stanley. Good morning, Ernest," Mandy said sweetly. "Lobby please."

The doors closed and the elevator resumed its course.

"Are you coming to your welcoming party?" Mandy asked.

Stanley quickly turned. "Welcoming party? Yes, I think I will be. Elaine the Event Planner gave me the invitation at 6 am this morning."

Mandy laughed. "Yes, Elaine would do that. She gets very excited about parties."

Ernest cleared his throat. "Miss Mandy, I have come to learn something quite interesting, just last evening."

"Yes? What's that?" Mandy asked. Stanley's eyes were wide. It's not that he thought thinking Mandy pretty was a bad secret, it just was not an appropriate thing to say about a stranger.

"He's going to say I think you're pretty," Stanley blurted, preferring it be heard from the horse's mouth. There was no horse in the elevator, so he preferred Mandy heard it from his own mouth.

Ernest raised his eyebrows in surprise. "Oh, Mr Stanley? Do you think Miss Mandy is pretty? Well isn't that something to know? I was simply going to say that I learnt that newspapers make great fly swatters."

Mandy laughed. "Thank you for saying that Stanley, that's very sweet. And Ernest; I know what you are trying to do. You don't need to try and set me up with someone." Stanley instantly felt at ease. Mandy was clearly a sensible woman.

Stanley and Mandy arrived at the lobby and exited the elevator, passing Jarvis the Jobless who was completing his doormat sale with a shady looking doormat dealer.

They walked together through the lobby to the big front door. Damien the Doorman got up from his desk and opened the door for the pair. "Have a good day at work, Mandy and Stanley."

"Thank you, Damien. Same to you," Mandy replied brightly.

The consultant and midwife stood for a moment on the sidewalk.

Mandy pointed right. "Well, I'm going this way."

Stanley pointed left. "I guess I'll see you tonight at my party."

"I'd say that's a pretty accurate guess," she said with a smile.

And they parted to go their separate ways.

The whole day was a blur for Stanley; he arrived at work, read some memos, completed some memos, had some lunch, read some more memos, made a presentation, and made a memo for the next day to create fewer memos. Before he knew it, he was shutting down his computer and making his way back to Tayel Tower.

It was 5:30 pm when he walked through the front door of Tayel Tower, and even though the party didn't start till 7 pm, there were people bustling around setting up tables, hanging streamers, and connecting speakers. Elaine the Event Planner spotted Stanley walking through the preparations and approached him with a slightly concerned look (slightly, for her face was still intensely smiley). "I know it all looks like a mess, but I assure you in an hour the lobby will look great."

"Really, this is too much," Stanley said modestly. "I just

expected the party would consist of a few pizzas and some bottles of ginger beer."

Elaine's eyes widened and she immediately turned to yell at one of the ladies. "Aldene, walk to the service station and buy some ginger beer. Deborah, please ring Lulu's Pizza and order ten pizzas."

"That's not what I meant," Stanley said quickly. "I'm sure whatever you have planned will be great."

Elaine's smile became a little unsure (a little) of what to do. She yelled at the ladies again. "Deborah, don't worry about the pizzas. Aldene, hurry up with the ginger beer."

Exactly an hour and a half later, Stanley was standing in the lobby wearing a new change of clothes and holding a bottle of chilled ginger beer. It looked like almost everyone in the building had turned out to welcome the new occupant. The loudspeakers played rock and roll classics and pop hits from decades ago. Paul the Policeman was dancing away, while Russell the Realtor complained about the lack of culture in modern music to whoever was in his vicinity.

Charlotte the Chef had done what Elaine the Event Planner had promised; made a feast. There was roast lamb with rosemary and garlic marinade, fresh garden salads, couscous salad, chicken caesar salads and a selection of fresh fruits so colourful that at first Stanley thought they were fake. On the desserts table, there were caramel mudcakes, chocolate mousse cakes, little white chocolate and raspberry muffins, and a giant tray of sticky date puddings drenched in rich caramel sauce.

Everyone at the party had someone in particular that they talked to; no one really mixed or mingled. After talking to Perry the Psychic for a while, Stanley found himself standing alone against a wall. He was looking at his phone when a middle-aged, very fit man approached him. "Stanley, I presume? My name is Julian. I live on the fifth floor."

Stanley shook the man's hand. "Nice to meet you. I live on the ninth floor. What do you do for a living?"

Julian took a sip of his ginger beer. "I'm a reporter, a writer and an investigator. What about yourself?"

"That's quite a repertoire. I'm just a consultant for a consulting company."

Jarvis the Jobless walked past holding a whole leg of lamb he stole from the roast platter. Stanley didn't know how long it would take for him to get used to the antics and quirks of his neighbours, even if he had learned not to judge by appearance.

"So, what's your quirk?" Stanley asked Julian without thinking.

"Excuse me?"

Stanley realised how rude that must have been. He looked around the room. "I mean; almost everyone I've met in the building so far has a quirk or two. I don't mean to suppose that you aren't normal; I have only just met you. Sorry, it was a rude question."

Julian laughed. "I know what you mean, brother. I thought the exact same thing when I moved in two years ago. But you'll get used to it. Everyone that lives here has a purpose; a role to play. And everyone that lives here knows they have a quirk or two. So the real question should be, Stanley, what's your quirk?"

Stanley thought about this long and hard. "Maybe my quirk is I don't have a quirk?"

Julian shook his head. "Sorry, no can do. I've already got that quirk."

Stanley couldn't think of any quirks or peculiarities he possessed. "I like to work. Is that a quirk?"

Julian started walking towards the food table. "Maybe, but I doubt it. Don't worry about it. I'm sure we'll find yours soon enough."

As soon as Julian left, Stanley felt a light tap on the arm.

"Hey, you," Mandy said, holding a plate of salad. "How are you liking your party?"

"Yeah, it's great," he said with as much positivity as he could muster.

Stanley couldn't get what Julian had said out of his head. "That man, Julian the Journalist, just told me that everyone in Tayel Tower has a… quirk. Is that true? Do you have a… quirk?"

Mandy the Midwife smiled but shook her head. "Julian's quirk is he thinks everyone has a quirk, and he likes to label them because of it. But besides that, he's a pretty normal guy. I assume a little like you."

Stanley laughed, taking 'being normal' in as a compliment in this situation. "I assure you, I'm normal. At least, I think I'm normal."

The music from the speakers cut off as Damien the Doorman carefully stood up on a chair. "Quiet please, everyone," He called.

A hush came over the room. "Thank you for being here today to welcome the newest occupant; Stanley, into apartment nine-oh-nine." The building's occupants gave a round of applause. Stanley gave a reluctant little wave.

Damien held up his bottle of ginger beer. "We wish you

good times, Stanley, and we hope you pay your amenities fees on time."

Everyone raised their glasses of coke and bottles of ginger beer in the air as a salute.

"Pour one out for Stanley!" Jarvis the Jobless yelled from the back of the room as he poured his bottle of ginger beer all over the lobby floor.

"Now, do you want to say a few words, Stanley?" Damien asked.

Stanley felt the weight of every eye in the room upon him. "Everyone's been great so far. Thanks."

Damien, a little underwhelmed at the speech, shrugged his shoulders and shakily got off the chair. "Oh well. Party on."

The music started up again and everyone resumed talking.

"So what's your story?" Mandy enquired. "What's brought you to Tayel Tower? If I may ask."

"Well, I lived down south, graduated from university last year and got a job at a consulting firm here in the city. The company chose Tayel Tower for me to stay at. I'll probably be here for 2 or 3 years and then I'll move back to my home town with a promotion. Not a very exciting story. How about you? What brought you to Tayel Tower?"

Mandy finished her mouthful of lettuce. "Well, I also graduated last year, but in midwifery, and got a job at the City South Hospital, where I did my placement. My family lives in the country, and so I moved here into Tayel Tower late last year."

They chatted pleasantly for a little while about their occupations; nothing deep or meaningful. Eventually, Mandy left to help Elaine fetch drinks from the lobby storage rooms. Julian the Journalist came back to Stanley, holding a plate piled with lamb and watermelon.

Stanley still wanted a conclusion on the subject of quirks. "I was talking to Mandy the Midwife," he said to Julian. "And she said that you are the only one with a quirk, and your quirk is thinking everyone else has a quirk."

Julian stifled his laughter through a bite of lamb. "She would say that. You see, Mandy's quirk is she denies that anyone in the building has a quirk!"

Stanley rolled his eyes; he gave up. He spent the rest of the night having a much more interesting conversation with Julian about journalism abroad. Julian had apparently been everywhere and seen many things. As it turned out, at the end of the week Julian was heading away to cover the celebration of birthdays among Antarctician penguins.

Soon enough, the older residents of Tayel Tower began to disappear up the elevator to their apartments. And it wasn't long until the working residents also retired to their homes. Soon the only people left in the lobby were Clare the Cleaner, Damien the Doorman, Jarvis the Jobless, and Stanley. He did not want to be rude and leave the party early before it had clearly ended. But now he was tired and ready for bed.

Stanley walked to the elevator and pressed the up button. The elevator bell dinged and the doors opened to reveal Ernest the Elevator Operator.

"Ernest, do you even sleep?" Stanley asked through a yawn.

Ernest shrugged his shoulders, "I sleep when no one needs to use the elevator."

At the ninth floor, Stanley walked slowly down the hallway, fishing his keys out of his pocket. He was too tired to notice Perry the Psychic sitting on the hallway chair.

"Goodnight, Stanley?" Perry asked.

Stanley jumped out of his skin, dropping his keys. "Was that a question or a statement?" He asked, picking the keys up again.

"Well from the look of you with Mandy the Midwife, I'd say it's a rhetorical question."

Stanley held his tongue. If he was honest, he would like to get to know Mandy the Midwife better; she appeared to be one of the only 'normal' residents.

As Stanley walked inside his apartment, he looked across the hallway at apartment 910. "Perry, who lives across the hallway, in nine-ten?"

Perry looked at my door. "Oh, a writer named Wray lives there. But don't expect to see him anytime soon. He likes to stay cooped up in there; he rarely goes out and about."

I always go out and about.

Stanley nodded his head and retired to his apartment.

Perry looked out the large hall window at the brightly lit city below, then left via the stairwell.

And I went into my own apartment; nine-ten. It was true; Stanley and the other occupants of Tayel Tower wouldn't see me any time soon. But I'm certainly not invisible; it's simply that no one notices me. Not being noticed does come in handy when you are wanting to write about other people and their lives; but less helpful for making friends. As Stanley would come to learn, the residents of Tayel Tower do all have their unique characteristics, eccentricities, habits, idiosyncrasies, peculiarities, and individual quirks. No one noticing me? That is everyone's quirk.

Wray Wrigley's

TAYEL TOWER

Book 2

THE DONUT DENIERS

CHAPTER ONE
THE SECRET SOCIETY

I do wish there were more societies, groups, leagues and alliances in the world.

I know there are already a good number of clubs that can satisfy the social needs of almost everyone on earth, but I would still like to recommend a couple more:

A society for people who own hamsters but wish they didn't. These poor people often have had hamsters thrust upon them from children who promised to care for the creatures but failed to follow through. Other people bought hamsters under the assumption the critters would be fun and fuss-free, only to find the hamsters are conniving, lackadaisical, uneducated little fluff-puffs who spend their days simply pooping, eating and sleeping. And then when a hamster's owner is looking for fun and love in return, what do they receive? Nothing. The hamster will just sit there, staring at you as if you are brick wall covered in a teenager's graffiti; worth glancing at once or twice for the patterns, but ultimately perceived as disgusting. I would have once liked to join this society.

Another good club would be for people who find value in giving strangers titles that are far too familiar than is appropriate. "Hello, brother!" a car salesman greeted me with yesterday. This car salesman was not, in fact, my brother. If he really was my brother, I would have been most surprised, given our contrast in appearance and vast difference in age.

"Morning, sweetie" or "Afternoon, honey" or "Are you interested in a car today, darling?". All these greetings from that car salesman would mean he would fit perfectly into the proposed club for people who find value in giving strangers inappropriate titles.

Tayel Tower, unbelievably, had a society that was membered by dozens of neighbours. This society was a secret society and therefore was not supposed to be spoken about except in monthly meetings and behind closed doors. I am not a member of this secret society myself, but given the nature of the Tayel Tower residents, maintaining a secret society was far beyond their capabilities.

"Paxton! Was I organising food for tonight's secret meeting?" the ladies of Tayel Tower were often yelling across the lobby and down the halls.

"Quiet, Rosemary!" Paxton the Pacifist would say back, his face red and his whisper loud and harsh. "It's a secret meeting. The emphasis is on 'secret'. We are a secret society with secret meetings."

"I know, I know," Rosemary would reply. "But do you think people would prefer blueberry or choc-orange cheesecake?"

Paxton the Pacifist was the founder and leader of this secret society and took his role very importantly. A General for the people, he was elected by himself because he felt he could do the job best, and he quickly realised no one else was as committed to the society's main characteristic; secrecy.

You may think that such a small society formed by a bonified pacifist must have a small following, made up of only the retired and lonely people of Tayel Tower. I wish I could say that was the case; the secret society had hundreds of active members from across the city and surrounding suburbs.

Paxton's nephew had taught the older man to use a computer, and Paxton had become absolutely enthralled by the new technology. He started a website for the secret society and advertised its existence on dozens of forums, conspiracy sites and blogs. People who liked anonymity were enthralled by being a member of a secret society such as that of Paxton's. Over 2 years since its founding, membership signups to the society had grown to 400 something, apparently. (The exact number is unknown, or so I'm told: a 'secret'.)

"I hear you run a secret society," Stanley said to Paxton one afternoon as the elevator began ascending.

"No, I don't," Paxton denied abruptly. "Where did you hear that?"

"Len the Lemon Seller told me. I didn't ask. He just walked up to me and said 'Paxton the Pacifist runs a secret society.'"

Paxton shook his head in dismay, but then appeared a little proud. "It's a secret."

"So you do run a secret society?" Stanley asked.

"No, I don't," Paxton again sharply denied, but then relaxed. "It's a secret."

Stanley nodded his head. He added 'secret society' to the list of reasons not to get too involved in the lives of the Tayel Tower residents. The concept didn't take him by surprise in the slightest; his week so far living amongst his neighbours was starting to create a resistance to surprise. His survival mantra was simple: keep his head down, work, work, work, get the promotion and pay rise, then move back to the suburbs. He was young and still optimistic about his future.

"Would you be interested in joining the secret society?" Paxton asked.

"Oh, no thank you," Stanley said very quickly.

"It's very little commitment. We meet once a month and annually for the convention. It would be good to have more, younger members like yourself."

Stanley shook his head. "No thank you. I can't commit. I'm not that good at commitment. I'm not really the committed kind."

Paxton looked disappointed. "Well, okay. That's good because I was joking. The secret society doesn't exist."

"I understand," Stanley said politely.

"It doesn't exist?!" Ernest the Elevator Operator exclaimed. "Where has everyone been going on the second Thursday of every month? Is there a party I'm not invited to? That's outrageous."

"No, it does exist, and you're most welcome to join," Paxton said to Ernest. He turned to Stanley. "But it doesn't exist."

Stanley stepped out the elevator on the ninth floor. The hallway was filled with a warm yellow glow from the setting sun. He always did like sunsets. He walked to the large window at the end of the hallway and gazed out over the city. The cars in peak hour tailgated and beeped below; the birds heading home from their days at work chirped "goodnight" and "see you tomorrow" to each other in their birdy language. Stanley and walked into his apartment, placing his backpack on the coatrack and got changed into a tracksuit.

He opened his pantry and looked inside, hunting for dinner. A long day at work had made him ravenous. Ask any single person, and you will find out just how creative they can be with creating dinner out of the ingredients they have. Tonight, he used a packet of ramen noodles, a chicken breast and some peanut butter to make chicken peanut satay noodles. He was quite honestly proud of his little creation. It wasn't going to win any Michelin stars, but it would win his stomach's gratitude and respect.

Stanley flicked on the television, bowl of noodles in hand. He was searching for something to watch that wasn't news or game shows when the apartment phone rang. He stared at the phone, unsure of what to do. The phone had never rung before. The only time he had used it was to call down to Damien the Doorman the day he had moved in.

The phone gave a cheerful ring, but at this hour of evening, Stanley felt it was a little chilling. Stanley looked at his mobile phone to see if anyone had tried calling him there first. No missed calls. Slowly, Stanley put down the bowl of noodles on the coffee table and walked over to the phone. The caller ID was 'Anonymous'. He picked up the phone.

"Hello?" he said.

"Hello, is this Stanley?" the male voice on the phone asked.

"Yes."

"Oh good. My name is Samuel and I am a salesman; I live on the 2nd floor. I believe we met briefly when you were moving in. How are you this evening?"

"Good thanks," Stanley said. "How can I help you?"

"Ah, well it's more of a question of how I can help you! You see, it has come to my attention that a lot of my neighbours are missing key 'this's' and 'that's' that would greatly enrich their lives."

"Thank you, but I think I have all the 'that' I need for the moment."

"Ah, you say that, but indulge me for one moment: do you have trouble going to sleep?"

"No."

"Do you have trouble remembering where you leave things?"

"No."

"Do your shoes smell?"

"Not particularly."

"Do you smell."

"Sometimes, but I shower. I really need-"

"Yes? What is it you need?"

"I really need to go and finish eating my dinner."

"I hear you, I hear you, but what you're really trying to say is 'I'm unhappy with my life, and I need something to make it better.' When you realise that, give me a call, okay?"

"I sure will. I will call you when I need something to make my life better. Goodnight," Stanley said as politely he could. He sighed and went back to the couch. He picked up his bowl of noodles, which were still reasonably warm.

There was a game show playing on the television from

his earlier browsing, but Stanley couldn't be bothered changing the channel. He was raising the fork to his lips for a second bite of noodles when the phone rang again. Stanley rolled his eyes but didn't move beyond that. He let the phone ring. And ring. And ring. After a dozen rings, the phone went silent. Stanley relaxed and resumed eating.

The phone rang again.

Stanley dropped the bowl onto the coffee table and grabbed the phone out of its holder.

"Yes?" he said impatiently.

There was silence for a moment.

"Oh, er… please state your name," the voice said on the phone said

"Is this Samuel the Salesman?"

"I don't know sir, you'll need to tell me. Please state your name."

Stanley had no idea what was going on. He hung up the phone. After a couple of seconds, it rang again. Stanley picked it up. "Who is this?"

"Please state your name," the voice repeated.

"My name is Stanley. Is this a telemarketer? Please take me off your list."

"This is not a telemarketer, this is your invite confirmation. Stanley, we look forward to seeing you at the secret society conference on the 20th of this month."

"Paxton?"

"Paxton? I thought this was Stanley."

"This is Stanley. I didn't apply for any conference. Please take me off your list."

"What conference?" the voice asked.

"The secret society conference!" Stanley yelled.

"I've never heard of it," the voice said.

Stanley hung up the phone and immediately went to Paxton the Pacifist's apartment, which was right next door. He loudly knocked on Paxton's door.

"What?!" yelled Paxton from inside. Paxton was not a fan of being interrupted for anything.

"It's Stanley!"

The door whipped open. Paxton held an inconvenienced expression. "Oh, hello Stanley. What can I do you for? I hope you know I'm not really the type of neighbour that trades sugar or flour."

"I just got a call confirming my invite to a secret society conference."

Paxton broke into a smile. "Oh good, glad to hear you can make it."

"No, I will not! I'm not interested in getting involved. I did say that. Remember? In the elevator?"

"I apologise then," Paxton said with a wink.

"Why did you wink?"

"Because I'm sorry you won't be able to make it to the conference."

"I'm highly confused," Stanley said.

Paxton looked up and down the hallway. "You're pretending not to want to be in the secret society. Fantastic work," he said in a low voice.

"I'm not pretending," Stanley said, also quietly. "I did not move to Tayel Tower to get involved in any of my neighbour's activities. I only wish to live in peace, go to work, get my promotion and move away again. I hope your conference goes well, but please take me off any membership list. Goodnight."

Stanley went back to his own apartment, closed the door, sat on the couch and ate his luke-warm noodles feeling lonelier than ever.

CHAPTER TWO
CURIOSITY AND MENTAL HEALTH

Stanley stared at his ceiling, wide awake. It was 2 am in the morning and he hadn't been able to sleep a wink. It may have been the chicken peanut satay noodles, but Stanley felt something much more; curiosity.

He was curious as to why more people didn't try chicken peanut satay noodles more often. He was curious about what Samuel the Salesman could offer him that would make his life so much better. He was curious as to who was on the phone the second time, and he was curious about why the secret society existed, and what they did.

'Secret societies don't form for no reason,' Stanley thought to himself.

He climbed out of bed and opened his laptop on the kitchen table. He did an internet search for 'Secret Society Tayel Tower'. The search results were dozens of references in shady looking black coloured forums, and a website with the title 'Don't Know What You're Talking About'.

It was a primitively designed website with no thought and understanding of graphic design or usability. The homepage had a stock picture of a cartoon man holding a giant question mark and the following text:

Hello and welcome to the secret society. If you do not want to join the secret society, please leave now and do not mention this website to anyone. We would further ask that you destroy your laptop, computer or phone. Here is a link for hammers you can buy. If you are still reading this, we hope it means you are looking to join our secret society.

Our secret society has been active for over 2 years now and has hundreds of active members. Our members are (for the most part) lovely people who would love to get to know you. Some are right hamsters.

Our secret society has a belief system that is central to who we are and what we do:

1. Saxophones belong in hell.

2. The earth is probably flat.

3. Peas should only be consumed through scooping, not stabbing.

4. The hand-sanitation industry is conspiring with the doctors' union to make you too sanitary so that you get sick easier.

5. Never mention the doughnuts.'

Stanley stared at the screen, eyes wide.

'This has to be a joke. How can hundreds of people be signing up for this secret society?' He thought to himself.

A bright red pop-up came onto the website. Our next meeting will be held in apartment 108 of Tayel Tower, Tuesday at 7 pm. We'd love to see you there. Please enter your name and email address to attend.

Stanley hated that he was so curious. He entered his name and email address and pressed enter.

****

The next morning, Tuesday morning, Stanley felt tired and groggy. He had managed to sleep for about 4 hours but felt like he had gotten no sleep at all.

"Morning, Ernest," he said through a yawn as he stepped into the elevator.

"Good morning, Stanley," Ernest replied, ever cheerful. "Ground floor?"

"Ground floor."

There was another man already in the elevator. He was dressed in a smart, buttoned-up shirt, dress pants, and held an expensive leather briefcase by his side. He looked and smelled exactly like a doctor. Stanley and the man exchanged a nod of the head. The elevator stopped at the 5th floor and on hopped Mandy the Midwife. Mandy the Midwife was a bubbly, joyful soul who could light up any room with her smile.

"Good morning, Ernest. Good morning, Dr Patrick. Good morning, Stanley," she said standing in the middle of the three men.

"Morning." "Hello, Mandy." "Morning, Mandy," the three men replied in chorus.

"Ground floor?" Ernest asked.

"Ground floor," she replied. Mandy turned to the doctor. "How is today looking?"

"Yes, it will be a busy one. I did manage to sleep in a little, but I have full blocks of patients today."

"And how is today looking for you?" Mandy asked Stanley.

"Well… uh, there is a couple of client reports I need to get done before Friday," Stanley said, feeling quite inferior to the doctor.

The doctor stuck out his hand. "I don't believe we have met properly; only in passing at your welcoming party. My name is Dr Patrick."

"Yes, that's right," Stanley said as they shook hands. "You worked in… podiatry?"

"Psychiatry," Dr Patrick the Psychiatrist corrected.

"Same thing, isn't it?" Stanley attempted to joke. Everyone in the elevator looked at him with raised eyebrows.

"Sorry."

"And what do you do for a living?" Dr Patrick asked.

"I'm a business consultant."

"Oh, that's great. And do you enjoy it?"

"Yes, I love it, it's so rewarding." Stanley lied. He enjoyed his work on most days, but 'love' was stretching it.

"It's wonderful to work, doing what you love," Mandy said with her wonderful smile. Everyone in the elevator nodded their heads.

The elevator stopped at the first floor, and on came a woman. This woman was dressed almost identically to the doctor (but more feminine), and instead of an expensive briefcase, she held a simple black backpack.

Everyone shuffled to let the woman in.

Stanley couldn't describe it, but as soon as the woman stepped in, the atmosphere in the elevator grew icy cold.

"Good morning, Dr Paige," Mandy said cheerfully.

"Good morning, Mandy. Good morning, Ernest. Hello; Stanley, isn't it?" Dr Paige asked.

"Yes, nice to meet you, Dr Paige," Stanley said, shaking the woman's hand.

"You can just call me Paige," the woman said with a smile, but that smile quickly disappeared. "Morning, Dr

Patrick."

Dr Patrick just 'humphed' in return. The silence was awkward. At the lobby, the passengers piled out of the elevator.

The two doctors walked briskly out of the lobby onto the street outside, continuing their silent conversation.

"What's the story there?" Stanley asked Mandy as they walked leisurely through the lobby.

Mandy shook her head. "You can only imagine. Dr Patrick is a psychiatrist, trained in medicine to help people with their mental illnesses. Dr Paige is a psychologist, trained in psychology to help people through therapy. Dr Patrick thinks Dr Paige, and all psychologists for that matter, give patients hope where only medicine would solve the issue. Dr Paige thinks Dr Patrick over medicates patients, where simple therapy and counselling would suffice."

"Wow," Stanley said.

"It's really nothing personal between them; it's just their professions."

"I'm guessing they're not married," Stanley laughed.

"Even worse," Mandy laughed. "Brother and Sister."

They exited the lobby and paused on the footpath.

"Which one is better, in your opinion?" Stanley asked. "Psychology or psychiatry?"

Mandy shrugged her shoulders. "I haven't been trained too much in that side of medicine, but I think it would really depend on the individual's situation. But if you ever want to hear a heated debate between them, just attend a secret society meeting."

Stanley's legs almost gave out. "You're in the secret society?"

Mandy shook her head. "I attended once, but it wasn't very good for my health."

Stanley was confused. "Your health? What do they do…"

Mandy looked at her phone. "I should get to work. I'll see you later."

They were unsure of whether to exchange a hug, handshake or hi-5. The silence lasted too long so they just said "bye" and parted ways.

Stanley was utterly confused about how a secret society could be bad for one's health, but he was curious to find out more.

****

"Stanley!" Richard Richardson said loudly, coming into Stanley's office. Richard Richardson was Stanley's enthusiastic, non-empathetic boss who had chosen Tayel Tower for Stanley to live in.

"Hello," Stanley said, looking up from the report he was chiselling away at. Richard Richardson took a seat on the other side of the desk and leaned back, hands behind his head and his eyes closed.

"Was there something I can get you?" Stanley asked, after a long silence.

Richard Richardson seemed to snap back into reality. "Apologies, it was a long night. I was proof-reading a report for a bakery that is doing very successfully lately. But, anyway, I do need to have a little talk with you."

Stanley sat up a little straighter. Anytime a manager says, "we need to have a little talk", the subsequent conversation is generally not favourable.

"As you know, I think you are a great asset to our team

here, but I feel it is important to note that we value hard work."

Stanley's mind raced, trying to think of what he had done wrong. Richardson held up a hand, reading Stanley's expressions. "You haven't done anything wrong. Your reports that I've seen are fantastic; our clients love you. But I.T. has shown me that you spend a long time using the internet for your own interests during work hours. You spend at least an hour a day searching for long-stay hotels, apartments to rent and bus routes from the suburbs."

Stanley had no defence.

Richardson once again leaned back. "I know what you are doing. You are looking to move out of Tayel Tower."

"I'm not sure how much longer I can live there," Stanley said in desperation. "I know that you said you think I can handle it, but I really think Tayel Tower might be inhibiting my ability to focus on work."

Richardson stared intently at Stanley. "If you really think it's going to affect your work, we can go tonight and have a look at Rustania Apartments. They're much shabbier, but it's separate units. You should have fewer distractions there."

Richardson stood up and went to the door. "I'll come and pick you up at Tayel Tower at 7 pm. Be out the front."

"Oh, I…" Stanley began, but his boss had left, closing the door behind him.

Stanley stared blankly at the wall. The secret society meeting was at 7 pm, his potential escape to freedom was at 7 pm. To run away from Tayel Tower or dive right in? That was the question that plagued Stanley for the rest of the day. He got nothing done.

His need for adventure and curiosity pulled him towards the secret society. What did they do? Why were their meetings so unhealthy? What was the worst that could happen if he stayed where he was? He had begun to make friends at Tayel Tower; Mandy the Midwife was so lovely to him and she seemed to be able to survive the chaos. Why couldn't he?

'What was the worst that could happen?' The question swam around Stanley's mind like an Australian in tomato sauce.

****

The time was 6:55 pm. Stanley stood outside the door of apartment 108. He took a deep breath.

At the end of the workday, he had timidly told Richard Richardson that he wouldn't need to go looking for a new place of residence; Tayel Tower would be fine. His boss had been ecstatic that Stanley was facing his problems head-on, but threatened that there wouldn't be another chance to move. The next move would be to a suburbs branch with no promotion or pay rise.

Stanley gave one knock upon the apartment door. Someone inside opened it an inch.

"Password?" a female's voice said through the gap.

"Um…" Stanley began. The door instantly closed. He didn't remember seeing or hearing anything about a password. The elevator doors opened at the end of the hallway and outstepped Patrick the Psychiatrist. Dr Patrick walked past Stanley, nodding his head in acknowledgement, and gave a knock on the door.

The door opened. "Password?"

"Password?" Dr Patrick asked. "There's no password!

Open the door, Paige!"

Reluctantly, the door opened all the way to reveal Paige the Psychologist, who looked at Patrick with contempt and disgust. "Come in," she said as cold as a toucan on a ski trip.

The door closed briskly again behind Patrick.

Stanley stepped up to the door once more and gave a knock.

The door opened quickly, and Paige almost picked Stanley up in a joyful bear-hug. "Hello, Stanley! It's so good that you could make it! Sorry, I thought you were Patrick when you first knocked. We don't really have a password."

Stanley was very taken aback by the warm reception.

"Please, go straight through to the living room and help yourself to tea and coffee."

Stanley walked down the short hall into the living room. Every apartment in Tayel Tower was architecturally the same but decorated to the unique desires of the owner. Paige the Psychologist's apartment was painted pastel green with calming photos of forests and vases of fresh flowers scattered about the rooms.

It also would not be amiss to mention the giant pile of donuts in the corner of the living room. Think of the biggest pile of donuts that you could possibly fit in the corner of a living room, and double that. Stanley didn't even know where to look at this monstrous pile of chocolate, raspberry jam, sugar and cinnamon, caramel, and glazed deep-fried holey delights. Stanley looked at the other people already in the living room, they all just walked around the donut pile as if it were a hat stand. Tanish the Taxi Driver walked over to the pile and picked up a donut.

"What are they for?" Stanley asked with wide eyes.

"What is what for?" Tanish asked, taking a bite out of a cinnamon donut.

"The donuts. There's so many…" Stanley suddenly recalled rule 5 on the secret society website: 'Never mention the donuts'. He let his voice trail off as Tanish the Taxi Driver quickly walked away and sat on the couch. Now he understood why Mandy the Midwife had said the secret society meetings were bad for one's health. Stanley sat down on a kitchen chair and watched as people, some residents, many strangers, filed into the apartment. By quarter past 7, there were a good 30 people squished into the apartment. They chatted happily amongst themselves, no sinister conversations as one might assume at a secret society meeting.

An older woman sitting next to Stanley munched away at a glazed donut. "They say it's going to rain tomorrow," she said to him. "I don't believe them."

Stanley just smiled and nodded.

"They also say that there is too much sugar in my diet." She took a bite from the donut. "I don't believe them either."

Stanley gave a polite smile. Then, he had an idea.

"I hear they say the earth is spherical," he said quietly to the lady.

The lady leaned away a little. "Are you crazy?" She looked Stanley up and down. "Of course it's spherical, you pancake. How do you think seasons could possibly work on earth if it weren't spherical?"

Stanley was quite surprised by the response.

"What are your thoughts on Saxophones?" he asked.

"Saxophones are pure evil," the old lady said with her

nose in the air.

"Eating peas?"

"Eh, you can eat peas however you want."

"Hand sanitiser?"

"Don't overdo it, I say."

"What are you eating?"

The lady looked at Stanley as if he just said she was fat. She left the chair in repugnance and went to the other side of the room.

Paxton the Pacifist stood next to the pile of donuts and clapped his hands together. "Grab a seat. Hurry up." He had with him a notepad full of notes.

Everyone looked for a place to be, whether it was sitting on the floor, on one of the chairs or standing against a wall. People filed past the donuts, grabbing one before finding their places.

Stanley looked around the room at the other attendees. There was no pattern to the age or genders of the members.

Paxton looked out upon his congregation. "Welcome, one and all to the secret society. Thank you for being here once again. Before we begin, let me point out that we have a new member here tonight: Stanley."

Everyone looked at Stanley; it was like the welcoming party all over again. Stanley gave a little wave.

Paxton continued. "Now, Stanley here works as a business consultant, and so you'll be happy to know that he has offered to help run next week's secret society convention."

This was certainly news to Stanley. Everyone in the room gave him smiles and nods. Elaine the Event Planner swallowed her mouthful of raspberry-jam donut. "I can't wait to work together on the convention! I have so many ideas."

Stanley didn't know what to say or do. He was fuming inside at Paxton. He had no intention on following along, but he felt trapped amongst the congregation.

"Now, speaking of the convention," Paxton said. "You'll be pleased to know we have an amazing three-hundred people registered to attend. We were going to hold it in the lobby, but it looks like we are going to need to move it to the convention centre. Vanilla Café has been contacted with the updated attendance numbers. Also, we have some great speakers lined up. I've been in contact with the zoo, the City Symphonic Orchestra, the Royal Farmer's Association, The Amateur Geographer's society, and my second cousin who works as a hand and elbow model, so there should be some great lectures."

Stanley's inner fuming continued to build like a volcano. He was normally a very measured man, but no one likes being told what they are doing without having a say in the matter. He stuck his hand up.

"Yes, Stanley," Paxton said.

"What... is this?" Stanley asked.

"This is the secret society," Paxton answered. He proudly looked around the living room. "Can anyone here enlighten Stanley about who we are?

A young man piped up. "This is the secret society with a name that is yet to be decided."

A woman added. "This secret society's purpose is to create belonging and purpose and introduce intellectual thought into life."

Paxton smiled. "Did you have a look through our website?"

Stanley nodded his head.

"Well, then you would have also seen our five-point belief system. One: Saxophones belong in hell."

"I still quite enjoy the saxophone!" a man yelled from the back of the room.

Paxton ignored the man. "Two: the earth is probably flat."

Almost everyone in the room rolled their eyes.

Paxton continued to ignore them. "Three: peas should be consumed through the use of a knife and fork."

"What?" the old woman that Stanley had initially sat next to exclaimed. "I thought peas were best consumed through scooping, not stabbing."

"So did I!" Paxton said. "But times are changing!"

There were confused murmurs amongst the congregation.

"Four: the hand sanitation industry and doctors are working together to make us sicker."

"Here, here!" Paige the Psychologist said in agreement.

Patrick the Psychiatrist shook his head. "You people do realise how maniacal that sounds, surely?"

"Of course you'd say that," Dr Paige said. "Knowing how much you love giving unnecessary prescriptions."

"Oh, what? So when someone comes in with hormonal imbalance you want me to just sit with them and envision sandy beaches and lush rainforests until they feel better?"

It was Dr Paige's turn to roll her eyes. "You know that's not what psychologists do."

"I do know what psychologists do: not much."

"Oh, how dare you! We help millions of people…"

As the psychiatrist and psychologist continued to argue, everyone else in the room groaned and used it as an opportunity to refresh their donut supplies from the huge donut mountain or grab a drink from the kitchen. The congregation remained silent, allowing Patrick and Paige to do their debating.

"… and what's next? Giving the patient high-fives until they are miraculously healed?"

"Alright, and we're going to resume now," Paxton said from the front of the room, once everyone was again seated. Paige the Psychologist and Patrick the Psychiatrist were both red in the face, glaring at each other.

Paxton continued his speech to Stanley. "And that is the five-point belief system that we live by. As you can see, not everyone agrees with every aspect, but that is what makes our group engaging and lively."

"And what of the fifth point?" Stanley asked, knowing full well what it was. Everyone in the room looked at Stanley as if he had just jumped out of a bin and declared himself 'King of Hugs'.

"The fifth point," Paxton began through a deep frown. He reached over to the donut mountain without looking and pulled out a glazed donut, which caused some pastries higher up to tumble down. Paxton the Pacifist held up the donut. Everyone in the room held up their donut.

It was as Stanley sat there, surrounded by people silently holding donuts, either glaring or looking at him with dismay, that Stanley realised he was far out of his comfort zone. He should have gone with Richardson to look at Rustania Apartments.

Stanley nodded and excused himself from the room.

He left the apartment and went down to Tayel Tower's lobby. The lobby was near empty at this time of night bar Damien the Doorman, and Stanley felt very alone.

He sat on one of the lobby couches and stared into space, wondering what he should do about his situation. All he wanted was to get through life without confrontation. He made up a resolution in his mind and heart to never be curious or adventurous again. Somehow, his curiosity had led him into being conscripted to helping at a secret society convention where everyone was surely bonkers; some believing conspiracy theories; others believing in the ignorance of science. All of them, donut deniers.

"Hello there," a voice said behind Stanley. He turned his head to see Mandy the Midwife.

"Am I intruding?" she asked.

Stanley smiled and shook his head. "No, no."

"I had a late shift today and grabbed some dinner on the way home." She flopped down on the couch opposite Stanley. "I am tired!"

"Me too," Stanley said. They sat there, staring off into space for a moment. "Anything interesting happen today?" Stanley asked.

Mandy shook her head. "No, nothing too crazy. One baby was due today, but the little one was comfortable where he was, so he'll probably make an appearance early tomorrow. How has your day been?"

Stanley shrugged his shoulders. "Fine, I guess. I went to the secret society meeting tonight."

Mandy sat up straight with a giant smile. "You went?! How was it?"

Stanley pointed upwards. "They're still going. They

were all… crazy. They couldn't agree on what they believe, and the one thing they all believed in was crazy in itself."

"Point five?" Mandy asked. Stanley nodded.

Mandy leaned back in the couch, shaking her head with a smile. "They certainly are a funny bunch. You're lucky you didn't hear about point six."

"I didn't know there was a point six."

"They got rid of point six pretty soon after the society was formed. Point six was 'bring a turtle'. The combination of points five and six made the meetings far too crowded; one of them had to go. The zoo had a lot of donations that week."

Stanley couldn't do anything more than give a laugh. "But what is the point to it all? I can't see why they bother meeting at all if all they do is disagree with each other."

"The point, I think," Mandy said, "is they are forming what they believe. To tell you the absolute truth, Paxton was the one that came up with the belief system to begin with. Their process and sense of existence comes now with working out which points to keep, which to change and which to get rid of. Slowly, over time, they will arrive at their final conclusions. They might never conclude what their group is about or what they stand for, but it is the process that excites people. Some of their beliefs are highly primitive, such as thinking the world is flat, but others are forward thinking, such as the doctor conspiracy."

"You believe in the hand-sanitation conspiracy?" Stanley asked.

"No, it's completely ridiculous," Mandy replied. "But that's not the point. The point is that they are debating it and continuing to form their beliefs, and that's the purpose for coming back to the meetings every week."

Stanley was genuinely impressed by Mandy's wisdom and insight. It had taken Mandy many weeks to figure it out for herself, after her own attendance to the secret society.

"You're quite smart," Stanley blurted out. Mandy blushed and shrugged her shoulders. "I could be wrong. They could all just be crazy. But it seems that their purpose is finding their purpose."

Stanley nodded. It made sense to him now.

He looked at Mandy sitting across from him and felt a little jump in his heart. She was smart, joyful and, as everyone now knows, Stanley thought she was 'pretty'. But now he was beginning to think that she was beautiful.

Stanley had not wanted to get more involved in the happenings of Tayel Tower, but if there's one thing that causes a person to go far deeper into a situation than planned, it's an attraction. Attraction and curiosity. Curiosity to many questions Mandy had raised in Stanley's mind. He hoped many questions could be answered at the annual Secret Society Convention.

CHAPTER THREE
ARGUMENTS IN FAVOUR
OF A FLATTER EARTH

Running a secret convention is much cheaper and easier than running other types of conventions. For one, there are minimal marketing expenses; no banners need to be printed and no flyers need to be handed out. All the money that a secret convention saves on those efforts, they can spend on something that they feel is much more necessary and appropriate.

Stanley stood outside the loading entrance to the City Convention Centre. He wore a plain black t-shirt and an orange baseball cap on his head, as was the volunteer's uniform. A large, white truck backed up to the convention centre loading dock. It stopped just short of the roller doors and the driver hopped out holding a clipboard.

"Delivery of donuts here for the Boring…Bank… Numbers… convention?" the driver said. Stanley was about to turn the man away when he realised that the Boring Bank Numbers Convention was the name Paxton had probably ordered the donuts under.

"Yes, that's here," Stanley said, signing for the order. The invoice said 'Vanilla Café' in big letters at the top of the page. The driver opened the back of the truck. The refrigerated truck was filled to the brim with white boxes; each box filled with a dozen donuts. There were the same types of donuts as Stanley had seen at the meeting, as well as chocolate chip, strawberry frosted, sprinkled, bear claws, maple logs, cronuts, ones topped with cereals; donuts topped with marshmallows; donuts topped with crumble; double choc, triple choc and quadruple choc donuts!

"You folks ordered a lot of donuts," The driver said with a big smile, happy to have the business.

"Yes, well…" Stanley stammered, unsure of how to explain what was going on.

"They're here!" yelled a volunteer. In no time at all, a chain formed of people taking boxes and boxes of sugar and deep-fried pastry into the convention hall.

The unfortunate coincidence of the day was that a weight-watch convention was happening in the hall next door to the secret convention. As the donuts crossed through the foyer, the people attending the other convention had to watch sweet, delicious, colourful, scrumptious delicacies float right past their noses. There were many tears and sobs throughout the rest of the day.

Stanley received the final box from the driver. "Thank you, have a good day."

The driver jumped into the cabin. "Mate, that's just the first load. Five more to go."

If you imagined how big the pile of donuts was at the meeting, think of a pile 5 times that size. Volunteers laid down a tarp in the corner of the hall, near the stage, and began piling the donuts up. The pile of sweets grew bigger and bigger until a tall ladder was pulled out to continue the

process. When there was simply no room to add more donuts under the convention centre roof, the leftovers were
stacked behind the pile, a dozen boxes high.

As the secret convention attendees from across the city
and suburbs entered the hall, they stared in amazement at
the holey wonder. But no one said a thing about it. After
staring at it for a moment, the attendees would pretend like
there was nothing there.

I believe the point of the donut pile was to make it ir-
resistible to talk about. Anyone weak-willed and unaware
of the secret society's beliefs would immediately mention
them.

A man in an electrician's uniform walked into the hall
from a back entrance, avoiding the registration desk. He
happened to come alongside Paxton the Pacifist.

"Wow. Are we allowed to take a donut?" the electrician
asked.

Paxton looked the man up and down. "No. Go away."

The electrician left the hall, turning back at the last moment to take another glimpse at the sugary glory.

By the time the last registered attendee had arrived, the
donut pile was complete and people began walking past
and taking a handful, ready to sit and listen to the convention's opening address. Stanley took a raspberry-jam
donut and took a seat in the front row with the rest of the
volunteers. There were about 30 Tayel Tower residents in
attendance (far more than were at the meeting), many of
them helping as fellow volunteers, as well as about 350 other attendees. The environment was alive and people were
buzzing with excitement, partly aided by the sugar.

Loud music pumped over the speaker system. The music wasn't heavy-rock, inspirational funk or groovy hits like you would expect at a conference; it was classical waltz of Strauss and Tchaikovsky. Many of the attendees raised their eyebrows in surprise at the soundtrack choice. Paxton the Pacifist was swaying back and forth in time with the violins.

As soon as the time was 9 am, the conference began. The music was cut mid-song.

"Sit down!" yelled Paxton the Pacifist into his microphone from the stage. The attendees silently found their seats.

The lights dimmed and a projector lit up, casting a giant map of the earth on the screen.

"This… is a map of the earth," Paxton commentated dramatically. "It is the home to 7 billion people. It is home to even more trees and ants and pumpkins. We like earth."

There were murmurs of agreement from those sitting around Stanley. The slide changed to show a picture of a city.

"This… is a city. Many people live in a city. People work and play in cities. It is home to less trees, less ants but the same number of pumpkins. Cities are good for growth. Cities are good for industries. Cities are good for business."

"Here, here!" said an attendee near the back. Stanley was utterly confused as to the point of this opening speech.

A spotlight from somewhere high above shined on Paxton. "Welcome, my friends, to the 2nd annual secret society convention."

The crowd cheered and applauded.

"My name is Paxton Evans, and I am your host for today. Today we are talking music, love, life, purpose, elbows, and business. At the end of the day, we may leave this convention having achieved no purpose; getting no closer to knowing who we are. At the end of the day, we may leave having united ourselves as a superpower with more purpose than a herd of lions ordering a pizza. But either way, we will progress our understanding of what it means to be… a secret society."

The crowd cheered and whooped. Stanley realised Mandy was spot on; this secret society was formed solely to find a purpose. The joy and enthusiasm of the crowd was infectious. Stanley gave a couple of claps.

"For this opening discussion, we want to discuss point two of our beliefs," Paxton said. There was a mix of groans and cheers from the audience. "Can anyone yell out point two?" Paxton asked.

"The earth is flat," a lady yelled cynically.

"Ah, no," Paxton said, shaking his head. "Point two is 'the earth is probably flat'. You may have missed it, but 'probably' was inserted at the end of last year's conference.

"Now, to discuss this point, I did have a member of the Amateur Geographer's Society lined up, however, they just called and said they read the directions wrong and are now in Brazil. Instead, I have lined up someone who is a member of our secret society. He is only a new member, but full of great knowledge. Stanley?"

Stanley, comfortably leaning back in his chair, looked up at Paxton, not understanding. Was he meant to introduce this member? Paxton looked down at him in anticipation. The crowd all looked at Stanley in anticipation.

It dawned on Stanley; Paxton wanted him to talk about whether the earth was flat.

"Come on Stanley," Paxton said. "Everyone give Stanley a hand as he gets up here."

The crowd cheered. Stanley had no way to escape. The awkwardness of remaining seated was far worse than getting up on stage. Stanley rose from his chair and walked up the steps onto the stage. A soundman handed Stanley a microphone. Stanley gave Paxton a look of panic and confusion.

"Stanley here is a business consultant," Paxton introduced. "Can you tell us what a business consultant does?"

Stanley raised the microphone right up to his mouth. His voice boomed loud and deep through the hall. "I consultant, I mean consult, businesses. Help them with strategies and stuff."

"Great," Paxton said. "And, can you tell us, regarding point 2, do you think the earth is flat or round?"

Stanley once again put the microphone right to his mouth. "Round."

The crowd gave their assortment of 'boos' and cheers at the answer. With that, Paxton left the stage without saying another word and sat in the seat where Stanley had been. Stanley was left alone and vulnerable and up on the stage, armed only with a microphone and his brain. Was this all just a horrible prank? Was Paxton evil like a hamster? Or maybe Paxton was forgetful and thought he had asked Stanley to join the group, and to help at the convention, and to speak at the convention.

After a good half-a-minute of awkward silence, the house lights came on. Stanley looked out over the crowd of expectant faces. He certainly wasn't nervous about public speaking; he had taken classes on communication at university and part of his job was giving pitches and speeches to his business clients. Now seemed a perfect opportunity to answer a question: were these people genuinely curious, or completely crazy?

"With a show of hands, who here thinks the earth is flat?" Stanley asked.

Only three people put their hands in the air: Paxton the Pacifist, another man who Stanley had never seen before, and Patrick the Psychiatrist.

"Alternatively, who thinks the earth is round?"

Most of the audience raised their hands.

"And who is undecided?"

A handful of people timidly raised their hands.

"Okay. We have three sides: people who think the earth is round, others who think it is flat, and some undecideds. Because those that believe the earth is flat are a minority, could you three that raised your hands join me up here?"

Paxton, Dr Patrick and the other man made their way onto the stage and stood next to Stanley. The stranger was the first in line.

"Sir, I don't believe we have met, what is your name?" Stanley asked.

"Last name: Yardley. First name: Oscar," the man replied.

"Oscar," Stanley began. "What evidence could you present in favour of the earth being flat?"

Oscar, a man in his late fifties, received the microphone from Stanley.

"Well, you see, I don't know a hundred per cent if the earth is flat or round, because I've never been into space, so I can't see it. Therefore, I believe that the earth is probably flat unless proven otherwise."

A lady in the audience stood up. "The mere fact that you are standing on this earth means it must be round because of gravitational pull," she called out.

"Yes," Oscar replied. "But the earth could be a table top. Gravity would still work on a tabletop."

Stanley moved to Patrick the Psychiatrist next. "Patrick, isn't it?"

"That is correct," said Dr Patrick standing tall and confidently.

"What is your argument for the earth being probably flat?"

"Just is, I think," Dr Patrick replied haughtily.

Stanley was a little surprised by the lack of thought. "You are a graduate of medical school, a scientist in your own right, and, not to be rude, you think the earth is flat because it 'just is'?"

Dr Patrick shrugged his shoulder, unoffended.

Paige the Psychologist stood up from the front row. She rolled her eyes. "He just says he thinks the earth is flat because I think the earth is round."

Dr Patrick lit up. "Well, if a psychologist thinks the earth is round, then I need to get a second opinion! Where did you learn about the earth? In a cute little self-help book with a picture of a dentist's dream on the front?"

"You are so immature, Patrick. Maybe you should take a spoonful of your own medicine to help with your own problems!"

"Oh, so you agree that medicine might be good then?"

"Most of your 'medicines', as you call them, are just sugar!" Dr Paige exclaimed.

"No, they're not! And a spoonful of sugar helps the medicine go down!"

"The medicine go down?"

"The medicine go down!"

I won't lie, their argument at this point had turned into using ugly, obscene, offensive, long medical terms that I can't remember too clearly. But they seemed to understand their conversation and the correct rebuttals to argue.

After a good minute of them fighting and shouting across the hall, the audience began to silently get up and head over to the donut mountain, grabbing a hand full of treats before silently returning to their seats. Even Oliver, Paxton and Stanley walked off stage and grabbed some round pastries before resuming their positions on stage.

Stanley was licking his fingers of sugar and cinnamon as the fight seemed to draw to a close.

"...and surely even you can see that all those therapy hours are just for profits," Patrick argued.

"Things take time; quick fixes don't last. Medicine is a quick fix, therapy gives lasting results."

"What do you mean..."

Stanley was mistaken; the fight was not drawing to a close. "And, we'll need to leave it there," Stanley said into his microphone. There was no response from the pair.

Paxton used his own microphone. "Finish!" he yelled. Dr Paige stopped mid-sentence, a little shocked.

Paxton took a deep breath. "You two need to give each other a hug, get over your differences, go grab a jam donut and..."

The gasps were audible. Paxton also gasped, when he realised what he had just said. He had mentioned the donuts. Even Stanley was in shock and didn't know what to do. Nobody knew what to do.

After at least twenty long seconds, Stanley said into his microphone "And why do you think the earth is flat, Paxton?"

And it was in that moment, as Stanley stood on stage at a secret society conference, asking a man why he thought the earth was flat, near a donut mountain so large the tops were burning under the lights, to an audience who all held donuts in their hands and a hate of saxophones in their hearts, having just pretended that mentioning donuts was equivalent of an unmentionable sin, that Stanley realised he had become deeply involved with the people of Tayel Tower; exactly what he hadn't wanted to do.

Wray Wrigley's

TAYEL TOWER

Book 3

WHY BIRDS FLY INTO WINDOWS

CHAPTER ONE

A VERY PRETTY WALL

Looking out the window from the ninth floor of Tayel Tower was like looking upon an artwork. Not a very good artwork, the piece showed limited imagination, but the detail was fantastic. In the mornings, Stanley liked to stand and look out his kitchen window to take the world in. When he was on street level he wasn't too fond of the city. He felt out of place, an impostor; as if he was a child dressed up as an adult. But from up high in his apartment, the city could be put into perspective. Everyone was just like him; trying to make their way in their world, discover who they were, earn a promotion, find love, work out what to have for breakfast. Looking down upon the city from his apartment in the mornings, Stanley felt that everything could be okay that day.

On a certain morning mere weeks after he moved in, he finished gazing out the window, picked up his work bag and headed out to the elevator. The elevator doors slid open and there stood Ernest the Elevator Operator.

"Good Morning, Mr Stanley," Ernest said, giving half a smile.

"Morning, Ernest," Stanley replied. "Ground floor please". The elevator began its slow descent. The elevator in Tayel Tower was incredibly inconsistent in its speed between floors. This was often the reason people could have such long conversations in it. Some argued that even the stairs were quicker. Ernest didn't like those people. He had said on a number of occasions to Stanley that those who prefer the stairs obviously had something sinister to hide.

"How did you sleep, Mr Stanley?" Ernest asked.

"Fine, I guess," Stanley answered, wondering whether that was too personal a question. He decided it probably wasn't. "How did you sleep, Ernest?"

"I slept like a teddy bear!" Ernest exclaimed.

"And… do teddy bears normally have a good or bad night's sleep?" Stanley joked.

"I would presume most teddy bears have a good night's sleep, wouldn't you? But I feel like some teddy bears would not get a good night's sleep, being squished and all. I slept badly; I slept like a teddy bear being squished," Ernest complained.

"Well that's too bad," Stanley said empathetically but also wondering if Ernest purposely made the elevator slow so that he could have a decent conversation with the passengers.

"Do you know why I didn't get a good night's sleep?" Ernest asked.

"Why?"

"Arnold the Artist from Room 202 is why. All night I had to take him up and down, up and down. I asked him where he was going at such strange hours, and he told me that he could not sleep!"

"Well, I'm sorry to hear that, for the both of you."

Stanley had only previously had brief interactions with Arnold the Artist, who was by all admissions a brilliant, artistic genius. But as many brilliant, artistic geniuses are, Arnold had little time for conversation with those he considered inferior and was often short in conversation.

The elevator stopped at the 5th floor. Mandy the Midwife hopped on board with her smile that made Stanley's heart warm.

"Good morning, Miss Mandy," Ernest exclaimed, with three-quarters of a smile.

"Good morning, Ernest! Ground floor, please. Good morning, Stanley."

"Good morning, Mandy," Stanley replied, giving a smile in return. If only the amount of 'good morning' wishes given in an elevator could have influenced how that morning was to unfold.

"How did you sleep, Miss Mandy?" Ernest asked.

Mandy looked at the top of the elevator as she tried to recall how she slept. "Alright, if not excellent, I believe, Ernest. How did you sleep?"

"Like a teddy bear!" Ernest exclaimed.

"Oh no! I'm sorry to hear that," Mandy said softly. Stanley wondered how Mandy knew 'slept like a teddy bear' was bad.

"What kept you up?" she asked.

"Arnold the Artist from Room 202 kept me up all night, wanting to go up and down, up and down. I asked him what he was doing in the middle of the night, and he insisted he couldn't sleep!"

Mandy the Midwife expressed a mix of care and anger.

"Well, that's just unfair. You should take the morning off after peak traffic and take a nice long nap!"

Ernest the Elevator Operator suddenly stood up straight and proud. "No thank you, Miss Mandy. It is my duty as elevator operator of this building to service customers at any time of day or night, except for between 5 and 7 pm on Thursday nights when I play Yahtzee, and International Hairy Llama Appreciation day. It's in my work contract."

"International what?" Stanley asked.

The elevator arrived at the lobby and the doors slid open with a 'ding'. Stanley and Mandy took a step out into the spacious building lobby, and would have stepped further, but were blocked by around a dozen of their neighbours, all standing in front of the elevator, but with no intentions of using the carriage. The neighbours were, however, looking up. Dozens of pairs of eyes stared above the elevator. Stanley and Mandy, curious as to what these people were seeing, turned around and looked up also.

"That really is a nice piece of wall," Stanley said sarcastically, looking up at the empty patch of wall above the elevator.

"Oh, the painting's gone," Mandy explained with wide eyes.

"The painting?" Stanley asked.

Leonard the Lemon Seller glanced down from the wall to Stanley. "Don't you remember, Stanley? The giant painting of the sky that used to hang up there?"

Stanley was confused. "Wait. That was a painting? I always thought that was a window..." As he said it, he realised it couldn't be a window to the outside. This patch of wall was in front of an elevator shaft.

Rosemary the Retired spoke from amongst the small crowd, but her big, sad eyes never left the wall. "Everyone thought it was a window when they first glanced at it. Even birds thought it was an open window. Many a bird has flown into the painting over the years. I'd say at least twenty-three."

"Twenty-three birds? How are there so many birds getting into the lobby?" Stanley asked.

"What's everyone looking at?" a man's voice from the back of the crowd asked. Stanley looked over and saw Jarvis the Jobless standing with a pigeon on his shoulder. The pigeon looked confused, as pigeons often do. It cooed. The whole crowd turned around in anger and annoyance.

"Jarvis, get that bird out of here!!" They all cried.

Jarvis turned and sulked off, talking to his pigeon as he went. "Come along, John Silver Twenty-four."

The crowd all turned again and stared up at the blank wall where a painting once hung.

Stanley looked at his watch, "Well, I must be off. Have a good day everyone."

He signalled for Mandy to lead the way, but she didn't budge. "Don't you understand?" she asked.

Stanley paused. "I honestly can't say I do."

"That painting, of the sky, was called 'Sky' and was painted by Jacques Perot. Have you heard of Jacques Perot before?"

Stanley shook his head. Mandy looked a little shocked, "Perot was world famous! He has works in The Louvre, the New York Metropolitan Museum of Art, and he lived in this very building in the early 20th century. He painted this work exclusively for Tayel Tower, but no one outside the residents and staff of Tayel Tower knows about it, and we don't want anyone to know about it, otherwise, it could get stolen. It's potentially worth millions of dollars!"

"Or even worse," Rosemary the Retired piped up. "People may want to come and see it!"

"So everyone thinks this painting has been stolen?" Stanley asked.

Everyone nodded their heads.

"It's probably just been taken down to be cleaned or restored," Stanley suggested. "Couldn't we ask Damien the Doorman? Surely he'd know."

Damien the Doorman, a short fellow, voiced up from amongst the crowd. "Nothing was scheduled, Mr Stanley."

Stanley was a little surprised, but time was getting on and he needed to be at work. "Ah, well, do let me know what happens." He began walking to the front door when a police car pulled up outside. Two lieutenants stepped out of their car and came quickly into the building. They pointed to Stanley. "Stay here please," one of the lieutenants said.

"I'm going to be late for work," Stanley said.

"I'm sorry, sir, but there has been a call about an alleged theft. No one leaves."

Stanley gave a big sigh, and let his bag swing from his shoulder to hang at his side. Another police car pulled up with more officers. Stanley pulled out his phone and called the office of RKJO consultancy. He really hoped his boss, Richard Richardson, wasn't in yet, to avoid the need for any awkward conversations. He was still working to get into Richardson's good books and being late wasn't 'good books' worthy. Richardson's secretary answered.

Stanley exhaled. "Hello, this is Stanley…I'm going to be late into work today, there has been a robbery at my apartment building and the police aren't letting anyone leave… I'm not sure, maybe 10 am?… Thank you."

Stanley walked back over to the crowd. The police had created a perimeter around the elevator entrance. Damien the Doorman directed an officer to where a ladder was stored in the maintenance closet.

"Are robberies a common occurrence here?" Stanley asked Mandy.

Mandy shook her head. "Not that I know of; not since I've been here. Rosemary, does Tayel Tower have a history of theft?"

Rosemary the Retired turned as if she had seen a ghost. "Someone stole my appendix, but I think it was Leah the Librarian."

"That was me that took your appendix, Rosemary," Devon the Doctor said. "But you said I could have it, remember?"

Rosemary thought long and hard. "I would like it back please."

Devon rolled his eyes and reached into his bag, pulling out The Knitter's Appendix, a thick book, and gave it back to the woman.

"I didn't know you knit," Mandy said.

Devon nodded his head. "If you can sew a major artery closed, you can certainly crochet a scarf."

"So robberies are rare, but everyone this one must have been an inside job?"

Rosemary nodded. "No one else knew the painting had any value."

'Great,' thought Stanley. 'Now I need to watch out not just for neighbours who might be crazy, but also some who may be thieves.'

By his own instinct, he felt like he could trust Mandy the Midwife. Devon the Doctor also seemed to be trustworthy, and Rosemary wouldn't have been able to make it up a ladder to take the painting down. Stanley lowered his voice. "Do any of you suspect anyone?"

Mandy gave a knowing glance to Devon. Devon gave a knowing glance back. Rosemary just came out with it. "Vincent the Villain."

Stanley couldn't believe what she said. "Vincent the Villain? Is 'villain' his occupation?"

"No, of course not," Mandy said. "He actually works as a shampoo scent tester, but trust me when I say; he's a villain."

Just then, as if on cue, the stairwell door opened and out stepped a man. This man was in his early 30's, and walked confidently, almost haughtily, through the lobby. But that wasn't the most interesting thing about this man. This man had the most luscious, silky, shiny, voluminous hair one could imagine, and a nose with such size that it would make a plastic surgeon faint. Stanley immediately guessed who this was by the occupation. Vincent the Villain saw the crowd gathered in the lobby and came over. A couple of people, seeing Vincent approach, shuffled away. "What's happening?" Vincent asked.

"Have a guess," Damien the Doorman said, accusatorily.

"The painting's gone," Vincent observed, seemingly unconcerned.

"Yes, it is," Damien the Doorman said. "And do you know where it is?"

"No. Should I?" Vincent replied. Everyone in the lobby silently stared at him.

"I don't have it," he said. "What possible use would I have for a stupid painting of sky?"

"You might want to sell it!" Len the Lemon Seller said.

"I don't need money. I promise you people; I don't have the painting. If I did have it, I would burn it. I would burn the painting and throw it into a river. I would then collect the burnt, wet painting, go to a laundromat, and throw the painting in with a stranger's load of washing. But I promise you, and believe me or not, I don't have your painting."

Vincent began leaving the building.

"You can't leave, sir!" a police officer said.

Vincent stopped and turned. "Officer: Do you have a warrant to arrest me?"

"No," the officer said sheepishly.

"Then I am going to go. If for some reason you suspect me of having anything to do with the painting, you will find me at the park, where I will be telling the mums at the kids swimming pool about the recent alligator sightings."

And Vincent left without being hindered further.

Stanley approached the nearest officer. "Does that mean I can leave as well? I really need to get to work."

"Do you have any information that could help us?" The officer asked, a little shaken by Vincent the Villain's abruptness.

Stanley shook his head. "Sorry, no."

The officer said he was free to leave.

****

There were no police to be seen when Stanley arrived home from work that evening. As he entered Tayel Tower, he looked above the elevator. The painting was still not there.

"Good evening, Mr Stanley," Damien the Doorman said from behind his desk.

"Good evening, Damien. Any news on the painting?"

"The police said the painting is bound to turn up within a year either on the black market or online."

Len the Lemon Seller, also on his way home from work, overheard. "Within a year?! Goodness gracious, that's a long time to have a blank piece of wall in the lobby."

Damien the Doorman shrugged his shoulders. "What else can we do but wait?"

"Well, there's a chance that the painting could be found next week or even tomorrow!" Stanley said optimistically.

"No chance of that," a voice called out from the lobby sitting area. It belonged to Arnold the Artist. "When a painting is stolen, the thief will keep it hidden for a while until everyone forgets about it. Then they will sell it on the black market to someone who will also keep it hidden for a while, who will sell it on, and so on and so on until it has had dozens of owners before some rich old pharmacist dies in a decade's time, and the painting ends up in an estate sale."

"That's a pretty specific scenario," Stanley enquired suspiciously. Arnold the Artist put his newspaper down. "I know how it works because it happened to me."

"Wait a minute," Stanley said. "What were you doing last night, Arnold? Ernest the Elevator Operator told me you were up all night, last night, going from the lobby to your room and back again."

"Are you accusing me of something?" Arnold challenged.

"Should I be?" Stanley asked, adrenaline rushing through his body. He wasn't normally the confrontational type, but it seemed like a good assumption to make. Arnold the Artist stood up calmly, but slowly boiled to anger as he talked. "I, Arnold Duthie, was an apprentice to Jacques Perot for over seven years—until the day he died! How dare you accuse me of stealing my master's painting!" Arnold the Artist slammed his newspaper down on the coffee table.

Stanley swallowed nervously, clearly inexperienced in confrontation. "My apologies, Arnold."

There was an awkward silence in the lobby. The dozen or so present, going about their evening duties, had paused to witness the heated exchange. Leah the Librarian, apparently undeterred by the outburst, yelled. "Hey, Arnold. Why don't you paint us a new painting we could hang on the wall until the old one is found?"

This vote of confidence appeared to calm Arnold down. "Well, I guess I—"

"Wait, why does he get to be the one to paint the new picture?" Mooney the Millionaire asked.

"Because Arnold's an 'Ar-tist'," Leah the Librarian enunciated.

"So what? I've dabbled in oil paints. Why can't I paint the replacement?" Mooney challenged proudly, wiping his nose with a ten-dollar bill.

"Oh, I've done some lovely paintings myself in my spare time. Would anyone like to see them?" added Elaine the Event Planner.

"Hey, let's have a competition!" Mooney suggested.

There were murmurs of agreement from around the room. Arnold looked around at his neighbours in disgust. "Wait, you would rather hang a painting done by an amateur than one done by a professional like myself?"

"I guess you'll have to do a better job and prove your abilities." Damien the Doorman said, not realising what an offensive challenge this was. Artists tend to be very proud people, and Arnold was no exception. His face turned red, his knuckles turned white. "Fine," is all he said, and he stormed away into the stairwell.

Stanley looked at Mandy the Midwife who had entered the lobby in time to hear about the art competition. She had a big grin on her face. "An art competition! This is going to be fantastic!"

"Do you paint?" Stanley asked her. She shook her head. "Not since I was at school! But this will be fun!! Will you do it with me?"

"You mean a painting, together?" Stanley asked.

"Sure! Why not?" Mandy said with a grin.

Stanley didn't particularly like art. He didn't hate art, he could appreciate the fine work of a painter or sculptor, but he had no experience with being an artist himself. Even in kindergarten when the kids were painting pictures, Stanley would be in the sandpit, delegating sand castle construction duties like a foreman. But now, with Mandy suggesting they do a painting together, Stanley suddenly felt very interested in art.

"Let's do it," Stanley said, smiling back. "Let's do this art competition!"

CHAPTER TWO
THE ART COMPETITION

If a passer-by was to enter Tayel Tower the following night, they would have thought they had happened upon a community art class. Spotted around the Tayel Tower lobby was 26 canvases and 27 'artists', all competing for the coveted trophy of having their piece of art hanging in the foyer above the elevator for all to see. There were the old ladies, Rosemary the Retired and Leah the Librarian, with their equally old looking brushes and art smocks; there were Stanley and Mandy sitting together with their brand-new art supplies and a big, clean white canvas. The business consultant and midwife were having a lively discussion full of laughs about whether they should paint a picture of a fluffy white duck or a giant donut, even though neither believed they could paint anything at all. Arnold the Artist looked at the couple with contempt. Positioned closest to the elevator, Arnold had his expensive oil-paints neatly laid out, his canvas primed with white paint and his paint brushes, handcrafted from the hairs of the finest hogs in Italy by women who were possibly the descendants of Leonardo da Vinci, sorted by size in pots.

Damien the Doorman shakily stood on a chair (as he was an older gentleman who did most things shakily) and addressed the crowd of artists.

"Well, it is now 7:30, so it is time to get started. There is a two-hour time limit, to create an even playing field for all artists. Please remember not to include any nudity or profanity in your pieces."

Jarvis the Jobless, standing behind his canvas, raised his hand.

"Yes, Jarvis?"

"Is a bird without clothing considered nude?"

Damien the Doorman stared at the man with a blank expression. "I'm not sure."

The doorman turned to the building's resident artist. "Arnold, is painting a bird that has no clothes on considered a nude painting?"

Arnold the Artist rolled his eyes. "Yes," he replied. The sarcasm was lost upon the doorman and Jarvis. Jarvis gave a deep sigh, got up from his chair and walked briskly up the stairwell.

Damien the Doorman looked at his watch, "And, you may begin."

Some people began drawing on their canvas with pencils; others began painting straight away; others still just stood in front of their canvases, attempting to envision what their respective masterpieces would be.

"So, have we decided on donuts?" Stanley asked. "A big chocolate iced donut with colourful sprinkles? I think a lot of residents would appreciate it." For some reason, donuts had been at the forefront of Stanley's mind a lot recently.

"But can't you just imagine a cute duck sitting above

the elevator, smiling at everyone that passes under him?" Mandy suggested with her gorgeous smile.

Stanley laughed. "Do you know how to paint or draw a duck?"

"Do you know how to paint a donut?"

"Well, yes. It's a circle with another circle in the middle."

Mandy grabbed Stanley's arm in excitement. "What if we paint a duck eating a donut?!"

"You really want a duck in this painting, don't you?" Stanley laughed, picking up his pencil and attempting to draw the scene of a duck eating a donut. When he had finished his drawing, it was really an unfortunate sight. The sketch of a duck Stanley's hand produced had a few deformities that only a parent could love. The duck's father appeared to have been a giraffe, producing a son with a long, stretched neck, and the duck's mother appeared to have been a rhinoceros, producing a son with thick, tree-trunk-like legs. The donut looked good though.

The stairwell doors flung open and Jarvis the Jobless ran through the maze of canvases carrying a miniature suit of armour. He clothed John Silver 26, a pigeon, in the suit of armour and quickly began his painting of the non-nude bird (although the bird still did not possess pants, and was therefore unlikely to be accepted into some restaurants).

Arnold the Artist picked up his pencil and began drawing an outline, but his pencil never touched the canvas. Some of the artists standing behind Arnold saw this strange action and wondered if they were doing it wrong. They began imitating the professional, holding their pencils in the air, but not drawing on their canvases. Arnold the Artist took his pencil away from the canvas and stared at it as if he could see the finished outline in the emptiness in front of him. After being deep in thought for a good minute, he shook his head and took the blank canvas off the easel, replacing it with another blank canvas he had sitting with his art supplies. The artists behind him looked at each other and rubbed out their invisible pencil lines.

Arnold the Artist picked up a tube of crimson red paint and squeezed a dollop onto his mixing board. He added a dollop of deep blue, vermillion, black, and white paint to his mixing board. The artists behind him with mixing boards of their own did the same. Graeme the Gardener didn't have a mixing board and so just used a magazine that was sitting on a lobby coffee table nearby.

Arnold the Artist picked up one of his dozens of paint brushes, a medium sized one, and held it as if it was a magic wand. He dipped the brush into the black paint. The amateur artists did the same, watching with deep fascination the apparent 'professional' way to paint a picture. Arnold the Artist's paintbrush hovered above his canvas, not moving an inch. The five amateurs behind him stood in the same position with aggressive anticipation. The professional's paintbrush moved a little to the left, so did the five behind him. Suddenly, the professional's paintbrush began moving in a flurry over the canvas, applying paint here and there. The artists behind him began frantically trying to mimic the movements, almost scared of what their hands were doing; Graeme the Gardner was going so quickly he stabbed his brush straight through the canvas. "Damnit," he yelled.

Stanley and Mandy mutually agreed that Stanley's duck drawing was an insult to nature, so he rubbed it out and

Mandy had a turn. She even surprised herself with her interpretation of a duck that she produced. It certainly wasn't going to win the 'Miss Duck' award, but if a real duck was to see it, he would think to himself 'Yep, that's a duck'. Similar to if a duck attempted to paint a human; the painting would not win the Pulitzer prize, but if a human was to see it, he'd acknowledge the painting had attributes that make it recognisable as a painting of a human.

They finished their pencil outline and moved onto painting. Stanley began painting the donut light brown, while Mandy painted the duck bright yellow.

"How was work today?" Stanley asked as they worked at their canvas.

"Good, thank you. A little tiring, but tiring in a good way," Mandy answered with a smile.

"Did anyone give birth today?"

"Yes. There were two births, in fact. A boy around 10:30 this morning and a girl at three."

"That's nice. What were their names?"

"I believe the boy was Karl, and the girl was Janet."

"Karl's a good name," Stanley said as he started mixing together whites and brightly coloured paints, ready to make sprinkles for the donut.

"Yes, I don't mind the name Karl," Mandy agreed. "What would you name your son if you had one, one day?"

Stanley thought about this. "I would name my son 'Heyou'. That way I would never be able to forget his name. I could just say 'Hey-you! Come over here'."

Mandy laughed. Stanley liked Mandy's laugh.

"What about you?" he asked. "What would you name your son?"

Leah the Librarian's ears pricked up.

"Rosemary," Leah said in what was a poor excuse for a whisper. "Hey, Rosemary!"

"What?" replied Rosemary the Retired, annoyed that her concentration was being distracted from her painting of a deaf man.

"Did you hear what Stanley just asked Mandy the Midwife?" Leah asked.

"No, what?"

"Stanley just asked Mandy the Midwife what she would name her son!"

Rosemary dropped her paintbrush. "What?"

Leah the Librarian nodded her head. "Yes! Mandy the Midwife is pregnant!"

Both old ladies were equally shocked and disgusted. Rosemary shook her head. "Why, I never thought Mandy was that kind of person. She's a midwife as well! She should know all about…that!"

"Who's pregnant?" asked Len the Lemon Seller.

"Mandy the Midwife!" Rosemary replied in a very loud whisper.

Len the Lemon Seller couldn't believe what he was hearing. "What? Mandy the Midwife pregnant? But she's a midwife!"

"Did you say Mandy the Midwife is pregnant?" Belinda the Beautician asked. Belinda loved to gossip.

Len the Lemon Seller shushed her. "Don't be so loud! It's not my news to tell."

"What's the news?" another asked, and on and on the news travelled.

Mandy finished painting the duck. It turned out to be

quite a cute duck, very fluffy and yellow with a toothy smile on its face. Stanley's donut turned out just as one would expect a painted donut to look. It certainly wasn't going to win a 'Miss Donut' award, but if a real donut was to see it, he would think to himself 'Yep, that's a donut'. Similar to if a donut attempted to paint a human; the painting would not win the Pulitzer prize, but if a human was to see it, he'd acknowledge the painting had attributes that make it recognisable as a painting of a human.

Stanley stood back and looked at their work. "I think our painting is coming along very nicely!"

"It is definitely a duck and a donut!" Mandy laughed. She felt a hand on her shoulder and turned to see Mooney the Millionaire sporting a very forced smile.

"Congratulations, Mandy," Mooney said.

"Oh, thank you," Mandy smiled back. Mooney the Millionaire nodded his head, deep in thought and walked away. She raised her eyebrows in surprise. "Well, I guess someone else likes our painting as well."

Rosemary the Retired wobbled over to Stanley and Mandy's canvas and held her arms open for a hug. Mandy was confused but gave the older lady a hug anyway.

"It's just so wonderful!" Rosemary said in a whisper.

"Really, you think so?" Mandy asked.

"Oh, yes, I tell you, you never forget your first! And Stanley, I assume this is your first also?"

Stanley looked at the canvas. "Well, yes I think it is. Although I might have made one in high school. I can hardly remember what I did in high-school."

Rosemary the Retired gave a look that contained a buffet assortment of disgust, shock, bewilderment, and concern. She gave a very, very forced smile and returned to her canvas.

Stanley and Mandy looked at each other proudly.

"I think we might be onto a winner!" Stanley said.

At long last, the allotted two hours were up. Damien the Doorman stood on his chair with his watch held high. "... three, two, one and that's time! Everyone put your brushes down. Jarvis, put your paintbrush down. Take it out of your hands and put it on your easel. No, Jarvis! You cannot continue by painting with your fingers! Jarvis, you cannot use any part of your body to paint! Yes, your nose is part of your body!"

The 24 completed paintings were lined up along the wall, and the artists stood back to admire their works. Arnold the Artist was outraged. Damien the Doorman looked at a group of half a dozen paintings that all looked remarkably similar. "Hmm, I'm not sure about this lot here. It looks like you all just copied each other."

Arnold the Artist had painted a beautiful beach scene complete with palm trees, a big blue ocean, an inviting golden, sandy beach, and a little thatched-roof beach cottage in the corner. The other similar paintings were ok looking beach scenes, complete with trees of an unknown species, a big flat blue ocean, a dangerous quick-sand looking beach and little remotely square objects that could resemble a beach cottage if your head was turned 23 degrees to the left and your eyes were shut.

Arnold the Artist looked at the artists that had been behind him. "You all tried to copy me!" He accused. They amateurs avoided eye contact.

Damien the Doorman picked up one of the crude

beaches. "Is this one yours, Arnold?"

"No, that's not mine! My painting is this one. The one that is actually recognisable as a beautiful Spanish beach scene."

"Oh, well, it's very good. All of you that worked together on the beach scenes have done a really great job!"

Arnold the Artist looked angrier than a French frog.

Damien moved along to the next painting. It was a square picture of a mouse sitting in a chair at a long wooden table, eating a bowl of birdseed.

"Oh, I like this one. Who did this?" Damien the Doorman asked.

"That would be mine," Jarvis the Jobless said with his chest puffed up.

"I thought you were going to be painting your pigeon wearing a suit of armour," Damien replied.

Jarvis nodded his head. "That was the plan, but John Silver 26 didn't like the plan and flew away. So I thought to myself 'who else would be eating birdseed?' Why another bird of course! So I went outside and tried to catch another bird, but they were too quick! It was almost like they knew I was coming. I was close to giving up when I saw a mouse run by! I chased the mouse down the street and caught it after I bribed it with the promise of cheese. Whether the mouse understood this bribe or not is unclear, but I think it did because it posed for me without giving a single complaint."

Everyone stared at Jarvis with blank expressions on their faces. Damien the Doorman tried to think of more praise to give to the picture, but couldn't, so just moved along. He went through the paintings one by one. There were watercolour paintings of gardens, oil paintings of elephants, acrylic paintings of hill-side houses and gouache paintings of colonial ships. The Doorman arrived at the final picture.

"Oh, this is an interesting piece," he said, tilting his head to look at the completed painting of a duck and a donut. "Who did this?"

Stanley raised his hand a little and quickly put it down again. "Mandy and I did the painting."

Damien held the painting at a distance in outstretched arms. "Well, it's a very interesting piece, Stanley and Mandy. Was this inspired by any cravings you two might be having?"

The rest of the crowd laughed quietly. Stanley and Mandy looked at each other, confused by the joke.

"And such a lovely, cute little duck," Damien continued. "I don't know about the rest of you, but I think that this painting should be the one to hang in our lobby. It represents what we are: a family."

There were cries of agreements and nods of the head among the crowd.

"You can't be serious." Arnold the Artist's gradually grew louder and louder. "You really want to hang a picture of a duck and a donut in our building's lobby for us to have to look at every day? For guests to see when they come? It has no class; the painting technique is laughable; there are clearly white spots and the shadows are inaccurate!" By this point, Arnold's face was bright scarlet. The crowd was, on the whole, a little shocked and upset by the outburst.

"We weren't painting it with the idea of it actually hang up in the lobby," Mandy said quietly, feeling insulted. "We were just having fun."

Stanley also felt insulted but didn't say anything to the egotistical artist. Damien the Doorman was the only one that appeared un-phased by the outburst.

"Thank you for that professional evaluation, Arnold, but I think we might decide with a democratic vote."

The vote results are what could be expected when one of the competitors was an egotistical hot-head. One vote for Arnold the Artist's beach scene (from Arnold), one vote for Jarvis the Jobless' mouse scene (the man rightfully and fairly liked his own art), and the rest of the votes went to a painting of a duck and a donut that had no class, white spots, and inaccurate shadows. And yet everyone loved it when Damien shakily climbed up the ladder and hung it above the elevator for all to see.

CHAPTER THREE
IT'S BACK

The next morning, Stanley was woken by his alarm. He was normally awake before his alarm, however, last night was more eventful than what would usually take place on a weeknight and he had gone to bed quite late. Mug of tea in hand, he stood at his window, looking out at the cityscape that lay before him. He couldn't help but feel more connected to Tayel Tower than what he had the previous morning. Something he had created now hung in the lobby. And he had created it with a good friend he had met at the apartment tower.

He got his things ready for the day, packed his bag, and headed to the elevator.

"Good morning, Mr Stanley," Ernest the Elevator Operator said when the doors slid open.

"Good morning, Ernest. Ground floor please."

The elevator began its descent. Ernest looked positively bursting to say something. "Did you hear the news?" he asked.

"What news?" Stanley asked.

"It's back!" Ernest said excitedly.

"What's back?"

"The painting of sky from the lobby. It's back!"

Stanley was shocked. "When…how… who?"

"I don't know, but Terry the Teacher told me on his way back from his morning run."

Stanley couldn't believe the turn of events. He didn't believe any real art robber would steal a painting for a night and just put it back. He suddenly had an idea. "How did you sleep last night, Ernest?"

"Well, as you can imagine, sleeping as an elevator operator has its ups and downs," Ernest paused to give a moment for the joke to sink in. Stanley gave a smirk.

"No, but seriously I slept very well last night. I was only disturbed once to let Arnold the Artist down to the lobby and back to his room."

"Really? Did he say where he was going?"

"No, I don't think so. He didn't really say anything at all."

"Did he have anything with him?"

"Yes, he had a postal tube with him. He had the same tube last night actually."

Stanley quickly connected the dots, and the dots were making Arnold the Artist look mighty suspicious.

"Do you think it's possible, Ernest, that Arnold the Artist may have stolen the painting?"

Ernest, gravely concerned at the accusation, gave deep thought to the proposition. "No, the postal tube wasn't big enough to fit the painting. The painting in the lobby is quite big if I remember correctly."

The elevator doors slid open at the fifth floor and on stepped Mandy the Midwife.

"Good morning, Miss Mandy!" Ernest the Elevator Operator said.

"Good morning, Ernest. Good morning, Stanley," Mandy said cheerfully. How Mandy seemed to be permanently cheerful, even in the mornings, baffled Stanley, but her cheer was certainly infectious to him. Ernest once again looked ready to burst. "Have you heard the news, Miss Mandy?" he asked.

"What news?"

"It's back!" Ernest exclaimed excitedly.

"The painting is apparently back," Stanley added sceptically.

"What?" Mandy was shocked as well. She failed to hide her disappointment, as she knew that meant their painting had lost its place in the lobby.

Ernest nodded his head. "Terry the Teacher told me earlier this morning."

"I'm a little suspicious that Arnold the Artist has had something to do with this whole disappearance and reappearance act," Stanley said. He didn't know how to rectify the situation, and confronting Arnold the Artist made Stanley feel uneasy.

The elevator doors dinged open at the lobby and Mandy and Stanley were once again greeted by a dozen or so people staring above their heads. They stepped out and looked up to see what Ernest had said was true. The painting of blue sky was hanging on the wall as if it had never been moved. Everyone in the lobby looked disappointed by the return of the painting. Damien the Doorman stood with the duck and donut painting in his hands as if it was an urn of ashes.

"It's back," Damien said sadly. "I guess you can hang up this painting in your son's room, Mandy."

Mandy turned around quickly. "My son? I don't have a son."

Leah the Librarian gave a caring smile, "He'll have such a lovely painting he can look at."

Mandy didn't quite know what to say. Neither did Stanley, this was all news to him.

"What are you all talking about?" Mandy asked.

Before anything more could be said, Arnold the Artist stepped out of the stairwell, holding his head low. But Stanley spotted him. His heart began to race, he didn't know whether he should race and tackle the artist, throw a shoe at him, yell "thief!", or let someone else take charge.

"Hey, Arnold!" Stanley called across the lobby. Everyone turned to look. Arnold the Artist paused like a deer caught in headlights.

"The paintings back. What do you think of that?" Stanley asked, his voice giving a little squeak with excitement.

"Well, isn't that nice," Arnold said, continuing towards the front door at a quickened pace. Paul the Policeman, a resident of Tayel Tower, was standing amongst the crowd.

"Paul," Stanley said quickly. "I think Arnold stole the painting."

Paul the Policeman frowned. "That's a serious accusation, Stanley."

"Just ask him what he has been doing for the past two nights and corroborate it with Ernest!" Stanley said quickly, not sure if corroborate was the right word.

"Arnold, can you answer some questions before you go, please?" Paul the Policeman called out, just as Arnold was opening the front door.

Paul the Policeman couldn't keep Arnold from leaving, but clearly the artist thought otherwise, or the artist's guilty conscious kept him inside. Arnold stopped, took a deep breath, and turned around.

"Where were you last night?" Paul asked, pulling out a notepad and indicating that they should go and sit in the lobby seating area. Paul, Stanley and Arnold sat down. The rest of the crowd in the lobby silently pretended to go about their mornings in order to listen to the interrogation. Some pretended to check their mail, others pretended that the pot plants needed petting.

"Where were you last night and the night before?" Paul asked Arnold again.

"Last night, I went to bed."

"And the night before?"

"I went to bed."

"Ernest said you were up and down the elevator many times the night before," Stanley blurted out, feeling more confident next to Paul the Policeman. Paul waited for Arnold to respond.

"I needed some fresh air, I have insomnia," Arnold said confidently. Neither Paul or Stanley believed this for a moment. As Paul jotted down notes, Stanley attempted to put the puzzle pieces together.

With his heart beating quickly, Stanley piped up. "Can I put forward a theory?"

Paul gave a nod. "You can, but it can't be a direct accusation without evidence."

Stanley sat up straight, feeling like a true detective. "I think… I think that someone took the old painting, hoping it would be replaced with one of their own! And then when this someone's painting wasn't chosen in the art competition, they replaced it back with the old one, out of spite!"

Arnold remained tight-lipped and expressionless. Stanley was on a roll. "And I think that they used a postage tube to get the painting on and off the wall!"

Arnold broke his silence. "That's very specific details for a non-direct accusation. But it does sound like something Norman the Nurse would do."

Everyone in the lobby listened silently for an admission of guilt or innocence from the artist.

Arnold sighed. "It was a painting of a patch of sky! Who cares if the painter was Jacques Perot! It was just a patch of sky."

Arnold raised his voice. Everyone in the lobby was clearly listening anyway. "Perot painted it when he was old and senile for goodness sake! My paintings now are magnificent, and soon they will be worth just as much as Perot's! But just out of pity, you wanted to give the spot to Mandy and Stanley's painting because she's pregnant!"

Mandy, standing by Damien's desk, utterly confused, looked around. "Why does everyone think I'm pregnant?"

Stanley realised. "I think they overheard us discussing baby names yesterday."

She shook her head. "Once and for all: Everyone, I'm not pregnant and don't plan on being pregnant for quite some time now."

Paul the Policeman shook his hands to tell the other residents to leave, "Okay, that's enough. Arnold, we need to go have a chat somewhere else."

The stairwell doors opened and out stepped Vincent

the Villain, his heavenly hair blowing a little in the breeze from the air conditioning. He gave a little skip as he exited and looked straight up at the painting. "Oh hey, look at that. The painting's back."

Arnold the Artist stood up. "You devious schmuck!"

Vincent turned to look at Arnold, giving the most knowing of grins. "Oh hello, Arnold. Did you see the sky painting is back? Isn't that fortunate? You did say how much you disliked the duck and donut painting."

Arnold stared at Vincent with a look that could kill the innocent. Vincent stared straight back. "I put the painting back up last night," he announced to the room.

"You stole the painting?" Paul asked.

Vincent shook his head. "No, I put the painting back. I don't believe that's a crime, putting something back."

"We made a deal," Arnold said through gritted teeth.

"I know, but then I saw how much you hated the new painting, and how much the rest of you liked the new painting, and I thought putting the 'Sky' back would be funny. Once again, it's not a crime to put something back."

Vincent walked through the lobby, smug as could be. Stanley could see how Vincent lived up to the namesake of a villain. In one move, by putting back the 'Sky', no matter who stole it, he disappointed literally everyone in the building. Vincent passed by the sitting area. "Sorry, Arnold, bud. Some things are more important than others. The look on your face shows me I made the right choice. Life can be a real 'devious schmuck', can't it?"

Vincent the Villain went over to Damien the Doorman and took Mandy and Stanley's painting of the duck and donut. He held it out and looked over it. "It's pretty badly painted, but the subject matter is good. Can't go wrong with ducks and donuts." He placed the painting down against the wall and left through the front door.

Paul the Policeman led Arnold into the maintenance room and began questioning him out of earshot of everyone else.

Damien the Doorman looked up at the sky painting. "Well, what do we do?"

An object suddenly hit the painting with a 'thud', followed by an explosion of feathers raining down. A bird squawked loudly as it flew in the opposite direction away from what it believed to be an open window. The bird managed to find the open front door. Jarvis, breathless, appeared from the stairwell. "Has anyone seen John Silver 27?"

Everyone pointed out the front door. Jarvis went running, holding a miniature pirates hat and eye patch. He quickly turned, "Oh, and Sir Pigeon the Second? Have you seen Sir Pigeon the Second?"

"My pillow cannot get much fluffier," Clare the Cleaner said as she began sweeping up the fallen bird feathers.

It only took a few minutes for Arnold the Artist and Paul the Policeman to finish talking in the maintenance room, and Arnold calmly exited the building. Everyone looked to Paul for a result. The policeman shook his head. "No confession, not enough evidence, and even if there was as to who actually stole it, there is no evidence the painting left the building, so nothing can be done. Arnold and Vincent are legally innocent."

"What do we do with the sky painting?" asked Patrick the Psychiatrist. "We can't have birds keep flying into it, but it would seem a crime to hide it away in a storage room."

And that is how a multi-million-dollar painting of sky came to hang in the lobby in a corner by the bin, covered permanently by a pair of thick, purple curtains.

Additionally, that is how a painting with laughable technique, white spots and inaccurate shadows came to hang permanently above the elevator of Tayel Tower, and almost everyone in the building loved it.

Wray Wrigley's

TAYEL TOWER

Book 4

THE LOBBY LOTTERY
TICKET

CHAPTER ONE
THE WINNING NUMBERS

The television showed a man in an orange snow-jacket kneeling next to a small penguin. "Penguins are fascinating creatures. They are also quite familial in nature. Many penguins will mate with the same spouse their whole lives. Most penguins will also return to the same nesting site in which they were born and raised. Their mothers will often drop hints that it's time 'they got a place of their own' by pointing over at the other single penguins or offering to go with them to seek out available apartments."

Stanley was sprawled out on the couch and unmotivated to do anything productive after his day at work. He changed the TV channel. The picture jumped to a flashy, colourful game show set complete with an oily haired host and glamorous assistants.

"…and today we have some great prizes up for grabs. Janet, what could our contestants be going home with today?"

"Well, Tom, tonight our contestants are playing for a brand-new toaster! This toaster is state of the art with five slots for toasting your bread, nine settings of heat and a brushed stainless-steel finish. Valued at one-hundred and ninety-nine dollars, it's a toaster!"

"Wow, that is incredible! Is there anything else on offer for our lucky contestants tonight?"

"Yes, Tom. Our contestants could also take home... a loaf of bread! This loaf of bread was baked fresh this morning and would go down a treat with butter or honey. If a contestant was lucky enough to win the toaster and the bread, they could even make some toast!"

Stanley rolled his eyes. He changed the channel again and let the remote fall out of his hand onto the adjoining couch seat.

The TV show was just another colourful set with an even greasier-haired host. "...that's right. It's Monday night, which means it's time for the Millionaire Monday Super Draw! I hope you have your numbers ready because as you know the jackpot is twenty-nine million dollars!"

Stanley wished he hadn't let the remote fall so far from his hand that he would have to make a movement to retrieve it. He had heard about this lottery draw too many times from too many Tayel Tower residents that week. Stanley was not interested in gambling, but the Millionaire Monday Super Draw had been the Tayel Tower talk of the week, and residents were buying tickets by the dozens.

"You won't win if you're not in!" Russell the Realtor had exclaimed a few days earlier holding a thick wad of tickets.

"I'm fine with not winning," Stanley replied, opening his mailbox in the lobby. He was trying to mind his own business, but being a Saturday morning, there were too many of Stanley's neighbours to avoid.

"Are you saying that you couldn't do with a bit of extra cash in your pocket?" Russell asked.

"I do like extra cash in my pockets," Stanley said, "and that's why I'm not going to take my extra cash out and gamble it on a billion-to-one chance."

Russell shrugged his shoulders and sat down on a lobby couch to continue browsing through his tickets.

"Oh, it's just a bit of fun," Rosemary the Retired piped up from one of the other couches. "I have bought myself one ticket, but that's it. I wouldn't know what to do with the money anyway. I'd probably just buy myself another tea towel. I do need another tea towel. What about you, Mandy, did you buy yourself a ticket?"

Mandy the Midwife, who was walking past holding a coffee, shook her head. "Oh no. I don't gamble."

"It's not for everyone," Rosemary smiled. "I don't encourage others to gamble. That would decrease my chances of winning."

"Well, lotteries sure are for me!" exclaimed a voice. Mooney the Millionaire came trotting over to the lobby seating area like a prize-winning horse, holding giant stacks of lottery tickets in his hands and a giant grin on his face.

"How many tickets did you buy?" Stanley asked in shock at the mass of paper in the millionaire's possession.

"Only about two or three or four hundred. Enough to keep my status!" Mooney the Millionaire said proudly as he cantered through the lobby, waving the tickets around for all to see.

"What did he mean by 'enough to keep my status'?" Stanley quietly asked Mandy.

Mandy the Midwife sighed. "Mooney the Millionaire is

a millionaire, but only just. If he was to spend too much, he wouldn't be a millionaire anymore. He'd just be; 'Mooney', I suppose. He's proud that he is a millionaire and sees that as his crowning achievement. A bit sad really."

Stanley nodded his head in agreement.

"How was your morning stroll?" he asked Mandy, always happy to make conversation with her whenever he could.

Mandy breathed in deeply and smiled, "I love the autumn weather, especially in the mornings when the sun is beginning to warm everything up. It's invigorating." She turned excitedly to Stanley. "Hey, you could come with me for a morning stroll sometime, if you'd like!"

Stanley's heart leapt in his chest. He had grown fond of Mandy for many reasons over the weeks since coming to Tayel Tower. Every time they talked, he found new and exciting things he liked about her.

"I'm going to win the lottery!" a voice sang out loud and melodically in the lobby. The voice belonged to Deborah the Debt Collector. To say Deborah the Debt Collector was beautiful was an understatement. The single men wanted to date her, and the impressionable young women wanted to be her. Both husbands and wives wanted her out of existence, but for different reasons. It was said that she had collected more debts than any other debt collector in the whole country by simply asking nicely. The only thing un-beautiful about Deborah the Debt Collector was the fact that she knew she was beautiful.

"And what makes you so sure you have the winning numbers?" Russell the Realtor asked.

"I just know!" Deborah said proudly. It was clear to

Stanley that the lottery was bringing out the proud, arrogant side of people, even though they didn't have anything to be proud of.

"No one can know the winning numbers," he calmly pointed out.

"That's what you think," Deborah said.

"What are the winning numbers then?!" Russell asked, slightly agitated.

Deborah gave a precocious laugh. "You think I'm going to give away the winning numbers to a twenty-nine million-dollar lottery?"

Russell gave a grumpy 'humph'. "Yes, well; I have the winning lottery numbers as well."

"What do you need more money for? You're already rich," Deborah snapped at Russell.

"I want to buy some more investment properties," Russell replied. "What do you need more money for? You can get whatever you want!"

Deborah stared off into the distance. "I'm going to buy out all the apartments on the tenth floor and turn it into a penthouse!"

Perry the Psychic, who had been checking his mail, closed his mailbox with a bang that echoed through the lobby. Everyone present in the lobby turned to see what the matter was. Perry, visibly angry and upset, walked briskly across the lobby and up the stairwell.

"He must have got a bad letter," Rosemary the Retired said.

Damien the Doorman shook his head. "I don't know why he's angry; being a psychic and all. Surely nothing can surprise him? If anyone has the winning lottery numbers, it's Perry the Psychic."

Yes, everyone in the apartment building was obsessed with Monday night's lottery.

****

The greasy-haired lottery presenter on Stanley's television on that highly anticipated Monday night pressed a giant red button which released numbered balls into an oversized fish tank. Jets of air sent the flying around the tank. Eventually, one by one, balls fell down a shoot into a row.

"The first number is a… '6'."

There was a loud series of knocks on Stanley's apartment door. Stanley, startled from his tranquil, sleepy state, jumped up from the couch and whipped open the front door. He was greeted by the frowning face of his neighbour, Paxton the Pacifist, who appeared by the look in his eyes to have seen the apocalypse.

"Does your TV work?" Paxton asked in terror.

"Yes, why? What's wrong?"

"Mine just broke." Paxton held out a lottery ticket. "And the first number on my ticket is a '6'!"

Stanley sighed and stood aside. Paxton ran in and sat on the couch.

Two additional numbers were already on the screen, '20' and '18'.

"And the next number is a '45'."

Paxton jumped up on the couch. "I have a 45!" he yelled.

"Then we have a '19'."

Paxton the Pacifist angrily hit his fist onto the couch. Stanley made a mental note to ask someone why Paxton was referred to as a 'pacifist'. The next brightly coloured ball rolled into place. Paxton's eyes were glued to the screen, the lottery ticket in his hand held in a vice-like grip.

"And second to last is a '42'."

Paxton shook his head, dismissing the '42' as if it were a fly.

"And for the final number, we have an '11'. Oh, my apologies, I was reading it upside down. The final number is actually an… '11'. Yes, I am receiving confirmation that it is an '11'."

Paxton read the numbers on his ticket over and over, comparing them to the numbers on the screen.

"How'd you go?" Stanley asked.

Paxton screwed his ticket up, clearly disappointed with the result. "Two matching numbers. A couple of bucks; nothing." He got up from the couch and walked to the front door. "I'm going for a walk."

Stanley closed the door behind Paxton and went back to the couch. He stared at the lottery numbers on the screen, wondering what he would do if he was to win the lottery. A couple of minutes later he was engrossed in a badly acted TV drama, and then he was engrossed in sleeping.

****

The next morning, Stanley ate a mango for breakfast and felt good. Great in fact! It was a nice day; the sun was shining and the sky was blue. He still had to go to work, which is always a mistake on beautiful days. But what made this a truly beautiful day, in his mind, is that Mandy had asked him if he'd like to go on a stroll together. The knowledge that someone wants to spend time with you can be as good as medicine unless you have an infection that requires a course of antibiotics.

Now it must be said that Stanley did not believe in exercise. He did believe in generally living healthily; not eating too much junk food and not sitting on the couch all day. He felt he got a decent amount of exercise from his daily commutes to and from the office. Stanley, if he was being frank, despised people like Boris the Body Builder from room 305 who spent at least 8 hours in the morning exercising his lower half, and 8 hours in the evening exercising his upper half. It was even rumoured that on Sunday afternoons, Boris the Body Builder spent 2 hours exercising just his right pinkie finger. No one knew why.

Stanley, content with life, put on his shirt and tie, packed his bag with a sandwich, a packet of chips and an apple, and headed out to the elevator. Ludwig the Lawyer, a resident of the tenth floor, was already in the elevator as Stanley stepped onboard. "Good morning, Ludwig. Good morning, Ernest. Lobby please."

"Good morning, Stanley," Ludwig the Lawyer replied, beaming a smile bigger than Stanley's. The lawyer shook Stanley's hand excitedly.

"You're in a good mood," Stanley laughed.

"Ah, same could be said for you, Stanley," Ludwig said. "Did you have a bit of luck with the lottery too?"

Stanley shook his head. "Not with the money lottery, Sir. May I presume by your smile that you did?"

Ludwig the Lawyer put a finger to his lips. "Ah, I can't confirm or deny anything. But let's just say I wrote out a resignation letter for my boss this morning."

"I thought you owned your own law firm?"

"I do, but I also work as a children's entertainer on weekends," Ludwig said. "Squabbles the Clown is not going to be laughing after I give him the letter."

Stanley waited for a laugh. No laugh from the lawyer came. He shrugged his shoulders. "Well, congratulations."

They arrived at the lobby.

"I must be off, I need to find my accountant," Ludwig the Lawyer said as he rushed excitedly through the lobby and out the front door.

As Stanley stepped out, he noticed Damien the Doorman standing in the centre of the lobby looking at a piece of paper.

Stanley gave Damien the Doorman a little wave. "Morning, Damien!"

Damien the Doorman didn't look up from examining the small, white piece of paper. This behaviour was very unlike the doorman, whose career was built upon greeting people, with the occasional door openings.

Stanley tried again. "Good morning, Damien."

Damien, slightly startled, looked up. "What? Oh, hello Stanley. Come, look at this!"

Damien held up the piece of paper to show Stanley. The piece of paper was a lottery ticket.

"It's a lottery ticket," Stanley observed.

"I know," Damien said in an urgent whisper. "But it's a winning lottery ticket!"

"Oh, really? Congratulations," Stanley said, astonished at the chances of two people from the same building winning significant money at the lottery.

Damien the Doorman lowered his voice even more. "It's the winning lottery ticket! Twenty-nine million dollars!"

Stanley was all attention now. He too lowered his voice. "Really?! That's amazing! Are you going to quit your job and retire?"

"It's not my ticket. I just found it on the lobby floor."

"Finders keepers?"

Damien frowned at the proposal. "I keep it? No-no-no, I couldn't do that. This million-dollar lottery ticket belongs to someone else."

"What's that you said?" Leah the Librarian asked, overhearing, or more accurately 'overseeing'. The one advantage of getting older and deafer is you get more astute at reading lips and finding more excuses for going to bed early.

"I really wouldn't tell…" Stanley attempted to interject.

"I said I found the winning lottery ticket, but it belongs to someone else and I'm not sure who!" Damien exclaimed innocently.

"Oh, it must be mine!" Leah said. "But I don't know how. My lottery ticket was locked in my apartment's safe. One moment, I'll just go check." She turned on her heels and wobbled back to the elevator as quick as she could.

Stanley shook his head. "I really wouldn't tell anyone else in the tower that you've found the winning ticket. You should probably take it to the lottery office and report it. I'm sure they can find out who it belongs to."

The stairwell door opened and out popped Mandy the Midwife, wearing jeans and a green jumper.

"Good morning, Stanley!" Mandy greeted joyfully, beaming her infectious, warm smile.

"Good morning," Stanley replied, himself trying not to immediately talk about Damien's lottery ticket. "Off on your morning stroll?"

"Yes, I am. We should set a date for our stroll together.

How does next Saturday sound?

"Next Saturday sounds fantastic, I can't wait! I just need to go to the bathroom," Stanley said excitedly. Mandy blushed a little at Stanley's loud excitement and went on her way. Stanley admonished himself silently for announcing his need for the bathroom.

"Take the ticket to the lottery office," Stanley said to Damien the Doorman, walking to the lobby toilet. "There will be a riot otherwise."

And a riot there was.

CHAPTER TWO
COOKBOOKS

It is a phenomenon how news travels so quickly through the hallways of Tayel Tower. Some say Ernest the Elevator Operator is solely to blame. Others say there is an official committee of residents who devote their days to the exercise of spreading gossip. Suffice it to say, when Stanley had finished in the bathroom, the lobby was filled with a good dozen people surrounding Damien the Doorman's desk. These people weren't aggressive or loud; no, instead they all appeared to be kettles on the boil, slowly but silently bubbling away and heating up. Damien, his hand tightly gripping the ticket and shoved deep inside his pocket, was white as a sheet and overwhelmed by all the attention. A little colour returned to the Doorman's face as he saw Stanley appear across the room.

He dodged through the crowd. "Thank goodness you're back, Stanley! All these people claim the lobby lottery ticket is there's. I don't know what to do!"

The crowd of a dozen or so turned like hungry vultures to watch wherever Damien the Doorman (or more precisely the lottery ticket) went.

"Does the lottery ticket belong to you, Stanley?" Damien asked fearfully.

Stanley frustratingly denied it. "No, I already told you I don't gamble."

Damien grabbed the ticket out his pocket and shoved it into Stanley's hand. "Good. You're deciding who the ticket belongs to then."

"Wait, why does Stanley get to decide who the ticket belongs to?" Mooney the Millionaire, one of the members of the crowd, protested.

"I believe Stanley's a fair man," Damien said confidently. "And he already stated, in front of everyone here, that it is not his ticket. That makes him an impartial judge." Damien dusted the responsibility from his hands with a clap, slumped down in the chair behind his desk and opened the morning paper.

The crowd of claimants silently waited to see what the new holder of their fortunes would do. Stanley was utterly bemused and began feeling very vulnerable. There were neighbours standing in the crowd that he wouldn't have ever thought were liars. Aldene the Accountant had always seemed to be honest; Paul the Policeman surely would know better than to be a liar; Tanish the Taxi Driver, although he seemed to get confused easily, had always been very honest; Barney the Banker and Charlotte the Chef were successful people, workaholics to say the least, who surely had better things to do unless they truly thought they were the rightful owners of the ticket.

"So, you all claim that this winning ticket is yours?" Stanley asked.

"Some of you must be lying!" Charlotte the Chef accused of her fellow vultures. "Aldene, you told me yesterday that you never bought a ticket because you hurt your foot and couldn't make it to the lottery office before closing time!"

Aldene the Accountant, on crutches, looked at the floor nervously, "I sent Samuel the Salesman to the newsagent last night to buy one for me."

"Then how did your ticket end up on the floor here this morning?" Stanley asked.

"It must have fallen out of my pocket when I came to pick up the morning paper," Aldene explained.

Stanley sighed. He knew the right thing to do was to take the ticket to the lottery office and leave it for them to find the rightful owner. But then there was that little annoying bug called 'curiosity' that was beginning to buzz in his mind. How could all of these people pretend to have had the winning lottery ticket? A statistically one-in-a-gazillion chance, there had to be something else going on.

Stanley looked at the time on his phone. He was already late for work. "This afternoon, when I get home from work around six, I will be up in the roof garden. If you wish to make a claim for the lottery ticket, you need to come and present your story of how you lost the ticket. Mandy and I, two impartial judges, will attempt to decide who the ticket really belongs to. If no one claims it, or we can't make a confident decision, the ticket will be taken to the lottery office. Or destroyed." Stanley added the last sentence for a little drama.

There was not much the vultures could really do but agree to these conditions. They all grudgingly dispersed back to their regular morning activities. Stanley placed the multi-million-dollar burden in his pocket and took out his phone.

"What?" Mandy exclaimed after Stanley explained the scenario over the phone to her on his way to work. He felt bad dragging Mandy into the mess without asking her permission, but he knew he could trust her. And if he were being honest, Stanley considered it a good opportunity to spend more time with her.

"That's a lot of money," she said.

"If we can't decide, I'll take it to the lottery office, I promise. But it's just so strange, wouldn't you agree, that everyone wishes to claim the ticket?"

Mandy, deep in thought, nodded her head. "I do agree it is very strange. But I'm not sure I'll be much help."

"I've found you to be smart and insightful," Stanley said.

He heard Mandy give her wonderful laugh. "And you are curious and very bold, Stanley—signing me up to something before asking."

"I know, I should have asked, I apologise," Stanley said. "But you're in? You'll help me tonight?"

Mandy gave a sigh. "I will admit, you have made me curious as well. But I won't make a decision about the rightful owner unless I feel I'm one hundred per cent sure."

"Fair enough," Stanley said.

"I need to go, but I'll see you tonight. Have a good day!" she said brightly.

"Thank you, you too," Stanley replied with a smile and a skip in his step.

****

For Stanley, the day zoomed by faster than Jarvis the

Jobless on his way to a free muffin event at the local community centre. Stanley purchased a sausage roll for dinner on his way home and ate while he walked, thinking about what questions he would ask to those making claim to the ticket. Every ten steps, he patted his pocket to double, triple and quadruple check that the ticket was secure. He arrived home at Tayel Tower and, once again patting his pocket to check on the ticket, pressed the 'up' button on the elevator. Deborah the Debt Collector, who had been watching Stanley ever since he entered the building, walked briskly over and stood beside him. She was wearing a black, designer business suit with high heels and her dark hair styled into perfect, lush waves.

"Oh, you're going up?" Deborah asked.

"Yes, I am going up," Stanley smiled back.

"Me too!" she replied, beaming a perfect, white-toothed smile.

They both stood silently as they waited for the elevator.

Deborah stuck out her hand. "I'm Deborah by the way. My friends call me Deb. You can call me Deb."

Stanley hesitated but shook the outstretched hand. "You do know we've met before? A couple of times?"

"I know, but I don't think I've ever fully introduced myself. I work as a debt collector. What do you do for a living?"

"I work at a business consulting firm. As a consultant."

Deborah's eyes sparkled. "Oh, sensational! That is so sensational!"

The elevator doors dinged open and the pair stepped on board.

"Second floor please, Ernest," Deborah asked sweetly

of the elevator operator.

"Ninth floor, please," Stanley also requested.

Ernest the Elevator Operator, fulfilling his duties, pressed the buttons on the wall, with the precision and finesse that only a full-time elevator operator can.

"So what do you like to do for fun, Stanley?" Deborah asked.

"Um, I like to read-"

"Oh, I love to read too! Isn't that sensational?" Deborah cut in, beaming her smile.

"I also like to cook."

"Oh, I love cooking!!" Deborah chimed in brightly, almost singing. "Oh, my goodness. I have a sensational collection of cookbooks that I inherited from my auntie. You should come and check them out right now!"

Stanley was unconvinced that Deborah's enthusiasm for her Auntie's cookbook collection was genuine, but didn't want to be rude. "That would be nice, thank you, but I can't right now. I'm running a little late for something."

Deborah pulled playfully on Stanley's arm. "Oh, come on. It will only take a moment."

Deborah was obviously very keen to show off her cookbook collection. Stanley looked at the time. He could have a quick peek and be in the roof garden before 6 pm. "Just a quick look then."

"Yay!" Deborah exclaimed.

The elevator doors opened at the second floor.

"I've been getting interested in Asian cuisine recently. Do you like Asian food?" Deborah asked as they walked down the hall.

"I don't mind noodles," he replied.

Deborah took out her keys and unlocked the door to room 202. "So I hear you have a big decision to make tonight?"

Stanley nodded. "Yeah, I guess so,"

"Oh, I am not envious of your position! Working out who the ticket belongs to? I don't know how you'll do it."

Deborah made Stanley feel important.

"I have a pretty good idea how to work it out," he lied.

Deborah the Debt Collector gently touched Stanley on the arm. "You are so smart!"

The touch on the arm was meant to be a warm, inviting touch, but to Stanley, it felt cold. He suddenly realised what Deborah was trying to do; she was trying to find favour in him to get the lottery ticket! She had been amongst the crowd that morning.

Stanley gently shifted his arm away from her. "So, you mentioned you had some recipe books?" he asked.

Deborah ignored the question. "You know, Stanley… I was wondering… would you be interested in maybe cooking together sometime? Or we could just go out for dinner?"

Stanley crossed his arms defensively. There was no doubt now in his mind what was going on. His thoughts flashed to Mandy the Midwife. He wanted to go out for dinner with her, not this woman.

"Oh, ah. I'm not sure—" he stammered.

Deborah moved slightly closer. "Not like, on 'a date' or anything. Just a 'get together' where we can cook together. I can make dinner and you can make dessert?"

"I'm sure we could have a party with lots of our neighbours invited one day. Like a pot-luck dinner." He quickly added, "But I should go now, I'm really late. Thanks for showing me the cookbooks."

Even though he hadn't seen any cookbooks yet, Stanley briskly moved out of the apartment and back to the elevator. He pressed the 'up' button frantically. The elevator dinged open and he was greeted by the last person he wanted to see at that moment.

"Good afternoon, Stanley," Mandy the Midwife said cheerfully with her usually delightful smile. Her smile faded when she saw Deborah the Debt Collector standing outside her apartment with a devious smile. Stanley stepped on board the elevator, not quite sure what to say or how to say it.

"Level nine please, Ernest," he said quietly.

The doors closed. Stanley and Mandy stood next to each other facing the front, a silent elephant doing a jig between them. Stanley felt awful.

He took a deep breath and broke the awkward silence. "Weird story; Deborah the Debt Collector insisted that I look at her cookbook collection but then she started trying to ask me if I wanted to cook with her or go out to dinner with her but I said no of course well not 'no' but I said we could work it out one day instead I suggested maybe a potluck dinner but I really don't want to it was quite strange but I think she just wants to get the money."

Stanley's face was as red as a beetroot caught with a tomato.

"Right," was all she replied, without her usual infectious smile.

Ernest the Elevator Operator gave a cough to clear his

throat. "Elaine the Event Planner thinks you two will be married within a year. She wants to plan your wedding."

The elevator dinged open at Mandy's floor, the fifth. She stepped out quickly.

"Will you still be there to help me tonight?" Stanley asked. Mandy turned and gave the smallest, most pained smile that tugged at Stanley's heart. "I should be."

The elevator doors closed between them.

"Relationship troubles?" Ernest asked. "Because that looked very much like relationship troubles."

"We're not in a relationship," Stanley said coldly.

"I was in a relationship once," Ernest said, staring off into space. "We were young, met in school. We fell in love. Then her father fell into money and it was all downhill from there."

"The lottery?" Stanley asked.

"Hm?" Ernest responded.

"You said her father fell into money."

"Yes, he was a repairman at a bank," Ernest clarified. "He fell off a ladder into a pile of money. He seriously injured himself. His daughter needed to take care of him, and I and my love became distant. Money is a dangerous thing."

Stanley sighed.

"Did you hear about the big lottery last night?" Ernest asked.

"Yes. Yes, I have," Stanley said.

"Did you buy a ticket?"

"No, thankfully."

"I have had many residents come into the elevator to-day claiming that they won the top prize. There must be a lot of lucky residents in this building," Ernest said.

"The winning lottery ticket was found in the lobby this morning," Stanley explained, wondering if the elevator had begun to ascend. "I need to decide tonight who it belongs to. The claimants are beginning to go mad. You'd think the ticket was the last bottle of water on earth from the way they look at it."

Ernest nodded in agreement. "Money is a killer."

"I know. It tears people apart from one another and promotes a materialistic culture," Stanley said bitterly.

"No, I mean money is literally a killer. My uncle was a magician; accidentally swallowed a coin during a trick."

"He choked on the coin?" Stanley said.

"No, the coin wasn't the problem. It was the lion my uncle took the coin from that was the problem. The lion demanded the coin back straight away, but my uncle had already swallowed and couldn't pay."

Stanley made a note to himself to avoid conversations with Ernest in the future. They always left him with too many questions.

CHAPTER THREE
"IT'S MY TICKET"

On top of Tayel Tower was the rooftop garden. The rooftop garden was a collection of garden beds in which plants of various shapes, sizes and colours attempted to grow. The maintenance and upkeep of this garden were done by the residents of the building, but Boris the Bodybuilder over the years had come to feel a sense of ownership over the little garden. Since the building was opened decades ago, the garden had fluctuated between a thriving jungle and a patch of weeds. In the year when Stanley moved in, the garden beds consisted mainly of spinach plants and lettuce heads. Boris had attempted to grow potatoes, but Jarvis the Jobless had attempted to bury butter and salt amongst the potatoes to make chips, preventing any potatoes from growing.

To set up the garden for the interrogations, Stanley dragged a little metal garden table and three chairs together into the middle of the courtyard. The time was 5:55 pm and Stanley could already see the heads of residents poking out of the stairwell door to check if he was ready to hear their tales of misfortune. The sun would be set in an hour. Most people would have seen this as a hindrance, but Stanley saw the unstoppable setting of the sun as a fortuitous preventative measure against the hearings going long into the night.

Stanley took a seat. He tapped his pen nervously on the notepad he had brought with him, anxiously waiting to see if Mandy the Midwife would join him as a judge. His mind wandered, imagining what she must have been thinking after seeing him on Deborah the Debt Collector's floor. He was quite sure that there was a mutual attraction between Mandy and himself. If this lottery ticket (and consequently Deborah the Debt Collector) was the reason that their affection for each other ended, Stanley decided he would be quite disappointed.

The stairwell door opened at exactly 6 pm Onto the roof stepped Mandy the Midwife. Stanley stood up quickly. She didn't make eye contact with him until she sat down in the seat beside him. She gave a smile, not a big lovely smile like he was used to, but a smile all the same.

"Are we ready to do this?" she asked.

Stanley tried not to grin with glee like a koala who just found out heaven is in a eucalyptus tree. "I think we are."

He went to the stairwell door to invite the first resident onto the roof. He was quite surprised to see the millionaire applicants had already formed a nice straight line.

Barney the Banker, dressed in a suit and tie, was first in line. With a nod from Stanley, he walked onto the rooftop garden and settled in the chair opposite the two judges.

"How are you, Stanley? And you, Mandy? How are you both this fine night?" Barney asked, enthusiastically shaking their hands.

"We're doing swell, thank you," Stanley said, trying to be as expressionless as possible to show he was not going to be playing any favourites. "I will tell you upfront that you have only three minutes to make your case. How did your ticket end up on the lobby floor?"

Stanley started a timer on his phone. Barney, not expecting the time pressure, suddenly became much less confident. "Well, uh, you see what happened was this morning I started work at six. That's very early, I know, but I had a meeting. I was running a little late, but that was a result of having celebrated last night for my winnings! I placed my ticket in my pocket this morning, the safest place it could be, with the intention of putting my ticket in a safe at the bank later today.

"At seven, remember I was late for work, as I was running out of the lobby, Samuel the Salesman asked me if I had a spare dollar or two. I'm a generous fellow, as anyone can tell you. I fished around in my pocket, took out two dollars and gave it to Samuel. That's when my ticket must have fallen onto the floor."

Stanley hadn't written anything down on his notepad. The story seemed perfectly legitimate to both Stanley and Mandy. They thanked Barney and asked him to leave.

"Well it must be his," Mandy said once Barney the Banker had left the roof.

"He could be lying, or simply mistaken," Stanley said.

"For all the time I've known Barney, he's always been kind and honest," Mandy said.

Stanley nodded. "That is what I've wondered all day. Why are these honest people suddenly lying? We need to question some more of them."

The next resident was Samuel the Salesman. Samuel shook hands with the judges. "What a fine night this is. But might I say not quite a fine night like last night when I saw I would be a millionaire for every night onwards!"

Stanley informed Samuel he only had three minutes. Samuel stood up quickly from the chair and began dramatically telling his story, using his whole body. "Last night, after I heard that I won the lottery, I was over the moon with excitement! I immediately rang my friends, all fellow salesmen, and we went out for a late-night pizza to celebrate. I took my ticket with me, of course, to show it to all my friends.

"We had a great time, but amongst the festivities I left my jacket at the pizza bar, and my ticket was in the pocket of my jacket! I woke up this morning with the shocking realisation that my ticket was missing! I ran downstairs, hailed a taxi and went straight back to the pizza bar. Thankfully, there was a cleaner at the bar, so I was able to safely collect my jacket. I breathed a sigh of relief to find my ticket safely where I had left it. It wasn't until the taxi reached Tayel Tower again that I realised I had left my wallet in my apartment, and didn't have any money to pay the taxi driver! I saw Barney the Banker in the lobby, and being desperate as I was, I asked him for some spare change to give to Tanish the Taxi Driver, promising Barney I would pay him back later. I must have dropped my ticket on the floor as I headed back up to my apartment! I'm always dropping and losing things."

"Thank you, Samuel," Mandy smiled.

"Do I get my ticket back now?" Samuel asked, panting from his animated storytelling.

"No, we still have a number of other stories to hear, sorry," Stanley apologised.

As Samuel the Salesman left the table to walk back to the stairwell, Stanley and Mandy looked at each other once again, neither wiser than the other.

"Both Samuel and Barney's stories match up, but if both claimed to have lost the ticket, then one of them must be lying," Stanley said quietly.

"I agree," Mandy said. "Is Tanish the Taxi Driver in the stairwell? We ought to ask him to corroborate their stories."

By this point, Len the Lemon Seller had already entered onto the roof.

"We're sorry Len, but we wish to speak to Tanish first," Stanley said, as politely as he could.

"But it's my ticket! Once you hear how I lost it, you'll know it's mine!" Len protested.

"What was the message written on the back of the ticket?" Stanley asked.

Len thought hard for a moment. "Oh, ahh… 'Buy milk' was written on the back."

"It's not your ticket Len," Stanley said.

"How can you say that so quickly?"

"There's nothing written on the back," Stanley said with a cheeky grin, considering himself clever for tricking the lemon seller.

"What do you mean? Look at the ticket," Len said heatedly. Stanley pulled out the ticket and held it out to Len. Len looked baffled; there was nothing written on the back of the ticket. He left dejectedly to send in Tanish, who was, in fact, waiting to tell his story.

Mandy was impressed. "Well played."

Stanley smiled. "Thank you."

Tanish the Taxi Driver walked over to the table and sat down very calmly.

"You have three minutes," Stanley said, pressing the timer on his phone.

"It's not my ticket," Tanish said. Stanley and Mandy were both surprised. Stanley stopped his timer. "Oh? Whose ticket is it then?"

"The ticket belongs to my cousin-" Tanish began. Stanley sighed and pressed 'start' on the timer again.

Tanish leaned back in his chair. "I purchased it for my cousin yesterday because I owed him a couple of dollars. It was my way of paying him back. Anyway, last night I was doing the night shift, from 10 pm to 7 am. Just before I left for work, I watched the television and saw that I…I mean my cousin, won! I was overjoyed. It felt like I was on the moon! The whole night while I was on my shift, I didn't pick up one customer, just because I didn't want to. I knew that my cousin would give me a big sum of the winnings. In the morning I finished my shift and was driving home when I saw Samuel the Salesman hailing me. He told me he needed to get to a pizza shop right away. I asked 'why?', and he said for his jacket. I took him there because I like to help my friends, and then brought Samuel home again. I printed out the taxi receipt and placed it on the tray table, not realising that the lottery ticket was under the receipt. Samuel said he forgot his wallet. He ran inside the lobby, came out again with a couple of dollars and paid me. He must have picked up the ticket off the tray table with the receipt by accident and dropped it on the lobby floor."

Stanley and Mandy were flabbergasted. Every story they had heard so far (bar Len the Lemon Seller) matched each other person's story and explained how the ticket ended up on the lobby floor. The pair of judges dismissed Tanish and talked quietly but quickly, aware that the day had almost completely turned to night.

"We need a different approach," Stanley said, again tapping his pen on the notepad. "I'm not a police detective, and the only policeman in the building, Paul the Policeman, is biased by waiting in the stairwell to tell his story."

Mandy leaned her elbow on the table, deep in troubled thought. "My gut is telling me something isn't right here; these people aren't passive liars! What if they are all telling the truth? How do we know they didn't all happen to get the exact same numbers on their tickets?"

Stanley shook his head. "I did think of that, but that would mean there would need to be a pile of identical winning lottery tickets somewhere—" Stanley almost fell out of his chair; he had an epiphany. "Perry the Psychic!"

"What about Perry?" Mandy asked.

"On the day I moved in, I saw Jarvis the Jobless dressed as he always is: shabby. I asked Perry how Jarvis stayed jobless but could afford to live in Tayel Tower, and Perry explained it was all through lottery tickets!"

Stanley had another epiphany but to Mandy, his excitement looked a little like epilepsy. "And yesterday! Deborah the Debt Collector was implying she knew the winning numbers before they were revealed. Unless she's also psychic, Perry could have told her the numbers."

Mandy began making the same realisation as Stanley. "Is Perry waiting in the stairwell to make a claim after the ticket?"

Stanley ran over to the stairwell and whipped the door open. "Is Perry the Psychic here?"

The ten or so residents present looked around at each other, but Perry was nowhere to be seen. Stanley hastily told the waiting residents that interviews would resume the next morning, and amidst a hail of opposition ran back to Mandy.

"Do you know what Perry's apartment number is?" he asked.

"Room two-oh-seven I believe," Mandy said.

"We need to pay him a visit."

The two of them ran down the stairwell, dodging past angry residents, taking two steps at a time. They burst through the second floor's door and walked quickly to the door of Room 207. They were surprised to find the apartment's front door wide open. Stanley cautiously peered into the apartment. All of the apartment layouts in Tayel Tower were identical across the tower, but each occupant decorated their apartments in a rainbow of colours and vastly different arrangements and styles of furniture to suit their unique tastes.

Perry's apartment was white and empty. It looked almost exactly like Stanley's apartment the day he had moved in. There were cardboard boxes lining the walls. Empty nails on the wall stood above fresh wall paint where photos and paintings had recently hung. There were no decorations anywhere. The living room had a single couch in it, and on that couch sat Perry the Psychic, staring off into space.

"Hello Stanley, Mandy and Paul," Perry greeted his guests without turning his head.

The two guests took this as an invitation to enter.

"It's only Stanley and me, Perry. Paul the Policeman isn't with us," Mandy said calmly.

Perry quickly turned his head, genuinely surprised. "Oh? I guess I can't get everything right all the time."

Perry got up from the couch, moving to his bare kitchen. "I'm afraid I don't have much in the way of food at the moment, but would you like a cup of tea or coffee? Please, take a seat on a box or the coffee table. Nothing is precious but time."

Mandy and Stanley cautiously sat down on two sturdy boxes.

"I'm fine with water," Mandy said, feeling obliged to have something. She looked over at the kitchen and realised Perry had already placed a glass of water on the bench ready for her. Perry pulled a mug out of a box and prepared an unrequested cup of coffee for Stanley. "You know I know everything you're about to say to me. You know I know how this conversation is going to end. But please, ask away."

"Are you behind the lottery ticket fiasco?" Stanley asked firmly.

"Partly yes, partly no. Mainly no," Perry answered.

"Did you give some of your neighbours the winning lottery ticket numbers."

"Yes."

"Why?"

Perry leaned on the kitchen bench, arms folded. "Because they asked for it."

"They all asked you for the winning numbers?" Stanley asked in disbelief.

Perry solemnly nodded.

"That's so dishonest," Mandy said.

Perry gave a nervous laugh. "Don't you think I know? It was okay when it was just Jarvis the Jobless asking for the lottery numbers. He gave away all the winnings to charity. But the rest of the residents? All they want is 'a new microwave' or 'a new car' or 'to be rich'. The plan was to have them all win, and realise their winnings were far less split amongst a dozen people. Riches are relative; I can guarantee they would all be less grateful and boastful if their neighbours all had the same level of wealth."

Perry paused and took a deep breath. "It was a stupid, badly thought out plan. I'm psychic, but I failed to see that those people winning the money would result in nothing but more squabbles, and they wouldn't learn the lesson I thought I could teach. I failed. Therefore, it was my responsibility to right my wrongs and change things back to how they were."

"You stole all the winning tickets back," Stanley realised.

Perry nodded. "I foresaw where each winner put their ticket when they went to sleep and was ready to swoop in and take it from under their noses. All except Samuel the Salesman who left the ticket in a pizza shop overnight. That was the ticket you found. The rest have been destroyed."

Stanley frowned, processing all the information. Perry handed him the coffee mug. Stanley absent-mindedly took a big drink of the bitter brew, even though he didn't like the stuff that much.

"What should we do with the last winning ticket?" Mandy asked.

Perry looked up at the roof for a moment. "Give it to

the new couple. They'll know what to do with it."

"Which new couple?" Mandy asked.

"I'm leaving Tayel Tower for a holiday," Perry said sadly, ignoring the question. "I'm going to find a place where I'm not tempted to meddle in people's futures. Maybe a farm out in the country."

"It looks like you're leaving for good," Stanley said.

Perry nodded. "It will be a long holiday, I think."

"Perry, you don't have to leave—" Mandy started. But she could see from Perry's face, and the fact that his apartment was thoroughly packed, that the decision was made.

"Would you two be willing to help me take my boxes down to the moving truck that will pull up in about ten minutes?"

Stanley patted his pocket where the last ticket safely remained. Over the next half hour, the three of them transported Perry's boxes down via the elevator to the lobby.

"Where are you going?" Damien the Doorman asked of Perry. Perry handed the doorman a blank but sealed envelope. "Please give this to the owner for me."

The news that Perry was leaving travelled quickly through the tower. Dozens of residents meandered into the lobby to see where Perry was going. By the time Perry was putting his last box in the moving truck, there was a crowd gathered at the front door. They all looked to Perry, waiting for him to say goodbye. Perry felt awkward, but also that he should at least say something.

"I'll be out of your hair, for now. I'm going on a long holiday," he began. "I'm sorry for any trouble I have caused you. A couple of things: Jarvis the Jobless, here is a list of winning lottery numbers for the next couple of weeks."

Old Jarvis the Jobless stepped forward to receive the piece of paper. "That's all right, I'll ask Paige for the winning numbers while you're gone."

"I've already told you, and I will tell you again: I'm a psychologist, not a psychic, Jarvis," Paige the Psychologist said.

"Ah, but how do you know you will tell me again if you're not a psychic?" Jarvis pointed out.

Perry turned back to the crowd, pulling a piece of paper from his pocket. "Also, this here is last night's winning lottery ticket."

Much to everyone's horror, including Stanley and Mandy, Perry proceeded to tear the slip of paper to un-recognisable shreds.

There were cries of protest from the crowd, they were still unaware that there had been more than one winning ticket. "How dare you destroy my ticket! Who do you think you are!"

Deborah the Debt Collector stepped forward. "You are an evil man Perry the Psychic! This is all just a game to you, isn't it?!"

"Deborah, Deborah," Perry clicked his tongue. "Your sweet charming disposition can only go so far. Would you like to know why Stanley could resist your abysmal flirtations?"

"You are a—"

"It's because his future is already set on a path that only he can change."

Mandy looked at Stanley with renewed hope. Stanley looked at the floor, blushing.

Perry stepped towards Deborah. "And you know something, Deb? You will get married one day, and you and your husband are going to have a couple of beautiful children together, and you will look back and realise that your riches weren't in how you look, but they were in your pocket all along."

Young Deborah, her eyes wide and her heart tugged, looked up at Perry. "I don't quite understand that final metaphor. My riches are in my pocket? There's nothing in my pocket. Is it my phone? My riches are on my phone?"

Perry the Psychic gave Stanley a wink and walked out the front door.

Stanley stuck his hand into his pocket and felt the lobby lottery ticket where it had been all along.

Wray Wrigley's

TAYEL TOWER

Book 5

A VILLAIN'S CHRISTMAS GIFT

CHAPTER ONE
AN AUDIENCE WITH
THE VILLAIN

"Good evening, Stanley. Vincent the Villain is looking for you," Damien the Doorman advised from behind Tayel Tower's concierge desk. Stanley froze in his tracks like a tub of ice-cream caught in headlights.

"Vincent the Villain is looking for me? What should I do? Should I hide?" Stanley blabbered fearfully.

"Well, you could hide, but let me know where you are so I can let Vincent know."

Vincent the Villain, by occupation, worked in a beauty salon laboratory as a shampoo scent tester. This oddly specific occupation was quite lucrative. He was known throughout the hair-product industry for his keen sense of smell, thanks to his obtuse nose, and his long flowing luscious hair which provided a perfect platform for testing new hair treatments and aromas. Beauty product companies around the world paid through their noses to have Vincent fly to their locations and use his. Vincent, who had a very healthy income from this work but so much time on his hands, became known for his villainous antics.

For example, several years ago, Vincent, dining alone,

decided to pay for everyone's meals in a steak restaurant. The man's generosity flabbergasted the customers. Over the next month, however, he sent letters to each of the customers, addressed from the steak restaurant, claiming that they had not paid for their meals. The payment address in the letters was for the bank account of a pro-vegan advocacy group. The customers were confused and frustrated as they thought they paid for their meals. The restaurant was confused about why customers were getting letters from them that they didn't send, and the pro-vegan advocacy group was offended that they were getting donations with receipts for beef steak, BBQ lamb and chicken burger meals. Vincent did that because he was bored and came up with the idea while eating dinner.

On another occasion, Vincent snuck into a dog show the night before the event and replaced all the dogs with exact look-alike cats, going as far as to put the dogs' collars on the cats. He then moved all the dogs to a back room and set them up in a replica courtroom. There was one Chihuahua dressed as a judge, a jury of ten Labradors, two Pitbull lawyers, a gallery of various mixed breeds and even a Sheepdog dressed as the bailiff. And in the place of the accused? He paid an actor to dress up as a postman. Vincent did that because he was bored and came up with the idea while eating dinner.

"Do you know what he wants from me?" Stanley asked the doorman.

"No. He didn't say," Damien replied, opening the front door for some other residents. Stanley, fearful for his life, although he had no evidence that Vincent was interested in causing him bodily harm, walked quickly up the stairs to his apartment and double locked the front door.

It had been a long day at work. His boss, Richard Richardson, had been annoying Stanley and his colleagues all day. Stanley had three assignments on the go at the same time, all due within days of each other.

"How's the Vanilla Café optimisation project coming along?" Richardson had asked for the fourth time earlier that day.

"It's coming," Stanley replied, typing customer data into a spreadsheet.

"I don't want to lose this client. Vanilla Café is an important client. Their donut sales lately have been through the roof and they need to expand. Them expanding means more work for us," Richardson explained.

'More work for us' really meant more work for Stanley and the other newer employees. Although Vanilla Café was Richardson's client, and he would be getting any corporate bonuses from the work, the manager claimed that 'efficiency was key' and being efficient meant giving the work to others.

By the time Stanley got into his apartment that evening, he was so tired from staring at a computer screen all day that he just flopped onto his couch and closed his eyes. Villain problems could wait until the morning. He was awoken by the apartment phone ringing. The loud ringing made his skin crawl. His heart beating quickly, Stanley got up from the couch and answered the phone.

"Hello?"

"Hi. Is this Stanley?" a man's voice asked.

"Yes, it is."

"Hi Stanley, this is Samuel! How are you doing this evening?"

Stanley exhaled in relief. It was Samuel the Salesman, one of Stanley's neighbours in Tayel Tower. Being called by Samuel was still a nuisance, but it was better than being called by a villain.

"I'm fine thanks," Stanley grumbled. "Is there something I can do for you? I'm not interested in buying anything."

"That's fine. I'm not selling anything."

Stanley was surprised. "You're not? The past three times you've called this month, all you wanted to do is sell me things."

"Well, this time, I want to give you something."

"Give me what?"

Samuel the Salesman paused for dramatic effect before announcing his gift. "Time."

"What are you talking about?" Stanley asked.

"I'm here to offer you time," Samuel repeated. "What would you do with more time?"

"At the moment you're taking more time, not giving it."

"Exactly! You would get more things done!" Samuel said as if he was reading from a script. Stanley, having been through this rigmarole a number of times already, sighed and hurried the salesman along. "So, you'd like to give me some time for free. What does it involve?"

"Well, the time is free. The ten-in-one super-speed slic-er-dicer costs only sixty-nine ninety—"

Stanley stopped Samuel's pitch. "I'm not interested."

"How about an eleven-in-one maximum speed slic-er-dicer-improviser?"

"What does the eleven-in-one do that the ten-in-one

can't do?"

"Take more of your money," Samuel admitted. Stanley hung up the phone. The phone rang again. Stanley frustratingly picked it up again. "Hello?" he barked.

"Oh. Have I caught you at a bad time?" Mandy the Midwife asked.

Stanley changed his tone, relieved it wasn't a villain or a salesman. "No, no. I'm sorry, I thought you were Samuel the Salesman calling with another sales pitch."

"I can call back later or even tomorrow if you just need a night to yourself," Mandy offered.

"No, I can talk now, just as long as you're not going to try and sell me a twelve-in-one knife or water bottle or guitar."

"Oh, well I do have a nine-in-one guitar I was going to pitch, but I'll leave it for another time."

Stanley laughed and slumped back down onto the couch. "How was your day?"

"My day was good thanks; quite relaxing actually. There were just routine checkups today. Not many babies are due this week, which is strange for this time in the middle of the year. How was your day?"

Stanley explained how Richard Richardson was passing on all his work to subordinates, and that meant that Stanley had a full plate of reports and plans to eat through.

"It sounds like you need a break," Mandy concluded.

"No truer words have ever been spoken," Stanley sighed. "I didn't realise a desk job could make me more tired than when I worked nine to five on my feet in a factory."

"You worked in a factory? What kind of factory?" Mandy asked.

"My Dad is a foreman in a pasta factory. From when I turned fifteen, I helped on the pasta packaging line. It was one of the most boring, tedious jobs imaginable. It was my motivation for getting a university degree and looking forward to a better career."

"What was the motivation for choosing a business degree specifically?" Mandy asked.

"I initially wanted to start my own business one day, but I got picked out of university for the job at the business consultancy firm, and the rest is history."

"Why don't you start your own part-time business?"

"I would if I knew what kind of business to start. But enough about me. What motivated you to pursue nursing and become a midwife? Did you also work in a pasta factory?"

Mandy laughed with her sweet laugh that made Stanley smile. "I worked in a restaurant while completing my studies. My interest in nursing came from my aunt who is also a midwife. The stories she would tell me were often joyful, but also sometimes heartbreaking. I wanted to follow in her footsteps and help mothers and babies."

"That's a much more noble cause than my career motivation," Stanley admitted. They sat in silence, one waiting for the other to continue the conversation.

"Do you want to go on a break, with me?" Stanley blurted out, his mouth saying the words before his brain had processed it. He cringed, waiting for the rejection.

"That sounds fun!" Mandy said. "We could go to Vanilla Café and try one of their amazing chocolate croissants as we talked about last week."

"Tomorrow afternoon?" Stanley suggested excitedly. "I finish work at four-thirty."

"Sounds wonderful. I finish work at four, but I'll meet you at Vanilla Café."

"Vanilla Café it is," smiled Stanley.

The hastily wished each other a good night and ended the call, saving topics of conversation for the following day. Stanley couldn't wipe the smile off his face as he made a dinner of instant noodles. He really did like Mandy and thanked his mouth for speaking faster than his brain. His brain would have most likely ruined it by reminding him he still didn't want to become too involved with the people in Tayel Tower. Getting a promotion and moving away in a few years was still Stanley's goal.

He poured boiling water over his noodles and leaned against the bench, waiting for the noodles to cook.

His doorbell rang. Hopeful that it might be Mandy wanting to go on a date there and then, Stanley opened the apartment door.

"Evening, Stanley," a man with an enormous nose and long, shiny flowing hair said.

Stanley almost fell over backwards slamming the door in Vincent the Villain's face. He stood in his hallway against the wall, frozen like a lemon ice-block caught in a light bulb. Vincent the Villain knocked on the door again with three sharp raps. Stanley remained silent hoping the villain would quickly give up and leave.

"Hey, Stanley!" Vincent called through the door. "I'm looking for some advice."

Stanley stayed silent.

"It's very rude to slam the door on a client's face," Vincent said. "I wouldn't do that too often, or you may run out of clients."

Stanley cleared his throat. "What do you want?"

"I already said; I'm looking for advice. You are a business consultant, are you not?"

Stanley didn't know Vincent the Villain very well at all, but the mere fact that he was known as 'Vincent the Villain' was a red flag in Stanley's book.

"Are you wanting to harm me?" Stanley asked with his hand on the doorknob.

"Harm you? What are you talking about? Why would I want to harm you?" Vincent replied.

Stanley opened the door very slowly, checking that Vincent didn't possess weapons of any kind.

Vincent, aware that Stanley was on edge, raised his empty hands in a show of innocence. "I'm unarmed."

Stanley kept his hand on the doorknob in case he needed to close it again quickly. "What do you want advice on?"

"A business," Vincent replied. "I'm looking to start a business but have very little business knowledge."

Stanley thought up a convenient excuse. "Even if I wanted to help you, I'm not really allowed to do consultations unless you go through the firm I work for."

Vincent, seemingly getting tired of interacting with this jumpy Stanley, rolled his eyes. "It's not illegal for you to sit down and answer some of my questions."

Vincent could see Stanley was still not convinced.

"How much do you get paid per job at your firm?" Vincent asked.

"It doesn't really work on a 'per job' basis…"

"Just give me a figure for what you'd charge if I was

some random nobody off the street who wanted advice on starting a shoe shop."

Stanley picked an absurd number. "Probably thirty thousand dollars for a statement of advice."

Vincent glared at Stanley, not believing that price for one moment. Without averting his gaze, Vincent pulled out his phone and tapped away at it for a minute.

"There. Thirty thousand has been transferred to your bank account," Vincent announced.

Stanley's eyes widened. Thirty thousand was almost half of his annual salary.

"How do you know my bank account details?" he asked sceptically.

Vincent remained expressionless. "Not important. I am now a paying client. May I please come in?"

Stanley reluctantly let Vincent enter his apartment. Vincent headed straight the kitchen, flicked on the kettle, and pulled out two mugs as if he knew Stanley's apartment intimately.

"Would you like a cup of tea?" Vincent asked. Stanley slowly entered his kitchen but stood back as far back as possible.

"Sure," he answered.

"Seeing as it's late at night, I'll have a herbal tea," Vincent said, scrummaging through Stanley's tea box. "Would you like a caffeinated or non-caffeinated tea?"

"Non-caffeinated," Stanley said, leaning against the wall.

Vincent paused his tea-making to look Stanley up and down. "I don't know how business consulting normally works, but I'm pretty sure you should be asking me questions."

Stanley sighed and went to find his stationery. He figured the faster things moved along, the sooner he could eat his noodles, go to bed, and dream of donuts, croissants, and dates with Mandy.

They settled in the living room. Stanley sat on the couch on one side of the room with a pad of paper resting on the arm of the chair, and a pen being chewed nervously in his mouth. He was still hungry. Vincent, on the adjacent couch, lay across the couch with his legs hanging over the edge. He surveyed the details of Stanley's living room décor, sparse as they were.

"You need a bit of colour in here," Vincent observed.

"I only moved in a couple of months ago," Stanley replied.

"And look at everything you've accomplished in that time. You've joined a secret society, got a hideous artwork you painted hanging in the lobby, and you have in your possession over twenty million dollars that you don't know what you're allowed to do with."

Vincent knowing all this information was of grave concern to Stanley. Absolutely no one but himself, Mandy the Midwife and Perry the Psychic knew about the winning lottery ticket that Stanley possessed.

But Stanley kept a straight face, neither confirming or denying Vincent's stories. He looked at the time on his phone. "It's getting late so we should get started. What usually happens in the first meeting of a business consultation is the client and consultant just get to know each other. So, let me ask you a couple of questions. Firstly, what is your full name?"

"Vincent."

"Just Vincent?"

"No, just 'Vincent'. Just Vincent was my father's name," Vincent smirked. Stanley looked at the man with disdain, wondering why he had let him into his apartment.

"Okay, what is your background in business?" Stanley enquired.

"None."

"What previous experience do you have in business?"

"Very little."

"Do you have any education in business?"

"No."

"What type of business do you want to start?"

At this question, Vincent's face came alive with excitement. He swished his luscious hair out of his face and sat up straight.

"Stanley, I am a genius," Vincent began. Stanley leaned forward a little, suddenly curious for how devious this villain's business would be.

"Last night," Vincent continued, "I was bored and eating dinner at Charlotte the Chef's highly exclusive and expensive restaurant, Trio. All my best ideas come to me when I am bored and eating dinner. I was eating the main course, which consisted of a leaf burger and flies, when I began pondering why everyone is always so exhausted and stressed at the end of every year. I consider myself to be very unexhausted and very unstressed, dare I say 'happy' at the end of the year, while everyone around me wanders around looking like stressed up stress balls of stress. But where does my happiness come from? I have lots of spare money, so maybe wealth brings happiness? I also have very few friends and family, so maybe friends and family don't bring as much bring happiness as everyone believes they do? Then it dawned on me; what the true cause of exhaustion, stress and unhappiness is: Christmas."

"Christmas?" Stanley repeated.

"Christmas," Vincent confirmed.

"So, what's the business idea?"

"I'm getting there," Vincent said. "At Christmas, there is an obligation and social requirement to buy presents for family and friends. The more family and friends you have the more presents you need to buy, the more decisions you need to make, and the more money you need to spend. That is why everyone else is so miserable! They've had to spend their money and time planning Christmas. So, then I thought how can I give people the same happiness I feel at Christmas?"

"Let me guess. By eliminating or kidnapping family and friends?" Stanley said quickly.

Vincent looked at Stanley like he was a madman. "No. That's a dumb idea. Who would do that?"

Stanley, embarrassed, scribbled his pen onto his pad of paper.

Vincent took a gulp of his tea. "My idea is to become Santa Claus."

CHAPTER TWO
THE DATE

"What do you mean 'become Santa Claus'?" Stanley asked.

"Santa Claus? You know, the mythical Christmas guy? I want to do his job," Vincent said, swigging back the rest of his tea.

"And what's the villainous aspect of the idea?"

"Villainous aspect?" Vincent shook his head in disbelief. "Who said anything about there being a villainous aspect to my business?"

Stanley, embarrassed that all his assumptions were being shut down, slowly said; "Well I just assumed, since you are known as Vincent the Villain, there would be some kind of villainous aspect to your business idea."

Vincent raised an eyebrow. "I'll let you know I don't appreciate being called Vincent the 'Villain'. It's very negative. How would you like it if I called you 'Stanley the Scoundrel' or 'Stanley the Scheming'?"

Stanley could see the man's point. "I apologise. I shouldn't have jumped to conclusions."

"That's okay," Vincent said, standing up and looking out the kitchen window across the night-time cityscape.

Stanley had heard that a real villain never knows or believes that they are a villain, but he did lower his guard. Maybe Vincent was just a 'mischief-maker', which in Stanley's hierarchy of evil falls below 'villain', but above 'nuisance'.

"So, you want to be Santa Claus?" Stanley asked, resuming the course of the consultation. "And how is being Santa Claus going to generate income?"

"I'm getting there," Vincent smiled mischievously. "As I was saying, there is an obligation at Christmas for people to buy presents for their friends and family. Parents have the unfortunate obligation of buying presents for their children."

"I would argue that some people, especially parents, enjoy giving presents at Christmas, and it's not an obligation for them," Stanley said.

"Yes, I'll give you that; presents at Christmas are a joy for some, but they're not my target market. Most parents find presents at Christmas an obligation. Therefore, my idea is to bring joy back into Christmas by removing the present-buying process that parents go through. Instead, with my business, which I've given the working title 'SAN-Ta', parents pay a flat fee, fill out a form about their child's personality. After a rigorous review by a trained team of present choosers, a present will be sent to the child on Christmas morning, and the parents won't have to think anything more of it."

Stanley had a million questions and struggled to know where to begin.

"Are you serious?" seemed like a good place to start.

"Am I serious?" Vincent replied. "Do you think I'd waste an hour of my time coming to you and making up a silly business idea? Of course I'm serious. I can see on your face you think my idea has merit. Does it not?"

Stanley wrote 'Santa' on his notepad.

"That's capital S-A-N-T with a little 'a'," Vincent said, peering over at Stanley's note.

"Why the little 'a'?"

"It's an acronym."

"What does it stand for?"

"I don't know. I'll come up with it later."

Vincent went to the pantry and found a packet of chips which he then opened and began munching on.

"So, to clarify," Stanley yawned. "Parents will pay you, say a hundred dollars or thereabouts and fill out a form profiling their child. You will hire employees who will evaluate each child's profile and pick an appropriate present for them. You will then order the present and ship it to the child's house."

"I was thinking parents would pay more like ten dollars," Vincent said between crunches.

"What present could you find and ship that is less than ten dollars?" Stanley asked. "Shipping alone could cost ten dollars."

"There are plenty of presents that can be ordered and shipped for less than ten dollars," Vincent said. "There are pens, phone cases, little teddy bears, pet rock kits. All sorts. Don't you worry about that."

"But parents normally spend more than ten dollars on their kids' presents. They'll feel cheap if they just pay someone else to buy their child a sub-ten-dollar present."

Vincent silently stared at Stanley, smiling through his snacking. Stanley waited for Vincent to agree or disagree.

It dawned on Stanley that what he had just said confirmed what Vincent was theorizing; parents felt obligated to get their children expensive presents.

Stanley cleared his throat. "I see…"

Vincent bounced up straight, sending some of his chips flying. "You're brilliant, Stanley!"

Stanley didn't know what he had said that was brilliant.

"You are right about the price. We'll make the cost a hundred dollars."

Stanley was surprised at this sudden change of plan. "But I thought you were just advocating that parent should pay less—"

"Nope, I like it," Vincent said. "Parents will pay a hundred dollars and I will scour the globe to find the perfect present for their sweet little children. Plus, as you said, shipping can be expensive."

Before Stanley could say another word, Vincent left the apartment, taking his bag of chips with him.

Stanley sat in his chair, stunned at what had just occurred. The mere fact that Vincent the apparent villain had come up with an idea that wasn't villainous scared Stanley even more. His neighbours at Tayel Tower were adamant that Vincent was a villain, but if they were wrong about that, what else were they wrong about? Were they all just a horrible group of people?

He locked his apartment door carefully and flopped onto his bed, falling asleep before he had time to put on his pyjamas.

****

"How's the Vanilla Café optimisation report coming along?" Richard Richardson asked holding a donut.

"I'm almost done. I need to finish going over their donut sales," Stanley explained, getting very tired of the question. "There is a lot of numbers here for a lot of varieties of donuts."

"Well, come on now. The others have finished with their sections of the report. It's only you left." Richardson took a noisy 'scrunch' of his jam filled donut. "Have you tried their donuts? They're amazing!"

"I've had one or two," Stanley said, trying to ignore the falling donut crumbs.

Richardson continued to enjoy his donut, hovering over Stanley's desk. "By the way—"

Stanley almost hit the desk in annoyance. "Yes?"

"When you've finished on Vanilla Café, I have more client projects to begin on. There's a bird company that thinks they've found oil in the middle of an Australia desert, and a mining company whose sales are projected to go through the roof at the end of the year. They're both due at the end of next week. And in case you haven't heard, I'm going on holidays as of this very moment and won't be back until the hour before the reports are due."

Richard Richardson left Stanley alone. The knowledge that Richardson was leaving was a relief. He could handle the work, just not the interruptions. Stanley, exhausted from his day of hard work, like the doctors that tried to determine how Beethoven died, watched the time slowly tick over to 4:00 pm.

His head and heart finally had a reason to be joyful: His date with Mandy the Midwife was in just half an hour! Everything was suddenly exciting, except for doing more work, so in the fifteen minutes before leaving to walk to the café, Stanley searched the internet for first date etiquettes.

The advice he found was less than helpful:

Question: Should you take a gift on a first date?

Answer: A gift is appropriate, but only in moderation. A box of chocolates is fine, a puppy is not. A bunch of flowers is fine, a brand-new car is not. A bottle of olive oil is fine, an engagement ring is not.

Question: Who should pay for the first date?

Answer: Paying for the date is appropriate, but only in moderation. If the date went really well, well enough that the couple is married before the date is finished, it is customary that the couple shares the cost of the date, but you must also pay for everyone else in the café, as it is now your reception. You may also request that the other café patrons give you gifts since it is now your special day.

If the date went just okay, it is appropriate for the man to pay the bill. He should, however, be sure that everyone else takes notice, especially any disgruntled female café patrons who need to see 'what a real man looks like'.

If the date went horribly, it is appropriate to pretend that the meal or coffee has just given you food poisoning, and you require immediate assistance from a medical professional. Choking or collapsing on the ground also provides closure to the date, and in most cases, cafes do not charge patrons that have almost died from eating their food.

"What are you up to?" someone asked behind him.

Stanley almost fell out of his chair. He turned to see Vincent the Villain eating a donut he had stolen from the break room.

"What are you doing here?" Stanley asked.

"I came to see how you were doing on the business plan for SANTa," Vincent said casually.

"Who let you up here?"

"The receptionist. This isn't the Buckingham palace under heavy guard."

Stanley began packing his belongings into his backpack and shut down his computer. "I'm sorry Vincent. I haven't had a chance to look at the SANTa business plan yet. I've got three other projects that need to be finished first. I will get to yours on the weekend."

"And how much is this firm paying you to do those three projects?" Vincent asked as Stanley walked past.

Stanley looked around fearfully to see if any of his colleagues had heard Vincent's question. He was fully aware that accepting a client without going through the firm was breaching rules. With no one else within earshot, Stanley lowered his voice. "Look, I want to help you with your business planning, but no amount of money can create time out of nothing. You asked for my helpless than twenty-four hours ago."

"Well, where are you going now?" Vincent asked, following Stanley outside.

"I'm going to meet a friend," Stanley said.

"Mandy?" Vincent asked.

"Yes," Stanley snapped.

They exited the office building. Stanley paused and turned to face Vincent. "I promise I'll look at SANTa over the weekend. I promise."

"I can't wait to hear about it," Vincent smiled and went on his merry way.

Stanley again wished he had never opened his apartment door last night for Vincent.

Vanilla Café was a reasonably large café that served breakfast, lunch, teas, coffee, and cakes. It was almost always busy with a regular flow of business people between meetings, entrepreneurs having meetings, ladies having lunch dates, and timid men and women having first dates. As it was nearly closing time, the café was much quieter. There were only two or three tables being used.

Stanley entered the café and spotted Mandy in one of the booths. She spotted him across the room and her biggest, warmest smile that Stanley had seen, and it made his heart skip more beats than a sloth at a drum set.

It is at this point I feel I can skip over the next half hour of events. First dates, you see, are only interesting for the two people taking part in the first date. Topics of conversation like family, dreams, career aspirations, favourite movies and books etc. may be very telling about a person's world view, but in most cases, those topics of conversations are merely interrogations to find out if there is an alignment on the major issues of life.

Stanley and Mandy had a most enjoyable time over tea and chocolate croissants getting to know each other, going through the phases of judging each other based on looks; to judging each other based on their senses of humour, to judging each other based on ambitions, to judging each other based on their opinion of the appropriate length of men's hair. A couple getting to the stage of judging each other based on their opinion of how long a man's hair should be is about as solid a couple can be although few couples manage to reach this phase. If couples agree on this point, marital bliss is guaranteed. Couples that disagree on a man's head or beard length are able to live together, but counselling is recommended to achieve unity. Alternatively, just saying 'Yes, I agree, dear', also works quite well.

"So, are you saying, if I was to grow a beard, I would be less or more attractive?" Stanley asked with a cheeky grin.

Mandy looked intently at Stanley's bare chin. "I will admit, I do prefer beards. They make men look slightly older and wiser."

"It's decided then. I'm going to grow a long grey beard like a wizard," Stanley announced.

Mandy laughed. "But beards can't be too long."

Stanley pretended to be annoyed. "Well, you better decide quickly, because I've already started on my long wizard beard. You have to let me know your preferences before it's too late!"

They both took a bite out of their luxurious, buttery chocolate croissants.

I will vouch for these croissants. They are better than anything, no everything, you have ever eaten in your life. People travel from across the globe to sample one of Vanilla Café's pastries and when they do, it is like they have sampled heaven. Chocolate-Filled heaven with a dusting of icing sugar on top and extra wide pearly gates.

"Okay, so what about head hair? Do you think long head hair on a man is attractive?" Stanley asked.

"How long do you mean?" Mandy asked.

"Say, like Vincent the Villain's hair length."

"Vincent the Villain's hair is an exception to the rule. He needs to have that length of hair for his job. But his length of hair on any other man?" Mandy cringed.

Stanley nodded in agreement but began thinking about

Vincent the Villain. "What do you think about Vincent?"

Mandy shrugged her shoulders. "It's hard to know with Vincent. One day he's as innocent as anyone else, and the next day you hear he's locked Ernest out of the elevator or replaced all the instruments at the city orchestra with rubber chickens. If I'm being honest, I think he's just a socially awkward man looking for attention."

"I think you could be right," agreed Stanley. "Who first started calling him Vincent the 'Villain'? That seems... mean to call someone a villain. He told me he doesn't like people calling him a villain."

Mandy almost choked on her mouthful of tea. "He said that? He was the one that came up with it! He thought it was a very exciting title for himself."

All Stanley could do was give a nervous laugh at Vincent the Villain's deceptions.

"But anyway, enough about Vincent," Mandy smiled. "I'm really enjoying getting to know you better. Do you have any plans for this weekend?"

Stanley, for the umpteenth time that day, reprimanded himself for agreeing to help Vincent. "I'd really love to catch-up this weekend, I really would, but we're getting swamped at work. I have three projects at work due very soon, as well as a business feasibility report I need to do over the weekend."

"What is the feasibility report for?" Mandy asked. Stanley realised he should have left the final part out. He wasn't sure how Mandy would react knowing he was now employed by the socially awkward villain who was looking for attention.

"Oh, it's just a little project for someone—"

"Stanley!" someone called across the café. The blood drained away from Stanley's face until he was as white as the teeth on a dentist's training dummy.

Vincent weaved his way through the café tables. "And Mandy as well! How lovely to see you both. Do you mind if I pull up a chair?" He pulled up a chair. "How's my business report coming along?"

Vincent grabbed a glass off an empty table, proceeding to pour himself some water.

Mandy raised her eyebrows, connecting Vincent to Stanley's weekend project.

Stanley had turned from fearful to angry. He spoke as quietly and calmly as he could under the circumstances. "I already told you, not an hour ago, I can't work on it until later. Right now, I am having afternoon tea with Mandy. Please leave us alone."

"Has Stanley told you about SANTa?" Vincent asked Mandy.

"Santa?" Mandy asked.

"SANTa. It's the brilliant idea that Stanley and I came up with."

"You came up with the idea," Stanley corrected.

"No, I can't take all the credit," Vincent insisted. "You helped add the finishing touches. Stanley has a brilliant mind, Mandy. He's a real catch."

"Thank you, and I can't wait to hear all about the business idea, but another time, please, Vincent," Mandy said politely.

"So, it's brilliant," Vincent continued, ignoring Mandy. "You know how at Christmas how there is always pressure on parents to spend copious amounts of money and try and find the perfect gift for their children? Well, with SAN-Ta, we're removing that pressure by providing a service in which parents pay a fee, fill out a personality form, and then on Christmas Eve we'll send their child a present that best fits their personality."

"That sounds like an interesting idea," Mandy said.

"I know, thank you. But because I'm not much of a businessman, I've enlisted the help of our friend Stanley here. But I should warn you, Mandy, this man does not come cheap. Thirty thousand dollars for one measly feasibility report?" Vincent laughed and took a drink of his water. "I should hope you expect a pretty fancy Christmas present from him."

Vincent looked into Stanley's eyes and detected there was an immediate danger of bodily harm.

"Well, I won't keep you from your date," Vincent announced, rising from his chair. "Have a wonderful evening."

He left with a grin on his face, leaving Stanley to assemble all the broken pieces of information for Mandy.

"I said it would cost him thirty thousand dollars so that he would leave me alone. I forgot that he was rich and bored," Stanley explained.

"So, he actually gave you thirty thousand dollars?" Mandy whispered in surprise.

Stanley nodded. Mandy sat back in her chair, silent and expressionless.

"What do we do? He's paid me for work I don't want to do," Stanley sighed. "What if we give the money to charity?"

"We?" Mandy asked.

"I mean 'me'; I mean 'I'; What if I give the money to charity," Stanley stuttered. "The problem is it's not a villainous or even really a bad idea."

"Do you know that for sure?" Mandy asked.

"Well, no," Stanley admitted.

Mandy took a deep breath. "If it was my problem, I would give back the money and say I'm unable to complete the job."

"This is a neurotic villain we are talking about. I don't exactly want to be on his bad side," Stanley said.

"Is being on a neurotic villain's good side any better?"

Stanley knew Mandy had a point. She always had a point.

CHAPTER THREE

'TIS THE SEASON TO
BE A VILLAIN

Telling the story of Vincent the Villain's Christmas busi-ness and Stanley's dilemma about helping a villain requires a large time jump. In the time between Stanley and Mandy's first date and December 23rd, many interesting, exciting, dangerous, mind-blowing events happened at Tayel Tower that I will need to cover one day, but for now I will skip all of those tales to focus on the story at hand. The import-ant thing to know is Mandy and Stanley continued to see each other, growing very fond of each other, to the point at which they became known as a 'couple'. In this sense of being a 'couple'. Also, Stanley, in a stroke of genius, came up with an idea for how to get rid of Vincent the Villain as a client the week after he and Mandy's first date.

"I'm back!" Richard Richardson had announced loudly through the office. There was a collective gasp of everyone trying to hold in their groans.

"Welcome back!" Stanley said cheerfully.

"Thank you, Stanley. It feels great to be back. The wife and I went for a holiday to the coast. There was sun and sand and water; everything you'd expect the coast to have."

"Sounds brilliant!" Stanley exclaimed with a big smile as Richardson entered his own office. Before Richardson closed the door behind him, it was like a switch went off in the manager's head. His holiday smile turned into a working frown. "Are the reports done?"

"Absolutely they're done," Stanley confirmed. "All three projects have been completed and sent off. And I've even gone so far as to get you another client."

"Get me another client? Looking for a bonus are you, Stanley? Who is it?"

"It's this gentleman from my apartment building. He's a true entrepreneur at heart but has very little business experience. He needs a feasibility report for a Christmas-centric business idea."

"Does this man have money, or is he just some cherry picker?"

"He's a very wealthy man paying top dollar for our services. He's already paid twenty thousand dollars."

Richardson nodded his head, impressed with Stanley's initiative. "Twenty thousand is a healthy sum for a man with little business experience. Well, I'm sure you'll do a good job on the report." Richardson reached into his wallet and pulled out a fifty-dollar note. "This is your bonus."

Stanley declined the money. "The only thing, sir, is he's asked specifically for you to write the report."

"For me to write the report?"

"Yes, sir. I told him you've had a lot of success consulting for retail businesses around the Christmas season. He said he would only go with this firm if you consulted directly."

Richardson puffed up his chest proudly, like a man that

just won an air eating contest. "Well, he's not wrong that I've done very well with my retail clients around Christmas. Email me his phone number, and I'll get to work."

Convincing Vincent the Villain, on the other hand, wasn't quite as easy.

"...trust me when I say my boss, Richard Richardson, is the right man to help you with this business idea."

"But I thought you thought it was a good idea?" Vincent said as they rode up the elevator together.

"Yes, but I'm more of a numbers guy. Richard Richardson is more of a visionary; a strategic wizard," Stanley explained.

Vincent gave it a moment of thought. "No, I'm happy to use you. I've already paid you the money."

"And that's the great thing! If you go with the consultancy firm, instead of just me, you'll actually save money! The firm will only cost you twenty thousand dollars. You can keep the extra ten thousand for yourself or invest it into SANTa."

"I'd be happy to take an extra ten thousand dollars," Ernest the Elevator Operator added.

"What would you need an extra ten thousand dollars for?" Vincent asked Ernest. "You never leave this elevator."

"I have my hobbies," Ernest said defensively. "At the moment I've taken up a hobby in whale watching."

"Whale watching? Where are you watching whales?" Stanley asked.

"Here."

"Here?"

"Yes, here. It's incredibly expensive getting the whales

here. Hence why I could do with ten thousand. It would pay for the whales' petrol money."

Vincent and Stanley ignored Ernest.

"So, let me get this correct," Vincent said to Stanley. "You're willing to give up thirty thousand dollars, a good chunk of your usual salary I'm sure, because you think your boss, who probably gets paid triple your own salary, will do a better job?"

Stanley swallowed. "Yes."

The elevator stopped at the sixth floor.

The villain paused before exiting. "Pay your firm whatever it wants, keep the rest. I don't care."

"So, you're off the hook now?" Mandy confirmed.

"I'm off the hook," Stanley smiled. They had decided on the Tayel Tower rooftop garden as the location for their second official date together. Mandy had made some white-chocolate and raspberry muffins, Stanley provided chairs, and they were watching the sunset over the adjacent buildings.

"What do you want for Christmas?" Stanley asked.

"It's a bit far away to be thinking about Christmas," Mandy laughed sweetly.

"I know, but let's say Christmas is tomorrow. What would you want for Christmas tomorrow?"

Mandy gave the question a moment of thought. "I watched this wildlife tv show last night about pandas. I'd like a panda."

"A panda? Where are you going to keep a panda?" Stanley laughed.

"I think the Tayel Tower basement is empty. We could put him down there. I'd provide him with some bamboo to eat and could take him out for walks here on the rooftop."

"And what would this panda's name be?"

"I think I'd call him… Stanley."

Stanley almost spat chunks of muffin all over his date. "Stanley? Do I remind you of a panda?"

"No, not at all," Mandy smiled. "It would be pure coincidence. I think you and the panda would be best friends. You'd have so much to talk about."

"The panda can talk in this scenario?"

"Yes, I forgot to mention it should be a talking panda."

"I think this present is going to be beyond my budget. Is there anything smaller you'd like?"

Mandy looked at her date happily. "A framed photo of us could be nice."

Stanley's heart almost ran out of his chest and did a joyful decathlon.

"What about you?" Mandy asked.

"I never know what to ask for. In the end, my family often just gets me movie vouchers, book vouchers or shirts. Oh, I know!" he exclaimed. "I want a 'do not disturb unless you are Mandy' sign for my apartment door. It would also be nice to have a personal secretary to quell the flow of neighbours coming and asking for things."

"I know a pretty good secretary," Mandy said.

"Who's that?"

"Well, there's this panda I'm going to get for Christmas named Stanley who has a diploma in office management…"

It really is a good thing that love has a sense of humour because the studio audience of birds in the rooftop garden watching the date unfold wondered if they were missing the jokes.

****

Stanley didn't see or hear from Vincent the Villain in the months leading up to Christmas or hear any mention of the Christmas business apart from Richardson mentioning what a strange client Stanley had given him.

That was until December when the first billboards appeared. Stanley walked past the billboard of a crying child holding an empty box a few times to and from work before actually reading it.

'Don't let Christmas bring you down', the billboard read in gigantic candy-cane coloured letters. Stanley let out a nervous laugh when he saw the call to action at the bottom: 'Book SANTa to bring your kids joy today'. This was followed by a website address.

From then on, Stanley couldn't get away from SANTa. More billboards of sad kids with empty boxes and happy kids with boxes full of toys appeared all over the city, at every conceivable corner and on every blank wall.

Commercials for the service were broadcast on television, radio and the internet. Morning talk shows invited Vincent the Villain onto their programs to talk about the new service. It was the fastest growing, most talked about business of the year. There were even rumours that SANTa was going to sell shares on the stock market before their first Christmas!

Suffice it to say, the publicity and the laziness and anxiety of parents all over the city meant there was an influx of orders to SANTa. Richard Richardson was in his finest mood ever for the holiday season. Vincent, with little idea on how to grow or scale a business, was literally throwing money at Richardson to help him run the business and make the important financial decisions while Vincent stood as the face of the company.

"He's the best client ever!" Richardson exclaimed on the 23rd of December to Stanley, who was busy cleaning up his desk, ready for two weeks of holidays.

"This Vincent lad sure is enthusiastic! He can't help but pay more and more money to us for advice and help. He's easily paid the firm over three hundred thousand dollars so far," Richardson reached into his pocket and pulled out a $100 note. "Well done, Stanley. This is a Christmas bonus for your satisfactory work this year."

Stanley forced a smile as he accepted the tiny bonus, which he knew he was due in overtime pay anyway.

"How is SANTa going?" Stanley asked.

"It's growing like a tomato on steroids. It's received over twenty thousand orders so far, and the orders are coming in every day by the hundreds."

One of Stanley's colleagues, an intelligent, soft-spoken man named Colson, approached Richardson. "Sorry, sir. South Tip Mining is on the phone. They said they need you straight away."

Richardson briskly went back to his office to take the call.

Stanley picked up a shopping bag from under his desk. He opened the bag and pulled out a stuffed panda to take another look at it. He had gone to the shops with the intention of buying a nice hand cream or something for his girlfriend, but as soon as he laid eyes on the stuffed panda, he remembered Mandy the Midwife's request from months ago and changed his plans. He found a little frame as well.

He smiled as he held the panda in his hands. Life was good. He was glad he decided to stay at Tayel Tower.

Richardson's office door swung open violently. "Stanley, put down the zebra bear. You're staying on for another couple of hours before you go on holidays. South Tip Mining desperately needs assistance. They've apparently made some big deal and need you to go over the contract."

"They need me to go over the contract?" Stanley challenged, seeing as South Tip Mining was Richardson's client.

"Well, they need me to go over the contract, but I've got other things to do. I nominate you as my best man for the job," Richardson clarified.

Stanley rolled his eyes, placing the panda back in its bag (not recommended for real pandas unless it's a sleeping bag). He had hoped to get home and wrap Mandy's presents that night while maybe listen to a couple of Christmas tunes to get himself in the Christmas spirit. He was tired. He was done for the year. He only had two more years on the books, and he would be able to move back to the suburbs with the pay rise and promotion that he desired. That goal had been his only motivation for putting up with the characters at Tayel Tower until he met Mandy. He didn't know what his goal was anymore.

Stanley slumped back down into his desk chair and picked up the phone, dialling South Tip Mining's number and resolved to the fact he would probably be there in the office all night long.

****

Stanley's eyes grew heavy as he stared at the contract on his screen, reading it line by line to look for any errors and ensure the contract was fair.

His mobile phone vibrated. "Hello," he answered, not looking at the caller ID.

"Hello, darling," Mandy said sweetly.

"Hello. What are you doing calling so late?"

"It's only seven," Mandy laughed. Stanley looked out the window, realising he had only been there for less than an hour.

"I'm out the front with dinner. Will you unlock the door for me please?"

Stanley rushed to the front door of the now empty office building and opened it for who he rated as the best girlfriend on earth. They took the boxes of stir-fry noodles up to Stanley's desk and ate while Stanley continued to scan over the contract.

"So, what's the contract for?" Mandy asked.

"It's just a really basic contract for the sale of coal, but it's a multi-million-dollar deal which the mining company insists is urgent. I just need to make sure there are no mistakes, and that the mining company isn't getting taken advantage of."

"Who needs coal this urgently before Christmas?"

Stanley began scrolling to the bottom of the contract. "It's entirely possible it's a power plant looking to have reserves of coal in case there is an energy spike over the holiday break. Or maybe someone's just really cold."

He reached the bottom of the document and read the recipient. "Seasons And New Traditions, asparagus." He re-read the name a number of times in his head. "Asparagus? Surely that's a typo."

The realisation hit Stanley like a wave of nuts and bolts in a sea of washers and screws. He dropped his box of noodles on the desk and turned to look at Mandy, who, in a rare turn of events, didn't know what was going on.

"What's wrong?" she asked.

"Season And New Traditions, asparagus," Stanley repeated, accentuating the first letter of every word. Mandy's noodles almost fell to the floor but thankfully her lap was there to catch the box.

"What does Vincent need with thirty thousand tonnes of coal?" Stanley asked, but deep down he knew exactly what was coming next. He hoped it wasn't true, he prayed it wasn't true, but it turned out Vincent the Villain was a villain through and through.

****

In Christmas movies, Christmas morning is often introduced by the sound of jingle bells, kids running up and down the stairs to see what Santa had left in their stockings, and the happy laughter of parents seeing the joy on their children's faces. That Christmas, however, was introduced at 2 am in the morning by an army of dump trucks travelling from the coal storage field at the city power station to the suburbs. At each house where SANTa had been ordered, exactly one metric-tonne of coal was dumped in the driveway, in the front yard, or, when there was no other place for the pile of black, ashy coal to be dumped, it went on the sidewalk.

Stanley and Mandy, having no luck finding Vincent between their realisation and Christmas morning, were forced to simply wait to see the aftermath of SANTa.

Stanley felt responsible for allowing the villain to go about his villainous plan for so long.

"You weren't to know," Mandy said comfortingly as

they sat watching the news on Christmas morning, both wearing Christmas-themed shirts and matching elf ears. The news helicopter circled above the city, filming the piles of coal that littered the city streets.

"The signs were all there," Stanley said, shaking his head.

There was a knock at his front door. Stanley, still feeling sick at the thought of kids waking up with no presents and parents with a pile of coal at their front doors, opened his door. There was no one there. He looked down and found a single piece of coal sitting on the hallway carpet. His snapped his head to the left to see Vincent the Villain walking away.

"You!" cried Stanley.

Vincent stopped and turned. "No need to say thanks. Merry Christmas to you too."

Stanley felt helpless and angry. "How could you do that? You just ripped off thousands of parents and made thousands of children unhappy."

"First of all, I didn't rip anyone off. A tonne of coal equals around a hundred dollars. I even got a bulk discount from South Tip Mining. Secondly; yes."

"Yes, what?"

"Yes, I did make thousands of children unhappy."

"But why? What did they do to you?"

"Absolutely nothing," Vincent laughed.

"Then why did you do it?"

"Because I was bored while I was eating dinner one night. But, Stanley, I must say you're a little bit to blame for all this. Originally, I was just going to give a single piece of coal, but then you suggested the parents pay more money, and I thought what's funnier than one piece of coal? Tonnes of coal."

"That's just evil," Stanley said.

"I'm a villain: Vincent the Villain. What did you expect?"

And with that, Vincent the Villain left via the stairwell with a big grin on his face.

Stanley returned to his apartment and collapsed onto the couch. "I don't know if I can handle this much, Mandy."

Mandy frowned. "It's not your fault, my love. You can't take all the blame upon yourself."

At that moment, Stanley's phone rang. He had changed his ringtone to 'Santa Claus is Coming to Town', which sounded ominous in such a cheerless moment. Stanley looked at the caller ID. It was his manager, Richard Richardson. He rolled his eyes and let the phone ring.

"Are you going to answer it?" Mandy asked.

"It's Christmas. Not the time for a work call," Stanley said.

"Maybe he's ringing to say Merry Christmas?"

"Maybe he wants me to come into the office?"

"Maybe it's an emergency?"

"You can answer it if you'd like to," Stanley said, holding out the phone. "But you must do it in a panda voice."

Mandy laughed and answered Stanley's phone using her sweet, but very un-panda like voice. She listened for a minute or two, giving the occasional 'uh-huh' and 'I'll let him know'. Stanley, unable to hear the call, watched Mandy's face change through a mix of emotions that ended in serious concentration.

"Thank you, have a merry Christmas." She ended the call.

Stanley waited in silence expectantly.

"Richardson said due to your performance this year at the firm, the pay rise and promotion is yours. You can move out of Tayel Tower and back to the suburbs as soon as you're ready."

Wray Wrigley's

TAYEL TOWER

Book 6

INVOLUNTARY CRIMES
OF EATING

CHAPTER ONE
HEAVY THOUGHTS

'To be fit or not to be fit'. That is the question one must ask themselves when faced with a delicious looking chocolate-hazelnut tart. Who does one blame for this temptation? One's self for going out of their way to walk past the local cafe? Maybe the baker for deciding to bake chocolate-hazelnut tarts that day? Or maybe the inventor of the tart, Mr Tart, is to blame for causing the anguish of millions who see a rich, smooth, chocolate filling inside a buttery pastry shell.

Stanley chose to blame Vanilla Café for placing their premises between his workplace and his apartment at Tayel Tower. He stood outside the café pretending to message someone on his phone. He was really fighting with his inner soul in favour of buying and consuming a chocolate-hazelnut tart.

"It's a dilemma, isn't it," Jarvis the Jobless said, having stopped on the footpath next to Stanley.

"What's a dilemma? I'm just texting," Stanley said quickly, holding up his phone.

"I can see you're having the same dilemma about what

type of windows they use in the café," Jarvis said. "I'm 90 per cent sure they use double-glazed, but I'm also 10 per cent sure that double-glazed isn't a real type of glass."

"That's less of a dilemma and more of a question, isn't it?" Stanley asked.

"The question is whether they are trying to keep people out, or the pastries in," Jarvis said thoughtfully, giving the windows a tap.

"Probably both," Stanley said.

Jarvis the Jobless nodded his head approvingly. "Well, it's doing a pretty good job."

Jarvis' mouth dropped open as he watched the café door opened and a lady exit holding a sausage roll.

Stanley followed his eyes. "Surely you know that doors exist."

"Of course I know doors exist," Jarvis said. "They said they were all out of sausage rolls! That lady has a sausage roll!"

"Maybe they just made a fresh batch," Stanley suggested. "Go in and buy one."

Jarvis excitedly pulled out a fake moustache and glasses and put them on his face.

"What's the disguise for?" Stanley asked.

"They often refuse to serve me," Jarvis said. He walked up to the café door and knocked three times upon the glass.

Inside the café, the barista looked over at who was knocking and dropped his shoulders. The barista marched over to the door and whipped it open. "Sir! How many times must I tell you we don't accept fake moustaches and glasses as payment for sausage rolls!"

Jarvis moped away down the street leaving Stanley to

shake his head at the man's ideas. The barista nodded in Stanley's direction. "You know, you could come in and have a coffee while you play on your phone."

"Oh, no thank you," Stanley said, thinking of an excuse for his loitering. "I'm waiting for a friend."

"Okay," the barista said and returned inside. Now Stanley truly had a dilemma on his hands. He could stand where he was and wait for a friend to come along and turn his lie into a half-truth, or he could leave and miss out on the sweet taste of a chocolate-hazelnut tart.

"Stanley!" A man's voice called. Stanley turned from the tarts in the window to see Boris the Body Builder walking his way. Boris was fit. To say he was just fit was an understatement. He was 'ripped', 'buff', 'muscular', 'toned' and whatever other synonyms one could use to describe a penguin who just found out all the lady penguins hung out at a gym. Bodybuilding was Boris' life, but not his trade. He was a tailor and was known for making some of the finest suits in the city. Boris the Body Builder himself, like a penguin, appreciated suits and could always be seen wearing a three-piece suit of the finest materials available. It was said that the material Boris required to make suits that fit his ginormous physique was the sole factor keeping southern Europe out of a financial recession.

"Boris!" Stanley greeted back with a smile to his Tayel Tower neighbour.

"What are you up to?" Boris asked, shaking Stanley's hand.

"Oh, just texting," Stanley said, casually waving his phone around. "I was thinking of grabbing a pastry on my way home from work. Would you like to join me?"

"Oh, you know I love food," Boris said. "Easily the second-best thing after silk and working out. What were you thinking of getting?"

"Well, I had my eyes on a chocolate-hazelnut tart—"

"Oh no," Boris said.

"What's wrong?" Stanley asked, seeing the fear on the big man's face.

"A chocolate-hazelnut tart? Do you know how much sugar that has in it?" Boris asked in a quiet voice.

"Probably a lot," Stanley said.

"The amount of sugar and fat in a chocolate-hazelnut tart means you'd need to run a marathon to burn it off!" Boris said.

"It's alright if you eat it sometimes, isn't it?" Stanley asked. "Besides, I can run the epsilon marathon that's happening next week if I start feeling too heavy."

The epsilon marathon was a marathon race that took place in the city every year. Epsilon, which is the fifth letter of the Greek alphabet, could lead one to believe that this was the fifth year that the marathon was taking place, but that person would be wrong and should know better. The marathon did start with the alpha marathon, but that was thirty-two years ago. The organisers reached 'epsilon marathon' in their fifth year and liked the name so much that they decided to call it 'epsilon marathon' ever since.

"Yes, sometimes," Boris nodded. "I treat myself to a donut once every ten years. You don't know how unbelievably good a donut tastes when you only have one every ten years. Unfortunately, I ate a donut about six years ago, so I need to wait another four years before I have another."

"That's very disciplined of you," Stanley said. "Especially if you like food so much."

"Love food," Boris said. "I love food. Easily the second-best thing behind fresh cotton and working out. I have to keep going but we should get dinner sometime. We should go to Charlotte the Chef's restaurant, Trio. It's incredibly exclusive, but I know Charlotte personally. She lives in the same building as me."

"I also live in the same building as you," Stanley said. "I know Charlotte personally as well… doesn't matter, sure, we should get dinner sometime. I'd be interested to hear about what being a tailor is like," Stanley said.

"Okay, well enjoy your chocolate-hazelnut tart," Boris said, moving away quickly. Stanley sighed. His stomach had won. He entered the café and walked to the counter. "One chocolate-hazelnut tart, please."

The owner looked into the display cabinet. "I'm sorry, we're all out of chocolate hazelnut tarts."

"What?!" Stanley exclaimed. "I just saw some in there!"

He looked into the cabinet where the tarts had been, and where there were once pastries, only crumbs remained. He looked around the café to see who had taken the last of the tarts. Jarvis the Jobless sat at a table, a deliciously good-looking tart on his plate. Stanley left the café and continued walking home. To cope with his loss, he started wondering if missing out on the tart was life telling him that he should ease up on the desserts.

He was only a couple of blocks away from Tayel Tower when he saw a peculiar sight. Boris the Body Builder sat cross-legged in the middle of the sidewalk with his eyes closed. For such an odd place to be sitting, other pedestrians needing to walk a wide birth to avoid knocking into the muscular man, Boris appeared to be quite at peace.

"Are you okay?" Stanley asked the man.

Boris opened one eye. "No, Stanley, I'm not."

"Do you need an ambulance?"

"I don't think that would help," Boris said, closing his eye again and taking a deep breath in.

Stanley, aware of the many onlookers, kneeled next to the big man. "If you're looking for a comfortable place to meditate, you've chosen a very uncomfortable spot."

Boris opened his eyes. "I was walking away from the café when I had a heavy thought. My heavy thought was wondering if heavy thoughts carry weight. If I have too many heavy thoughts, will that cause me to gain good weight or bad weight? And where does the weight from heavy thoughts go? I assume the weight from a heavy thought goes from one's brain to one's chin, but I'm not sure. But if heavy thoughts do put on weight, I'm gaining a lot of weight, because I'm currently having a lot of heavy thoughts!"

Stanley felt deeply concerned for the man. "That's a really unhealthy way of thinking."

"So you agree with me then?" Boris asked.

"No, I don't agree that thinking is unhealthy. I think that you thinking thinking is unhealthy is unhealthy," Stanley said. "Why don't we walk back to Tayel Tower and you can go and relax at home. Maybe listen to some music or watch TV?"

"Does listening to music cause you to gain weight?" Boris asked.

"Not that I know of," Stanley said.

"Then where does the sound go when it enters your

ears? It can't just disappear can it?"

"I'm no physicist," Stanley said, "But I'm pretty sure sound waves don't carry any weight."

"I don't know," Boris said. "I've heard some pretty heavy songs in my time."

Stanley changed tact. "Well, maybe you should listen to some lighter music instead. Like country music."

"Oh no," Boris shook his head. "Country music once gave me tonsillitis."

Stanley stood up from the pavement and offered his hand to help the large gentleman. It was of little use to hoisting the 200kg man. Boris the Body Builder slowly walked alongside Stanley to their home.

"I just can't stop these weighty thoughts now. Do birds really fly?" Boris asked, watching a pigeon walking in the gutter. "Or are they just taking really big jumps from location to location? What is the purpose behind sleep? Maybe sleep was invented by the mattress industry to sell more products!"

"Do you know Paige the Psychologist?" Stanley asked.

"I know of Paige," Boris said. "I haven't talked to her personally though."

"Maybe you should get to know her. She could help you out with your heavy thoughts."

"I've talked to Patrick the Psychiatrist, Paige's brother," Boris said, "and he told me that psychologists are all 'voodoo mumbo-jumbo' and don't know what they're talking about."

"Well, then maybe you could talk to Patrick the Psychiatrist?" Stanley suggested.

"I don't know," Boris said. "I was talking to an anti-medication activist who said that psychiatrists are all about giving unnecessary medications."

"That sounds a little biased, doesn't it?" Stanley asked.

"Maybe," Boris replied. "But the anti-medication activist said he was a doctor of enlightenment, so he must have had some medical experience."

The two men walked, one after the other due to one of the men's oversized frame, through the front door of Tayel Tower. The lobby was bustling with people coming home from work, people pretending they were coming home from work, and Jarvis the Jobless attempting to build a cat-pyramid on a coffee table using six cats he had purchased after been told they had been trained for tricks such as replicating Egyptian monuments and rap battles.

Stanley spotted Paige the Psychologist checking her mail and excitedly pointed her out to Boris the Body Builder. Stanley led the reluctant man to meet her.

"Paige, this is Boris the Body Builder," Stanley introduced.

Paige shook the big man's hand. "Hello there Boris. How can I help you two gentlemen?"

Stanley looked to Boris to explain he wanted to sit down and talk about heavy thoughts, but the big man sheepishly stared at the ground.

"Boris was wondering if it might be possible to make an appointment," Stanley said. "I think it would be great if you could have a talk with him."

Paige the Psychologist nodded empathetically. "Absolutely. There's no shame in seeing a psychologist, Boris. We can have a quick chat about whatever you want. I'll just need you to ring my office in the morning and make an appointment—"

A man down the line of mailboxes gave a loud chuckle. The three turned to see Patrick the Psychiatrist taking out a pile of magazines from his mailbox. Patrick the Psychiatrist shook his head. "How typical. A psychologist requires you to make an appointment for a future date rather than helping a neighbour who is clearly in distress. Boris, my good friend, I'd be more than happy to talk with you right away. We'll see if we can help put your mind at ease."

"Excuse me, Patrick," Paige said, folding her arms. "No one asked for your opinion. Boris has come to me for help."

Boris held up a finger. "Actually, I—"

"Boris doesn't need a hug, Paige," Patrick said. "He needs empirically-evidenced scientific advice."

"You don't even know what his problem is," Paige said.

"I don't need to know what the problem is to know that science is better than whatever you're going to say to him."

Paige rolled her eyes. "Medication is not always the answer."

"No one said it is," Patrick replied.

"Actually, I think I would prefer to see Patrick," Boris said quietly to Paige the Psychologist. "I am a fan of science, even if I don't understand it all."

"I have a degree in psychology. As in the science of psychology," Paige said.

"Psychology is a science?" Boris asked.

"Yes!" Paige exclaimed. "Fine, you can have a session with Patrick, but I insist on also being present so that he doesn't diagnose you with some made up ailment and prescribe you a medication to meet his weekly quota of sales."

Patrick shook his head. "You are so ignorant, Paige. Fine, I will go against all oaths of doctor-patient confidentiality and let you sit in on our session. Which will be right now."

"Great!" Stanley said to Boris, giving the man a pat on the shoulder and beginning to move away. "They say two minds are better than one, I'll leave you in these four very capable hands."

"Can you come along too, Stanley?" Boris asked. Stanley stopped walking away. Roaringly hungry as he was, he didn't feel there was any way he could say no.

****

Patrick the Psychiatrist's apartment was dirty. Stanley had expected the psychiatrist, a doctor, to have a pristine clean apartment, maybe even sterile.

From the first step inside, Stanley could see that Patrick either spent most days at his office, leaving little time for organising his home, or he simply didn't have the desire to put dishes away from the drying rack, pick up his clothes from the bedroom floor, or neatly stack the sea of paper that covered his dining room table. To accommodate his guests and patient, Patrick did the bare minimum of clearing his jackets and science magazines off the couches to make room for four people to have a very unconventional counselling appointment.

Boris the Body Builder followed Stanley into the apartment, very unsure of the whole process he was about to go under, followed by Paige the Psychologist who had apparently felt the need to redo her hair and makeup for the event.

"Tea? Coffee? Anyone?" Patrick asked.

Stanley thought he was daydreaming for a moment. Patrick pulled out from his fridge a plate of three chocolate-hazelnut tarts. Stanley swallowed, imaging the tarts going into his belly.

They sat down on the couches. Boris sat in an armchair facing the other three. Paige armed herself with a notepad and pen while Patrick booted up his laptop, which he placed on the coffee table next to chocolate-hazelnut tarts. Stanley had to restrain himself from immediately taking a tart and downing it in one bite.

Patrick began the session with a smile. "Thank you for coming to see me this evening, Boris. Especially on such short notice."

Boris gave a small smile back.

Patrick leaned forward in his chair. "How was your day today? What did you do today?"

"My day was okay," Boris said. "This morning I went to the gym and then I went to work. After work I passed the book store, you know the one near Vanilla Café? In the window, I saw a book called 'Love Lamington', and I thought it looked like an interesting book, because I love lamingtons, but I'm trying not to eat sugar at the moment. This got me wondering if even reading about sugar would cause me to gain bad weight, which made me wonder if reading anything would cause me to gain good weight or bad weight, which made me wonder if even thinking about anything heavy would cause one to gain bad weight, and I can't stop thinking about such heavy thoughts, which makes me concerned I might be gaining a lot of bad weight."

Patrick and Paige both nodded empathetically in unison. Paige scribbled something down in her notepad.

"So, it sounds like you have concerns about gaining weight?" Patrick asked. "If you don't mind me asking, as a bodybuilder aren't you looking to gain weight? Isn't gaining weight helpful for building muscles?"

"Gaining good muscle weight is helpful," Boris said, "but it's really sugar that I'm worried about. Sugar makes me gain bad weight."

Before Stanley could make a subtle grab towards the plate of chocolate-hazelnut tarts, Patrick whisked the plate away and returned the tarts to the fridge. "I do apologise for putting those tarts out in front of you, Boris."

Stanley's heart sank as the pastries disappeared.

"No, bring the tarts back," Paige said. "It will be good for him to see that sugar is not evil."

"You're proposing he has a fear of sugar, and putting sugar in front of him is going to cure that fear?" Patrick said, shaking his head and sitting back down.

"I could eat one and let Boris know if the tarts are evil or not?" Stanley suggested.

"No, I can see," Patrick the Psychiatrist said, "that you, Boris, might have some concerns about your future, and your state of health. Do you feel you are healthy?"

"I'm very healthy," Boris said. "I don't drink anything but tea and water, and I don't eat any sugar apart from a once-a-decade donut. I exercise daily, sometimes twice or nine times daily, and I try and sleep at least three hours a day."

"Well, first of all," Patrick said, "I'm going to suggest you try and get some more sleep. Three hours a day isn't very much."

"But how else will I exercise for 8 hours a day and run

my business?" Boris asked.

"It's my suggestion that you sacrifice some hours, not all but some, hours that you spend exercising and use them to exercise your brain. By sleeping," Patrick said. "Now, if you're having trouble sleeping, there are Benzodiazepine medications that would help—"

Paige stood up. "Ah! There, you see?! It's been less than ten minutes and you're already wanting to prescribe him psychoactive drugs."

"I didn't say I am going to give them to him right now," Patrick replied. "If you let me finish, you would have heard me qualify my statement with 'after a few weeks of not being able to sleep, medication could help.'"

"Yeah, sure," Paige said.

Stanley stuck his hand up as if they were in a class. "Sorry to interrupt, and I don't purport to be an expert, but I feel I could mediate here so we can move things along, and possibly bring out snacks if we need to keep going for too much longer, but maybe we could find a middle ground to your diagnoses?"

"But we haven't reached Boris' core issue yet," Paige said. "I can't give a diagnosis until I know what's really causing the issue."

"When I was a child," Boris began, staring off into space. "My mother was a wonderful cook. My father struggled to cook toast in a toaster. I remember one day, when I was twelve or thirteen, my mother came down with the flu. She was bedridden. But even worse than that, it meant that my father had to cook me my dinner. He insisted on making salt and pepper squid. He poured over the recipe book, and once we cleaned up the milk that fell from the recipe book to the ground, he cooked us salt and pepper squid. He served it to us on a bed of lettuce leaves and garnished with two little pieces of chilli."

The psychiatrist, psychologist and Stanley were on the edge of their seat as Boris took a drink of water from his glass.

"But my father," Boris continued, "he mixed up salt and sugar. He had served us sugar and pepper squid. And that's probably why I have a fear of sugar."

Patrick the Psychiatrist and Paige the Psychologist exchanged a puzzled glance.

"I don't wish to assume that Patrick is as intelligent as I," Paige said, "but I think we would both agree that sugar and pepper squid has not caused the core issue here."

Patrick nodded.

"I feel like your core issue may have something to do with a fear of appearing out of shape, maybe?" Paige asked. "Is there someone in your life that you're trying to impress?"

Boris closed his lips tight and looked away. Paige nodded. "I thought that might be the case."

Patrick shook his head at his sister. "Wait, you're turning this into a 'lovesick' case? Boris only gets three hours of sleep a day! Being lovesick is not going to cause that kind of borderline insomnia." Patrick turned to Boris. "Insomnia is where people have trouble falling asleep."

Boris nodded. "I had a pet dog with insomnia. It didn't stop watching TV until four in the morning. Or maybe it was my Mum with insomnia and that just kept the dog up?"

Boris the Body Builder stood up from the couch, his

weight leaving a large impression in the cushions. "Thank you both for your appraisals, but I don't think I'm cured."

"Well, you're not going to get cured that quickly," Stanley said. "They're still looking for a cause."

Boris shook his head. "All this thinking about my childhood, and really specifically squid, is just making me feel increasingly burdened. I need to, as Stanley said, get my thoughts on lighter things, so I'm going to go and stare at the sun for a while."

"But the sun has set," Paige said.

"Well, then it won't hurt my eyes. Double win," Boris said. "Stanley, I'll book us a table at Charlotte the Chef's restaurant."

The big man opened the apartment door and left down the hallway.

"Well done," Paige said sarcastically to her brother. "You've scared the man away!"

"I scared the man away?" Patrick replied. "You were the one trying to pry into his love life!"

"I might head off as well," Stanley said.

"Well maybe if you didn't suggest hypnotic medications, he might have been more willing to share his problems!" Paige said.

"Is it alright if I grab one of those tarts to go?" Stanley asked as he inched towards the kitchen.

"I wasn't suggesting medication right now!" Patrick replied to Paige. "I know not everything needs to be solved with medications, but it is a perfectly legitimate last resort for patients!"

Stanley sighed and left the apartment, tartless, to leave the siblings to their bickering.

CHAPTER TWO
EXCLUSIVITY IS AN UNCOMMON WORD

Fine dining is not my scene. I am happiest in a diner in the dingiest part of town paying a reasonable price for a chicken schnitzel of a size that could be used as an umbrella or a bowl of chicken wings that would exceed the baggage limit of most domestic airlines.

As you know, I hate digressions, but I must mention that it is only because of effective marketing by the chicken industry that we eat chicken schnitzel, rather than pigeon schnitzel. The common pigeon farmers, of which I am happy to say I know a few of, remain livid over their industry's downfall. Pigeon, or 'squab' as the meat is often called, has its place in fine dineries or the fire of a homeless man while everyone else is pecking over chicken like it's mana from heaven. My point is that it is only by the skills of the chicken farms' marketing departments that most common pigeons are allowed to enjoy their lives to their fullest while chickens are literally 'chicken scared' because they are scared for their lives.

Charlotte the Chef; owner, founder, head chef and occasional entertainer at the restaurant Trio, did not serve chicken or any garden variety pigeon. No, at Trio, the bird on the menu was passenger pigeon; Ectopistes migratorius. If you do any research, you will find that the passenger pigeon is supposedly extinct. Their 'extinction' is, once again, thanks to the power of marketing. What better way to turn people off from eating a bird then to tell them it is extinct, and so they might as well eat a chicken? And what does that do to the price of passenger pigeons on secret menus around the world but make their price skyrocket. The passenger pigeon industry realised there would be no way they could beat the chicken industry, so they came up with a different strategy.

The passenger pigeon industry built a new habitat for the birds in the middle of Australia's dessert, far from human detection. They spread leaflets and flyers through all the trees which told the passenger pigeons of a wonderful new utopia built just for them where they could live out their lives free and safe. The passenger pigeon industry executives held information sessions about timeshares that were being opened in this Australian utopia to cater to the birds' precise needs. Most of the passenger pigeons thought this sounded wonderful and left their nests to live in luxury. In only a few years, there were only a couple of passenger pigeons that stayed behind who didn't believe that heaven was in Australia. Those passenger pigeons that stayed behind became lunch and dinner and leftovers for the next day. Soon enough the passenger pigeon was declared extinct, and the passenger pigeon industry had a party that continues to this day.

A passenger pigeon today is worth ten-thousand chickens, and only the most exclusive, expensive restaurants around the world can afford to serve it. Of course, they can never write on the menu that they are serving 'passenger pigeon' due to the non-disclosure agreements the restaurants must abide by. Most restaurants serve passenger pigeons under the name 'fancy squab'. At Trio, Charlotte the Chef serves passenger pigeon under a butter, garlic and thyme au jus with a side of potatoes that have been hand carved by local cattle ranchers into famous poets, a side dish known as 'poetatoes', which is a great solution for not having to reprint a misspelling on a menu.

If you were standing outside Trio, you wouldn't know it was a restaurant. Its entrance was merely a brown door at the end of an alleyway squeezed between two large buildings. Stanley had walked past three times before seeing a tiny sign nailed to the door that read 'Trio – Bookings Only'. Boris arrived wearing a dinner suit. The fanciest clothing Stanley owned was a suit he had been obliged to purchase for an uncle's wedding when he was 15. He didn't know why he still owned it.

"I'm sorry, I didn't know we were meant to dress up," Stanley said, looking down at his collared shirt and pants which were his work clothes.

"It's not a problem," Boris the Body Builder said. "I just always wear suits. Going out for dinner? I have a dinner suit. Attending a funeral? I have a funeral suit. Going swimming? I have a pair of shorts."

"Not a swimsuit?"

Boris shook his head. "Don't be absurd. Ties are not made for water."

Another restaurant patron arrived behind Boris in the narrow alleyway. The three exchanged awkward smiles and waited silently for the restaurant's door to open.

The third man broke the silence. "Hi, I'm Gavin."

Stanley and Boris introduced themselves and shook Gavin's hand. Stanley had to squeeze his arm between Boris the Body Builder's massive body and the alley wall to greet Gavin.

"So, are you two as excited as I am to go here?" Gavin asked. "I've had a reservation for over nine months now."

"Nine months!" Stanley exclaimed. "It's really that good?"

Gavin appeared almost offended. "Trio is the most exclusive restaurant in the world. How long were you on the waiting list for?"

"I made a reservation on Monday," Boris said.

"Monday, nine months ago? Gavin asked.

"Monday, two days ago."

"What makes Trio so special?" Stanley asked. "Why are people booking nine months in advance?"

"Well," Boris said. "It's called Trio because it's only open three days of the week, and they only have three seats in the restaurant, and they only do one sitting each day."

"That is exclusive," Stanley admitted. He leaned closer to Boris and whispered. "How much are we paying for this?"

"Well, it's ten thousand dollars per head."

"Ten thousand?" Stanley almost passed out. "That's more than I have in my bank account!"

"Don't worry. Charlotte the Chef doesn't charge if you're a Tayel Tower resident," Boris explained. "But be warned, in exchange for the free meal she often tries out her most experimental creations on us."

Stanley breathed a sigh of relief.

The door opened. A waiter in a white suit held the door open for the three men to enter. They arrived in a hallway where the walls, floor and ceiling were all covered in deep-red, lusciously soft felt. Only a painting on the wall of a turtle playing the piano was something different from the red.

The waiter led the men down the hallway to another door at the other end, the only other door in the hallway. This door was also covered in the soft red felt with only a golden door handle showing its function. The three men were guided through this door into the restaurant. The Trio restaurant dining area was little more than a closet. It was smaller than the dining area in Stanley's apartment. The room was dimly lit by a bare overhead lightbulb and was furnished with two tables and three chairs. The waiter seated Gavin at the table with a single chair and Stanley and Boris at the other table.

"I will be back with your menus," the waiter smiled.

"Why only three seats?" Stanley asked, seeing that the other table could easily accommodate another place.

"The restaurant is called Trio," Boris explained. "It wouldn't make any sense for there to be four seats."

"Then why two tables? Why not put three chairs at one table," Stanley suggested.

Boris frowned. "Would you really want to go out to a date with your someone special, only to realise you have to sit on the same table as a stranger?"

"Am I your someone special?" Stanley laughed.

"No, that was just an example—"

"Isn't this cool?" Gavin interrupted from over at his

table.

"Very cool," Stanley said.

The waiter returned with a menu. He handed it to Gavin. "Would you like to see our drinks list?"

"Oh, yes please," Gavin said.

The waiter fetched another menu from a shelf by the kitchen door and handed it to the gentleman. Gavin flicked through the drinks list, clearly looking for something he could not find. "Um, sorry, but is there any wine selections?"

"Oh, no," the waiter said. "Trio does not serve alcohol. It's too… cheap for our customer's tastes."

"Really?" Gavin said. "I've come across some extremely expensive wines in my line of work."

"Yes, but still," the waiter said. "These drinks, I'm sure you'll find, are far more interesting. Take the Sahara 1985, for example, on page two."

Gavin turned to that page and read the description. "A dry water with a light palate of airiness, a smooth finish. It's water?"

"One of the finest waters you can buy, harvested in the Sahara Desert from deep within the earth. Bottled in 1985 and currently at the perfect age to be paired with red meat, white meat or fish."

In disbelief, Gavin read from another description. "Ocean 1954 – A smooth, soft, full-bodied water with a touch of salt and pine."

"One of our most popular," the waiter said proudly. "Desalinated and delicious."

"But once again, it's just water?" Gavin asked.

"Well, to call a bottle of Ocean 1954 'just water' is to

call a filet mignon steak 'just cow'," the waiter said.

"Alright, if you insist it's that good," Gavin sighed.

The waiter retrieved two drinks lists for the other table. "And what can I get you, gentlemen, to begin with?"

Stanley, overhearing the strange beverages explained to Gavin, flicked through the two pages of drinks. It was all just water. Page 1 was cheaper, seemingly 'normal' waters, while page 2 contained absurd waters such as Tears of Pelican 1963 and Barossa Tap Water 1999.

Overwhelmed by the options, Stanley closed the drinks menu. "I'll just have table water, thank you"

"Would that be Irish, British, Chinese, Australian, Hawaiian or mystery table water?" the waiter asked.

"What's the mystery table water?" Stanley asked.

"That's from the rainwater tank out back."

"That will be fine," Stanley said.

"And for you, sir?" the waiter asked Boris.

Boris handed back his unopened drinks list with a knowing smile. "Surprise me."

Stanley could see why a restaurant that only served different kinds of water would appeal to a health-conscious individual like Boris the Body Builder. The waiter disappeared into another room and reappeared holding three identical glass bottles of water. He poured a glass of water for Gavin, a glass of water for Stanley and a glass of water for Boris. Stanley took a sip. The waiter's eyes went wide as he watched Stanley.

"Oh, I'm sorry," the waiter said. His face went red. "This has never happened before, but I believe I have mixed up your drink orders."

"Why?" Gavin asked. "What have I been given?"

"I accidentally served you the surprise water," the waiter said, appearing very distressed. "And I gave you, the gentleman who ordered the mystery table water, I gave you the Ocean 1954, and to you, the very well-dressed gentleman, I gave the mystery water."

"I'm sure it's fine," Stanley said, but also very aware that drinking decades-old water surely wasn't fine.

"No, it's not fine," the waiter said, gathering the identical looking bottles back up. "I am so sorry. This has never happened before. I think it was all the indecisiveness that confused me. Most customers are very confident about their beverage choices. Never worry, I will get you all clean glasses and new bottles."

"Don't worry about it. It's all good," the three restaurant patrons insisted to the sweating waiter, but he proceeded to rearrange their tables with new glassware.

Charlotte the Chef entered the dining area. She was a short woman, but her years working in kitchens had given her almost super-human strength to carry around bags of flour, heavy pots of soup and tankards of imported water. At that moment she had in her hand a 40-pound block of lead which she carried as if it was a loaf of bread.

"Hello, Boris and Stanley!" Charlotte the Chef said warmly.

"Hello, Charlotte," Stanley said, shaking the woman's free hand.

"Hey, Charlotte," Boris said, barely able to maintain eye contact with the woman for more than a glance.

Charlotte turned to Gavin. "It's always nice to have new visitors at Trio. Gavin, isn't it? My name is Charlotte and I am the head chef and proprietor of this restaurant."

"Very nice to meet you, Charlotte," Gavin said politely. "It's a very nice restaurant."

"Thank you," Charlotte said. "I built it myself. It turns out if you're good at following a recipe, creating anything from jewellery to a building becomes quite easy." She clapped her hands together. "Now, you might not know, Gavin, but when I have friends visit, I often experiment on them with some of my newest culinary creations. Would you also like to be a guinea pig tonight? If not, I'm very happy to serve my tried and true tasting menu. I'll also let you all know that there is a new dessert I'm trying out that was put together by one of my neighbours."

Gavin shrugged his shoulders. "I'm happy to be your guinea pig."

"Would you like to try some guinea pig?" Charlotte asked.

The question took Gavin by surprise. "Well… uh, I'm not sure."

Charlotte the Chef went back into the kitchen and came back with a cute, brown-haired guinea pig which she placed in Gavin's arms. "Did you want to try holding some guinea pigs?"

Gavin exhaled in relief, holding the cute little rodent.

The waiter brought forth two more guinea pigs and handed one each to Stanley and Boris.

"I like to allow patrons to cuddle a cute animal at the beginning of their dining experience," Charlotte the Chef explained. "Stanley, you are holding Fluffles. Boris, you are holding Lionel, and Gavin, you are holding Snuggles."

Fluffles twitched his little nose. Stanley, although not really a fan of rodents, couldn't help but smile. Charlotte took out a notepad and pen. "Now, Stanley, would you like Fluffles fried or roasted?"

Stanley held the poor creature close to his chest in horror at the thought.

Charlotte dropped her notepad on the table and laughed hysterically. "Oh, it gets everyone every time. I didn't think I could get you, Stanley, but I did."

Boris, having dined at Trio before, was also laughing at the absolute disgust on Stanley's face. "She got you good."

The waiter retrieved the guinea pigs back, most reluctantly from Stanley who still wasn't confident the 'Fluffles Pie' wouldn't be the second course. Charlotte the Chef returned to the kitchen to wipe her tears of laughter. After only a brief moment, the waiter brought out three brown paper packages, placing one on each of the three plates.

"This is bread," the waiter announced. "Inside your packages, which I kindly ask you to open now, you will find your deconstructed bread."

Stanley, still a little shaken by the guinea pig joke, opened his package to find a pile of flour, a small bottle of water, a packet of yeast and a thimble of oil.

"This is deconstructed bread?" Stanley asked. "This is non-constructed bread."

"Ah, it may appear like that," Boris said with a smile, "but try a spoonful of the flour on its own."

Stanley, still thoroughly sceptical, used a teaspoon to scoop up a morsel of the flour. Never having tried the deconstructed bread myself, I can't give a fantastic description for how the flour tasted, but from the surprised expression on Stanley's face, as he moved the flour around his mouth, this was not just normal flour.

"It tastes like bread," Stanley said.

The waiter nodded. "This flour is actually finely ground dehydrated breadcrumbs. When you combine it with the water, oil and yeast, it will turn back into bread. I will then bake the bread in the wood oven fire, and you will have your own hand-made bread to enjoy."

Boris the Body Builder had already begun gleefully combining the ingredients into a dough. The other restaurant patrons followed suit. Stanley kept his mouth firmly shut to keep from grumbling about how they were having to cook their own food. The waiter placed the piles of dough on a tray and took them away.

The three men sat patiently in silence. In the quiet, the faint sounds of sizzling and metal clanging could be heard coming from the kitchen. Stanley hadn't eaten since lunchtime, but from the slow-moving service, he wondered if he should have brought a snack.

"So, what do you do for a living?" Stanley asked Gavin to distract his mind from his stomach.

"Me?" Gavin asked. "I'm in finance."

"Interesting," Stanley said. "I'm a business consultant. What do you do in finance? Accountancy? Management?"

Gavin paused. "Well, as I'm sure you're aware, defining one's job can be quite difficult."

"I don't know," Stanley said. "I can define my job as sitting in an office talking to clients then writing up business plans and repeat."

Gavin laughed. "I guess you could say I work freelance in banks. Mainly in security and organisational planning."

"Wow," Boris said. "Are you one of those tech experts that build bank security systems?"

Gavin considered the description. "A better description would be I'm hired to test out the bank's security systems. What do you do for a living, Boris?"

"For a living, I am a tailor," Boris said. "For life, I am a bodybuilder."

"Ah, I see," Gavin said.

"What made you choose to be a bodybuilder?" Stanley asked.

"Out of all the hobbies I could have chosen, I just felt that bodybuilding would be the most beneficial for my future," Boris explained. "If I have this hobby now, it means later in life I can pursue other hobbies like chess or piano or collecting rocks that look like famous landmarks."

"Rocks that look like famous landmarks?" Stanley repeated.

Boris nodded. "It's a hard hobby. I only have Uluru so far."

The waiter re-emerged with three plates. Stanley's mouth began to water at the thought of whatever could be on those plates. And, unlike the deconstructed bread for which he was still unsure whether he approved of, the meals that followed were spectacular. There were little quiches made from seven different types of bird eggs; pinecone fries, which Stanley found to be quite chewy; 'fancy squab' served with poetatoes. Stanley had Plath and Shakespeare spuds. Every serving was small, but plate after plate of wondrous delights came from the kitchen onto their tables. Between chewing, Stanley and Boris discussed the tailoring industry and then the bodybuilding industry, then the chicken industry and the restaurant industry.

"…now there are all sorts of 'healthy' restaurants you

can go to," Boris continued with a piece of chicken pie on his fork. Stanley had wondered whether the chicken pie was served to replace a failed experimental dish or whether Charlotte the Chef was simply lying that is was chicken pie.

"I don't know," Stanley said, subtly searching through the pie for any clues to its contents. "I mean, this restaurant is incredible, but I'm just as happy sitting in a pub with a bowl of spaghetti marinara for dinner and an ice-cream sundae for dessert."

Boris shook his head. "There's sugar in ice-cream."

"I know," smiled Stanley. "That's why I eat it."

"Charlotte the Chef is always so nice to me," Boris said. "She knows I don't eat sugar, and so when I come here, she prepares desserts that look the same but don't have any sugar in them."

"Did I hear someone talking about desserts?" Charlotte the Chef said, emerging from the kitchen with three bowls. "I hope you're ready for your first dessert because it's a brand-new recipe from one of my neighbours. It's sugar-free caramel pudding!"

"Oh yes!" Boris exclaimed as a bowl of the sickly sweet, saucy pudding was placed in front of him. Charlotte the Chef waited with her hands behind her back to see her customers' reactions.

Stanley had a mouthful of the pudding. He raised his eyebrows in surprise. "This is delicious. And you say this is sugar-free?"

"Indeed it is," Charlotte the Chef said.

Boris downed the pudding in half-a-dozen mouthfuls. "This is amazing! You're an incredible cook, Charlotte."

"Thank you," Charlotte said. "But my neighbour made

this dessert. She insisted."

"Who is this neighbour that's such as good cook?" Stanley asked, spooning up the last of the sauce.

"Do you know Paige the Psychologist?" Charlotte asked.

Stanley looked down at the remnants of sauce in his bowl, then over at Boris' bowl which had been all but licked clean.

A concern came to him that he could not shake. "This isn't sugar-free."

Boris' eyes widened. He calmly placed his spoon down.

"Are you sure?" Charlotte asked. "Because I did explain to her that Boris doesn't like sugar."

She used her pinkie finger to take a small sample of the sauce from the edge of Stanley's plate and tasted it. She inhaled deeply, tasting the sugary sauce.

"Is she here?" Stanley asked, watching Boris closely in case the giant man collapsed to the ground.

Charlotte the Chef returned quickly to the kitchen and re-emerged with Paige the Psychologist at whisk point. Paige was wearing a chef's bleached-white shirt with evidence of caramel sauce on her sleeves.

"Was there sugar in the pudding?" Charlotte asked.

"Only a little bit, I promise," Paige said, holding up her hands in case she was attacked with the whisk. "I did it for Boris."

"What do you mean you did it for Boris?" Charlotte the Chef asked. "I specifically told you Boris can't have sugar. You must have snuck it in when I wasn't looking!"

"He can have sugar, he just chooses not to," Paige said quickly. "I am simply applying cognitive behaviour therapy to show Boris that sugar is nothing to be afraid of. I'm a trained psychologist."

"Surely what you've done would be considered a seriously unethical method of treatment," Stanley said.

"Boris is a strong man," Paige said. "I think he can handle us skipping a number of steps in the treatment process," Paige said.

Meanwhile, Boris wasn't listening to anyone around him. He sat in his chair staring down at his plate where his dessert had once been.

"Are you feeling alright?" Charlotte asked, pouring the man another glass of the surprise water, which was really Ocean 1972, another fine year for desalinated water.

"Maybe this was a good thing for me," Boris sniffed. "No, I'm not sure it was a good thing for me."

"You will be alright," Stanley said to reassure the man.

"I could be," Boris said with a distant stare. "But I fear I won't be. Sugar is…not healthy."

"I know, I know," Stanley said. "But it'll pass through your system, and then you'll be as good as gold."

"I don't know," Boris said, his eyes distant. "I need to run a marathon."

"No Boris—" Paige the Psychologist began but was silenced by the murderous glances of her neighbours.

"I'm going to run the Epsilon Marathon," Boris said with fearful determination.

CHAPTER THREE
THE TURTLE AND
THE RABBIT

The city streets around the marathon route were blocked off to all traffic. Hundreds of runners, walkers and soon-to-be oxygen tank users gathered behind the starting line. Boris the Body Builder was at the front and centre of the pack, his large frame in contrast to his mostly fitter fellow runners. Boris was wearing a running suit, which was very similar to his dinner suit but made with breathable materials. Stanley, not seeing any benefit to purchasing a proper running outfit, stood next to the man wearing an old t-shirt and shorts. He and Mandy had immediately agreed to participate in the marathon to support their friend. Stanley could see fortitude in Boris' face that made everyone around the bodybuilder feel very solemn and take the marathon seriously.

That is except for Rosemary the Retired and Leah the Librarian, who decided it would be great to do the marathon dressed in their nightgowns.

"Are you sure you ladies are okay to do the race?" Mandy the Midwife asked. "You do know that you are wearing your nightgowns?"

"We know," Leah the Librarian said. "We're making a statement. What we're wearing is no less silly than all you people in your fancy gym clothes."

"Here, here!" Stanley exclaimed.

Mandy turned to her boyfriend. "Are you saying I look silly?"

"No," Stanley backtracked, "I just mean… everyone else looks silly. You look great in your athletic wear."

Mandy stretched her legs to warm them up for running. Stanley copied Mandy, assuming she knew what she was doing. The old ladies copied Stanley, assuming that the young couple knew what they were doing.

"How are you feeling, Boris?" Stanley asked.

Boris nodded his head, staring off down the street. "I'm ready, Stanley. I'm ready."

"Before we run," Stanley said. "You do know that after you run the marathon, you're not going to be any further past your fear of sugar?"

"We'll see," Boris said.

Stanley and Mandy exchanged a concerned glance.

"We're worried about you," Mandy said softly.

"Please don't worry about me, Mandy," Boris said. "I'll feel as good as new when I finish the race."

Mooney the Millionaire was the starting official. He walked to the side of the street holding a megaphone and some sort of apparatus under his arm.

"Alright," Mooney announced. "I want this to be a nice clean race. Although we haven't done any performance-enhancing substance testing, I want everyone to be honest and put their hand up if they are cheating. No one? Good. Well, on the firing of my crossbow the race will begin."

"Mooney, you were meant to bring a starting pistol—" Elaine the Event Planner called. Before anyone could stop him, Mooney had already fired a bolt from his crossbow into the air.

"I don't own a gun," Mooney complained. "All I had was a crossbow."

"Run!!" Stanley yelled, and never had a marathon gotten off to a quicker start. The participants, organisers and even spectators ran for their lives away from the starting zone. Thankfully it was found later that the bolt actually saved a man's life, but that's a different story.

After they were clear of the starting zone, the runners slowed down to a jog. Stanley made an effort to run alongside Boris, who was already breathing hard.

"This is pretty great," Stanley puffed looking up at the blue sky. "Nice morning for a marathon."

Boris kept his head down. Sweat dripped from his brow as he focused on the task at hand.

"Look, I know it's not my business," Stanley continued. "But I really think you should go see a therapist. Maybe not Patrick or Paige, but someone else. I'm sure a therapist would know how to—"

"—thank you," Boris interjected, followed by a spluttering cough. "But I can work this out on my own."

Stanley didn't take the conversation further. Charlotte the Chef sped up a little to also run adjacent to Boris.

"Charlotte!" Boris said, giving the small woman a smile.

"How are you doing, Boris?" Charlotte asked.

Boris nodded his head, breathing heavily. "The sugar, I can feel it weighing me done. I'm usually a much better runner!"

"You're doing fantastically," Charlotte said. "I promise when we finish I'll cook you whatever meal you want!"

"Thank you, Charlotte," Boris said. "That would be nice."

Mandy and Stanley raised their eyebrows to each other. There was certainly a connection between the chef and the bodybuilder. Barney the Banker had sprinted from the start line, but his enthusiasm for his level of fitness was beginning to prove unfounded. More people were passing him until he was also in line with Boris.

"Boris, my friend!" Barney called between inhales. "Look at you go! You're a machine!"

Boris began running a little faster, a big grin on his face.

Jarvis the Jobless, a man no younger than the age of the earth, ran up from somewhere in the back of the pack.

"Oh, hello Boris!" Jarvis called. "Wherever you're going, you're going to get there very quickly."

Boris let out a laugh.

"But where are you going?" Jarvis asked, running along.

"I'm going to finish this race!" Boris said triumphantly.

"That's excellent," Jarvis the Jobless said. He turned to Stanley. "And where are you running to?"

Stanley pointed forward quickly, not wanting to waste any energy. "Same place. End of the race."

"Ah, excellent," Jarvis said. He turned to Mandy. "And where are you running to?"

"We're all running to the end of the race," Mandy explained.

"I see," Jarvis said. "Hey, did you know I just came from where there are all these checkered flags down further the way we're all going, and there was Vanilla Café handing out free chocolate-hazelnut tarts for the first five hundred winners?"

"Five hundred winners?" Charlotte the Chef repeated. "But there are only three hundred people in the race!"

The news travelled quickly through the racers that there were free chocolate-hazelnut tarts at the finish line, and everyone increased their speed. Some spectators jumped onto the course with a new interest in running. Everyone was salivating for the sweet treats but Boris the Body Builder, who had stopped dead in his tracks, causing several close-collisions behind him. His body wanted him to keep moving forward, but his fear kept him in his place. The other runners, oxygen deprived, didn't realise they had left Boris behind and continued the marathon.

"What are you doing, Boris?" Ludwig the Lawyer called from behind the spectator's line.

Boris the Body Builder was hardly aware of where he was anymore. He took one step forward, then rotated and started power walking back towards the start line. After a couple of meters, he pivoted again and began walking towards the finish line. He couldn't make up his mind. After a dozen spins, he stopped and sat down cross-legged in the middle of the street.

Minutes passed by and the spectators on the sidelines began drifting further down the course towards the finish line until the bodybuilder was by himself in the quiet.

Boris felt someone run straight into his back. He opened his eyes in alarm to see someone fly through the air over him, and three duffle bags go flying from the person's hand crash onto the bitumen. The person landed with a thud and let out an audible groan.

Boris the Body Builder leapt up and ran over to the person. "I'm so sorry! Are you okay?"

Boris turned the person over. Thankfully they were wearing a motorbike helmet. Boris opened the motorbike helmet to see a familiar face. "Gavin?!"

Gavin peered up at Boris in surprise. Gavin quickly did his best to stand up. "I gotta go…"

"Wait a minute," Boris said, gently holding the man. "Are you okay? You just tripped over me and I'm truly sorry for that."

"I'm fine, I promise," Gavin said. "I really need to get going."

"It's alright," Boris said. "The race isn't as important as making sure you're okay."

"The race?" Gavin asked quietly. He looked around, unable to see any evidence of a race. At that moment, Jarvis the Jobless could be seen in the distance cheering on a turtle and a rabbit he had borrowed from the pet store. He was trying to coax the rabbit down the race track with a carrot. Unaware of what turtles were a fan of, he was threatening the turtle with a recipe book of soups.

"I know, I know," Boris said, "not everyone sees the marathon as a race, but the important thing is everyone is trying their best. Everyone's race should be only against themselves."

"Yes, I agree," Gavin said, limping and gathering up his duffle bags.

"What are the bags for?" Boris asked, noticing that they seemed quite heavy as he picked one up and handed it to Gavin.

"Oh… these are from a job I was just completing. I was

testing out the security of a bank near here," Gavin said, holding the bags tightly on his shoulder.

"Oh, that's exciting," Boris the Body Builder said. "Did the bank pass?"

Gavin shook his head. "No, unfortunately not. But that's a good thing sometimes."

"So, you're not in the marathon?"

"No, I am in the marathon," Gavin said, nodded vigorously. "If anyone asks, I've been in this marathon from the beginning. You can see me in the marathon now. But I think I hurt my leg and should probably go home and rest."

"I was thinking of doing the same thing," Boris said. "Not because of my legs, but because they have chocolate-hazelnut tarts at the finish line."

"What?" Gavin asked impulsively.

"My fear of sugar," Boris said. Gavin remembered the peculiar scene at the Trio restaurant that had ended his dining experience abruptly and with a refund.

"Your fear of sugar is that crippling?" Gavin asked, throwing his motorbike helmet in a nearby bin. A police siren could be heard echoing through the city several blocks away. Gavin began hobbling quickly down the street with Boris following closely behind.

"I don't know what I'm afraid of," Boris said. "I just hear so many bad stories about sugar and I don't want to become another. I want to, you know, grow old with a family and run my tailor store until I'm a hundred."

"That sounds like a good goal," Gavin said.

"What's your life goal?" Boris asked.

"My life goal?" Gavin repeated, anxiously checking

over his shoulder. "Probably retire in ten years' time. Set up shop somewhere in a quiet town."

"And what's stopping you from reaching that goal?"

"I just have other interests. Too many things to do, and too many things to avoid," Gavin said.

Boris stopped. An epiphany washed over him.

His face to light up with a smile. "You're right!"

"We really should keep moving," Gavin said with a broken voice.

"I'm not living my life to the fullest, because I'm too worried about avoiding things! I avoid sugar like it's the plague," Boris laughed.

"That's a great way of summing it up, let's keep discussing it later—"

"And now we're avoiding finishing this race," Boris said. "I am because of sugar, and you are because of your leg!"

Gavin touched his leg dramatically. "I know. It really hurts!"

Boris the Body Builder, strong as a man that spends at least eight hours a day in a gym, hoisted Gavin onto his shoulders as if the bank-security tester was a child.

"What are you doing?!" Gavin cried.

"We're going to finish this race together!" Boris announced, surging forward down the race course.

"I'm really okay with not finishing the race," Gavin pleaded as he bounced along on top of the man's shoulders.

"I'm not okay with us not finishing the race," Boris said.

Boris the Body Builder ran down the streets with Gavin on his shoulders. Spectators watched in amazement at the strong man and his passenger. By the time the pair arrived on the home straight to the finish line, all the other racers had completed their marathons. The racers, chocolate-hazelnut tarts in hand looked back to see Boris charging down the main street with a very pale man on his shoulders.

Stanley received his chocolate-hazelnut tart with glee at the Vanilla Café cart. He was about to bite into the tart when the sight of Boris and Gavin startled him so much that he dropped the tart into the gutter. He gave a little whimper.

Everyone cheered and clapped to encourage the last two men. Not joining in the excitement and frivolity were six police officers who were standing behind the finish line. Gavin almost passed out when he saw the police ready with their cans of pepper spray drawn. Boris picked up the pace to the encouragement of the crowd. The two men crossed the finish line to a roar of celebrations.

"We did it!" Boris said triumphantly, taking Gavin from his shoulders and gently placing him down on the ground. Gavin looked for an escape route away from the police, but he was surrounded by cheering sweaty bodies.

One of the police officers stepped forward towards Gavin. "Sir, can you please answer some questions for me?"

Gavin instinctively placed his hands in the air.

"Did you see a man on the race track with a rabbit and turtle?" the police officer asked, taking a bite from a chocolate-hazelnut tart that he had procured from the Vanilla Café cart.

Gavin turned his hands in the air from being a stance of surrender to stretching his arms out. "Yes, sir. He was about two kilometres behind us."

"Right," The police officer said, signalling for his comrades to follow. "There's been a break-in at a bank, and a witness said he saw a man with a rabbit and turtle running from the scene."

The police officers started running back down the race course. Gavin exhaled in relief.

Boris the Body Builder was still elated as he was joined by Stanley and Mandy.

"Where did you go?" Stanley asked the big man. "You were beside us one moment, and the next you were gone."

"The tarts," Boris said, still catching his breath. "I didn't want to be near the tarts. But Gavin here taught me that I should not let sugar be what stops me from living my life to the fullest. A locked door? Yes, that could stop me. A rapidly flowing river? That could also stop me. Getting my feet stuck in cement and then needing to tie my shoelace—"

"We get what you're meaning," Stanley said with a smile.

"But I'm not going to let sugar stop me," Boris said proudly. He still looked apprehensively at the runners around him eating the tarts, but he was pleased with his progress.

"Good for you, Boris," Mandy said.

"Hey," Gavin said, beginning to back away. "Thanks for the lift, Boris. I'm going on holiday this afternoon to a far-off location, so I'll see you when I see you."

"Come here, brother," Boris said, grabbing Gavin into a big hug. Gavin squeaked as he almost had the life squeezed out of him. In the excitement, two small objects fell out of one of Gavin's bags.

"Oh, you dropped something," Stanley said, picking up

two small motorbike helmets. "What are these for?"

Gavin snatched back the helmets and tried to place them back in his bag, but the bag slipped open again. A rabbit, a turtle and a bar of gold fell out. Those in the vicinity looked from the animals to the bar of gold to Gavin and gasped. Gavin at the onlookers and gave a nervous laugh. The animals looked at each other and didn't say anything because their sounds weren't mutually understandable.

"You need to control those animal's diets," Boris the Body Builder said. "They were really heavy."

Gavin, unable to make any sort of escape from the mass of bodies surrounding him, accepted his fate and waited for the police officers to return and arrest him.

"I doubt I'm going to start eating sugar regularly, but maybe I should at least acclimatise myself to being around and talking about sugar," Boris said as the police led Gavin away. "So here I go; Stanley, how was your chocolate tart?"

"Wouldn't know," Stanley said sadly. "I dropped mine."

Boris charged through the crowds to the Vanilla Café cart. He returned to Stanley with a tart sitting neatly on a serviette. Stanley, with the deepest gratitude, received the tart like it was a newborn baby.

He carefully lifted the chocolate delight to his mouth and took a victorious bite of the pastry. But, after only two chews, the taste caused his satisfaction to disappear.

"These taste… different. I don't like them," Stanley said.

Charlotte the Chef handed a tart to Boris the Body Builder. "They're sugar-free."

Wray Wrigley's

TAYEL TOWER

Book 7

THE HOLIDAY

CHAPTER ONE
EVERYONE'S GONE

'International Hairy Llamas Appreciation Day' had to be the most inappropriately named holiday in existence. For one, it was not an internationally recognised holiday. If it wasn't for a couple of llama lovers the next state over from Tayel Tower, it could hardly be called an interstate holiday. Secondly, and probably most importantly, the day wasn't meant to have anything to do with llamas. The original holiday proposal was 'International Dairy Farmers Appreciation Day', but at the city council meeting the title got wildly lost in understanding due to a faulty microphone. The misunderstanding was horrible for the morale of dozens of local dairy farmers, but it turned out quite well for a man named Neil who owned two hairy llamas named Consuela and Rick. On this annual holiday, all the folk that lived in the city went out for the long weekend to the coast, the forests or the farms to take a break, leaving only a few essential people behind to run the operations required in the city. All the shops and offices would close. Even the police left and went on holiday as all the criminals did the same.

The Friday evening before International Hairy Llamas

Appreciation Day, there was a hustle and bustle in Tayel Tower as everyone prepared to leave to their respective holiday destinations for relaxation, recuperation and llama appreciation. Everyone but Mandy the Midwife, who had been assigned the weekend shifts at the hospital in exchange for the following week off, and Stanley who wanted to keep Mandy the Midwife company and frankly didn't understand what the holiday was for.

Stanley's act of chivalry and kindness, however, did not go unpunished.

"Are you writing this all down?" Damien the Doorman asked as he made sure everything valuable at the lobby front desk was packed away and locked in the drawers. "You need to lock up at nine pm, both the front and back doors, and then unlock them again at six in the morning. On Sundays, the roof garden needs to be watered. Oh, and don't forget to refill the roof bird feeder with bird seed."

"Birdseed. Got it," Stanley said, keying reminders into his phone.

"Also, don't forget not to refill the bird seed in the car park garden bird feeder," Damien said. "Jarvis the Jobless keeps taking the bird seed from there and laying it out in shape of a basketball court so it looks like the pigeons are playing basketball."

"Don't fill bird feeder in the car park. Got it."

"Are you not going away for the weekend, Stanley?" the beautiful Deborah the Debt Collector asked, holding an expensive oversized suitcase for her camping trip.

Stanley shook his head. "No, I'm just going to stay here for the weekend and catch up on some reading."

"Oh, that sounds nice," Deborah said. "Well, since

you're staying behind, I was wondering if you could do a little favour for me."

"What can I do for you?" Stanley sighed, getting ready to set another reminder.

"Well, if it's not too much trouble," Deborah said. "Could you please collect a debt for me? It's from a man who keeps eating in a restaurant and then asking for the bill to be added to his account. The man's account is over two thousand dollars now."

"Am I allowed to collect someone's debt?" Stanley asked.

"Oh, of course," Deborah said with a laugh. "Anyone is allowed to collect someone else's debt, as long as they're authorised by the creditor. It's just a question of if they can."

Stanley looked very unsure about the idea of becoming a freelance debt collector.

"Listen, it'll be easy," Deborah said. "I wouldn't ask you if I thought it was hard."

Stanley really couldn't be bothered feeling offended. "What's the person's name?"

"Ludwig the Lawyer from apartment ten-oh-three."

"Alright, I'll try, but no promises," Stanley said.

"Stanley! Stanley my good friend!" Vermont the Violinist called across the lobby. "I hear you are staying behind. Perfect. I have a package coming and it should be arriving tomorrow morning. You can sign for it and leave it at my door."

Before Stanley could reply, Vermont was out the front door.

"Will the post deliver parcels on tomorrow?" Stanley

asked Damien. "I thought the mailmen also went on holidays."

Damien the Doorman nodded. "Yes, absolutely the mailmen go on holidays; all but one. Every year one postman must stay behind. To decide who will stay behind, all the postmen play a giant game of rock-paper-scissors. Several years back one of the postmen, Lincoln, unfortunately, lost all his fingers in a letter writing incident. Because of this, he is very easily beatable because he can only play rock."

"That doesn't sound very fair," Stanley said.

"He's fine," Damien said. "The other mailmen buy him two roast chickens as consolation. Two birds with one stone."

"Hey, Stanley!" A man said in a loud whisper. Stanley turned to see Ludwig the Lawyer hiding behind a newspaper on one of the lobby couches. Stanley walked over to the man. "I'm apparently supposed to collect your debt for some restaurant," he said with little enthusiasm.

"Never mind that," Ludwig said. "I hear that you're not going on holiday. I was wondering if you could do me a little favour?"

Stanley didn't say anything.

"Excellent," Ludwig smiled. "I have a pet lizard named Shakespeare that needs to be fed three times a day. There is a box of crickets in the cupboard under his tank. Please feed him five crickets in the morning, five in the afternoon and seven at night."

"There's an easy solution to this," Stanley said. "I'll agree to feed your lizard if you pay your debt to Deborah the Debt Collector."

"When Vanilla Cafe actually serves me a decent cup of coffee, then I'll pay the debt," Ludwig said stubbornly.

"You've racked up two thousand dollars of debt over coffee?" Stanley asked.

"A large coffee and a piece of chocolate cake every morning," Ludwig said.

"What's so bad about their coffee?" Stanley asked.

"Every time I get it, it's piping hot!"

"And?"

"Since when is coffee hot?"

"Since the beginning of coffee production."

"I grew up drinking my coffee cold, the way it is meant to be," Ludwig said. "Nowadays everyone's serving coffee like they've just put boiling hot water through it!"

"I think you're wanting an iced coffee," Stanley said.

"No, iced coffee is coffee with icing sugar on top. I want a cold coffee," Ludwig said.

Stanley shook his head at the man's defiance. "Here's a deal for you. If you pay your debt, I promise next week I'll find you the cold coffee you're looking for and I'll feed your pet lizard, Shakespeare, three times a day."

Ludwig, with apparently little bargaining power, pulled out $2000 in cash from his wallet and handed it over. Stanley, rarely having seen that much cash in his life, quickly put the wad of $100 bills in his pocket.

"Why do you have two thousand dollars in your wallet?" Stanley asked.

"In case someone ever made me a good cup of coffee," Ludwig explained, also handing over the key to his apartment. "Thank you, Stanley. You're very helpful. I'm off to visit my sister's dairy farm to celebrate the true meaning of International Hairy Llamas appreciation day by playing volleyball with their pet llama, Hemmingway. Hemmingway's not hairy, but he sure does a mean spike."

The elevator doors in the lobby whooshed open. Outstepped Ernest the Elevator Operator with the biggest smile on his face. "It's 5 pm!" he shouted. "No more elevator operations until Tuesday 12 am!"

"Goodbye, Ernest!" the residents in the lobby called. After his announcement, he left out the front door with his backpack.

"So we have to press the elevator buttons ourselves this weekend?" Stanley faux-complained to Ludwig.

Ludwig shook his head. "Even when he's away he has remote access to the elevator controls through his phone. It was the only way the building management can ensure that Ernest takes breaks."

Elaine the Event Planner hurried into the lobby with her hands full of heavy-looking luggage.

"Do you need a hand, Elaine?" Stanley offered.

Elaine put her bags down and gave Stanley a big smile. "I like holidays as much as the next person, but they are quite inconvenient sometimes, especially when there's work to be done! I need to organise a whole pageant! It's very hard to see this pageant coming to fruition."

Although her smile didn't fade, it was clear to Stanley that she was stressed with whatever pageant or event Elaine was organising.

"You don't have to go away on holiday," Stanley said. "You could stay behind if there's lots of work to do."

Elaine shook her head. "This weekend is a holiday. Everyone else is going away, so I don't want to be one of those people that stays," she remembered Angus was staying behind, "not that there's anything wrong with staying, but you know… I hope you have a great weekend!"

The lobby gradually emptied out until there was only Stanley left standing in the eerily silent room. The elevator doors opened and out came Rosemary the Retired, followed by Mandy the Midwife who was holding the older lady's luggage.

"I hope you have a lovely weekend, Rosemary," Mandy said.

"Thank you, dear. My granddaughter is taking me down to their shack by the coast. It will be lovely."

Mandy the Midwife carried the luggage outside and put it in the boot of the waiting car, wishing it was her luggage and her car taking her away to a shack by the coast.

"Well, I guess it's just us," Mandy said to Stanley who had joined her on the sidewalk. They watched the car drive away.

"I guess it is," Stanley agreed. The city was quietening down as everyone drove away or caught buses to their holiday destinations. Mandy and Stanley both had smiles on their faces.

"We should do dinner together on Saturday night," Mandy proposed.

"That sounds wonderful," Stanley said, "but it will need to be after I've fed Ludwig's lizard, watered the plants on the roof, refilled the bird feeder, vacuumed the hallway of level five and made sure no one has stolen the painting of Sky. And dinner will need to be before I have locked all the doors, made sure all the lights are off, made sure there are no bats in the stairwell and tucked in Ludwig's lizard."

"I promise I'll help you where I can," Mandy said.

Stanley put his arm around Mandy. "Thanks for the offer, but I'll manage. You just focus on your work."

****

Stanley woke up startled; everything felt wrong. There no noise. He had gotten used to the sounds of people thumping around upstairs, the sound of cars and dogs far below on the city streets, the sound of Jarvis the Jobless and a capuchin monkey practising their drumming on pots and pans after watching junk-percussion videos online. He looked at the time on his phone; it was 7 am.

Stanley's heart skipped a beat. He had slept in and hadn't opened the building! Stanley leapt out of bed and ran to the elevator. He mashed the down button. The elevator slowly arrived at his floor and Stanley stepped on board. Doing something he had never been required to do before, he pressed the ground floor button. Nothing happened. He looked over the button panel, wondering if there was some extra key he had to press to activate the board.

"Good morning, Mr Stanley," a voice said over the elevator's speaker system.

"Ernest?" Stanley asked.

"Ernest indeed," Ernest the Elevator operator said. "Which floor would you like, sir?"

Stanley looked around for a camera. "How do you know it's me."

"It doesn't take a detective," Ernest laughed. "It does, however, take a little camera that's hidden in the button dashboard."

"How do I enable the buttons?" Stanley asked.

"What buttons? Oh, you mean the buttons in the dashboard?" Ernest asked. "They're fingerprint sensitive. They only activate at my fingerprint."

"Well that can't be very safe," Stanley said. "What if you die? Or there's a fire."

"If there's a fire, Mr Stanley, you shouldn't use the elevator," Ernest said. "If I die, then you really shouldn't use the elevator until a full investigation has been launched."

"But you can control the elevator from… wherever you are?"

"Absolutely! Which floor?"

"Ground floor, please," Stanley said.

The elevator began to descend.

"So, how is your day going so far?" Ernest asked.

"I haven't had any day yet. I just woke up. That's why I'm wearing my pyjamas."

"They're your pyjamas? I thought you'd just been in a time machine to the 1930s and stolen an old man's clothing."

Stanley looked down at his blue and brown pinstriped pyjamas. "I like these."

Ernest coughed. "Sorry, I better go now. My waiter is bringing me my coconut-banana smoothie."

The elevator arrived at the ground floor. Stanley could see a man in a postman uniform walking away from the front door holding a package. Stanley ran across the lobby as fast as his slipper covered feet would allow. He reached into his pocket, producing the keys that Damien the Doorman had given him. There were only half a dozen keys, so finding the correct one was no problem at all. The problem was the postman was already driving away.

"Wait!" Stanley yelled down the street. Thanks to the

lack of environmental noise, the driver, Lincoln the Post-man, heard the cry and looked in his mirror to see Stanley standing in the middle of the street in his pyjamas. Lincoln rolled his eyes and applied the brakes to the post van.

Stanley ran up to the driver's door. "Thank you, I'm so sorry. I overslept."

"I don't have all day, you know," Lincoln said cold-ly, reaching behind him to find Tayel Tower's mail. He dumped a large pile of letters into Stanley's waiting arms. "This is all the letters, and there's one package. It says high-ly fragile. If it breaks, you break."

Stanley was a little taken back by the man's bluntness, but on the other hand he was glad to see a postman taking his job so seriously. "Hey, Lincoln. I just want to say thank you for doing the mail when it's a holiday and all."

"Roast chicken," Lincoln said.

"I'm sorry, what?"

"To say thank you for delivering their mail, people buy me a roast chicken."

"I heard you get two roast chicken from your col-leagues," Stanley laughed.

"Roast chickens can be frozen," Lincoln stated. "You'll find an esky outside the post office. Please deposit the chicken in there." Lincoln drove down the street to the next building.

Stanley juggled the pile of letters and the package (a small cardboard box), back to Tayel Tower. Sorting the mail had not been on his to-do list and he did not look forward to the task.

"Hello there," Mandy said cheerfully in her exercise clothes. She gave Stanley a hug. "I didn't know it was pyjama day. I would have stayed in my pyjamas!"

"Good morning," Stanley said, always so happy to see Mandy's smile.

"Did Lincoln just leave the letters unsorted here?" Mandy asked, seeing the pile of mail at Stanley's feet on the lobby floor.

"No, it's my fault. I slept in and didn't unlock the front door."

Mandy, helpful and studious as she was, immediately began going through the pile, reading the names and placing the letters into the correct lobby post boxes.

"No, you don't have to help me," Stanley said. "I've got it. You go for your run."

"Nonsense," Mandy said, keeping at the sorting. She handed the box to Stanley. "I'll put these letters in, you take the package to Vermont the Violinist. Damien the Doorman's master key unlocks anyone's apartment."

Stanley gave Mandy a kiss on the cheek. "You're the best. I promise I'll make it up to you with dinner tonight. I was going to do roast chicken, but apparently I need to take it to—"

"Lincoln," Mandy said, shaking her head. "By the way, I wouldn't go too far into Vermont's apartment. From what I remember the one time I visited him, it's quite messy and he has many sharp tools everywhere."

For a curious man like Stanley, Vermont the Violinist's apartment sounded like an interesting adventure.

CHAPTER TWO

GRASSHOPPER

Stanley took the elevator up to the fifth floor where Vermont the Violinist's apartment was. He did his best to avoid a lengthy conversation with the vacationing Ernest the Elevator Operator over the elevator speaker system.

The small package was very, very light. Stanley wondered if it was empty. He gave it a light shake and did feel something move about inside. Stanley deliberated about whether he should leave the package outside the door or inside the door, eventually deciding he didn't want to be held responsible for the package being stolen. All of the apartments in Tayel Tower, although identically laid out, each reflected their occupant through the décor. If Stanley was a professional postman, he wouldn't have gone past the front door. He would have left the package against the wall in the hallway and then left on the rest of his route. But Stanley wasn't a postman, so he ventured further inside to take a quick peek.

Vermont had his apartment set out as a workshop. Instead of the kitchen table, there was workbench adorned with half-assembled violins. There was a block of shelves above the sink containing woods such as spruce, maple and rosewood. The living room contained a grand piano, which Stanley had no idea how they would have gotten into the apartment, and sheets upon sheets of sheet music covered most surfaces.

The other eye-catching piece of furniture in the living room was a glass enclosure. The enclosure had dirt at the bottom, a pile of lettuce leaves in a corner, but besides those things appeared to be empty. Stanley leaned down and peered around, trying to see what creature lay inside.

"What are you doing?!"

Stanley knocked his nose into the glass enclosure. He spun around, heart thumping, to see Vermont the Violinist standing in the bedroom doorway with a pile of laundry in his arms.

"Vermont! How are you?" Stanley said, standing up straight. "Sorry, I was just dropping off a package and this enclosure caught my eye. I thought you went on holiday?"

"I am on holiday," Vermont said, placing the laundry down on the workbench, not letting Stanley out of his eye-sight. "I don't need to go away to go on holiday."

"Very true, very true," Stanley laughed nervously, inching towards the door.

"Where's the package?" Vermont asked.

"It's inside the front door."

"And you saw my enclosure from down the hallway and around the corner?" Vermont asked with suspicion.

"I was just going to check…" Stanley did not have a good answer so told the truth. "I was just interested to see what your apartment looked like. I'm sorry."

Vermont relaxed a little. "Well, this is the apartment."

"It's a very nice apartment," Stanley said.

"Would you like a photo taken with my fridge?" Vermont asked gruffly.

"No, no. That should be fine," Stanley was quite close to the front door, but his curiosity still nagged him. "If I may ask, what is in the enclosure?"

"A grasshopper," Vermont said.

"Just one grasshopper?" Stanley asked.

"Yes. But that's why I purchased more. The package has more grasshoppers."

Vermont leaned over the enclosure, doing the same search that Stanley had done for signs of movement or life. Vermont appeared to grow increasingly concerned.

"Is everything alright?" Stanley asked.

"Did you see a grasshopper in here?"

"No, nothing. I didn't see anything," Stanley said.

Vermont began searching around the living room, moving piles of sheet music, even going as far as to lift the lid off and look inside the grand piano. Stanley didn't feel right leaving the man in such a flurry. "Did you want help looking?" Stanley offered.

"Did you leave the front door open?" Vermont asked, continuing his search through the kitchen.

"Well, yes, but only for—"

Vermont snapped his head up to look at Stanley with wide, angry eyes.

"It's only been open for a couple of minutes, I promise," Stanley said. "Not to be rude, but why is this one grasshopper so important? Didn't you say you've ordered more?"

"That grasshopper that has gone missing is the last

descendant in the line of grasshoppers owned by King George the fifth," Vermont explained.

Stanley then asked a question he often found himself asking when conversing with his neighbours at Tayel Tower. "What are you talking about?"

"There's no time to explain," Vermont said. "We must find that grasshopper! He could be anywhere by now!"

"Well, I'm sure he can't have gone too far," Stanley said. He realised Mandy the Midwife was probably wondering why he had abandoned the mail sorting. "I'll go have a look in the lobby for you," Stanley said. "I'll call you if I find the grasshopper."

"Its name is King George the Two-Hundredth and Twenty-Ninth," Vermont said.

Stanley paused at the front door. "You want me to call out the grasshopper's name?"

"No! What good would that do? Grasshoppers don't understand English," Vermont said, checking inside the half-made violins on the workbench. "And don't make any clicking or whistling sounds either. I still haven't worked out what they all mean. I am pretty sure I heard a group of grasshoppers talking smack about me a while ago."

Stanley left Vermont the Violinist and went back to the lobby where Mandy the Midwife was just finishing with the mail sorting.

"I'm so sorry for leaving you to sort the mail alone," Stanley said, looking at the last letter and putting it in the right mailbox to feel like he contributed. "I delivered the package to Vermont the Violinist, and apparently his grasshopper has escaped."

"His grasshopper?" Mandy asked in surprise.

"Yes. It's allegedly a descendant from grasshoppers owned by King George the Fifth or something."

The elevator doors opened and out came Barney the Banker wearing a big fake moustache and bushy stick-on eyebrows.

"Barney?" Stanley asked. "I thought you were going to visit a third cousin who owned old wine or something?"

"It was a second cousin who owns a gold mine," Barney said. "But I'm not Barney. Barney is my brother. My name is Brett and I am just collecting the mail for my brother."

"Then why did you come through the elevator?" Mandy asked, wondering how on earth Barney thought the thin disguise would deceive anyone.

"Well… I needed to collect something from Barney's room. He gave me his key."

"Well it's very nice to meet you, Brett," Stanley said, humouring the man.

Barney stood up straighter, glad to see his disguise was working. "It's very nice to meet you, Stanley and Mandy."

"If you're going to pretend to be someone else, you need to pretend not to already know our names," Stanley said shaking his head.

Barney rolled his eyes. "Fair point."

"But what are you doing here? Stanley asked again and then considered more important, "Does this mean I don't need to clean your windows?"

"My second cousin had to cancel, last minute," Barney said.

"Why the disguise?" Mandy asked.

Barney shrugged. "Well, you know. Everyone else has gone away on holidays and is having fun, and I didn't want to be 'that person' that didn't go away on holiday. So, I planned on staying in my room all weekend until everyone came back."

"There's no shame in not going on holidays," Stanley said. "There are other people that have stayed behind. Vermont the Violinist also said he's having a holiday at home."

"Wait," Mandy said in surprise. "Vermont the Violinist is actually here? He told me he was going on a weekend cruise!"

"He's definitely up in his apartment right now," Stanley said. "Who else stayed behind that said they're going away for the weekend?"

****

As part of Stanley's doorman training, Damien the Doorman had shown Stanley the building's alarm systems.

"Underneath my desk here is three buttons," Damien explained, running his hand along the underside of the concierge desk. "This first button doesn't do anything."

"Did it ever do anything?" Stanley asked, taking notes.

"Probably. It might have something to do with the cold war, I'm not really sure. But you can press the first button as much as you like to your heart's content," Damien pressed the button rapidly. "When I'm feeling restless, I sometimes press it in the hope that it does something, but nothing ever happens. The second button is the fire alarm. Although the building is fitted with smoke detectors and heat sensors, having a good old fashioned manual button just brings one peace of mind, doesn't it?"

"Wouldn't it be better to have the fire alarm button out in the open, where anyone can press it if there's a fire?" Stanley suggested.

"I feel like people would abuse that," Damien said. "Besides, you need the training to know when to press it."

"The training would just be, 'if you see a fire, press the fire alarm button', would it not? And then let the fire brigade come and deal with the fire?"

"Ah, no. You see, this fire alarm button doesn't alert the fire brigade," Damien said. "It used to when the fire station was located in the city square, but a couple of decades ago the fire station moved to the south side, and a shop went in where the fire station used to be."

"If it doesn't alert the fire station, then what does the fire alarm button do?" Stanley asked.

"It lets out a light pinging sound and enables the speaker system throughout Tayel Tower. That's so that you can let everyone know why you pressed the alarm."

"Right, got it. So, the second button is essentially an announcement speaker system."

"That's one way of putting it." Damien the Doorman moved his hand to the third button. "Now this third button is the announcement speaker system. It enables the speaker system throughout Tayel Tower and allows you to make announcements."

"Okay," Stanley sighed, lowering his phone in which he was recording notes. "So button one does nothing, and button two and three do the same thing."

Damien shook his head. "No. Button one did or does something, I just don't know what. Button two is a fire alarm that allows you to give an announcement explanation for why you pressed the alarm. And button three enables the speaker system. They are all very different."

"Does everyone know what the fire alarm sounds like?"

Stanley asked

Damien laughed. "I highly doubt it. There's hasn't been a fire here in years."

****

Stanley considered so many Tayel Tower residents lying about leaving to go on holiday a fire hazard and therefore worthy of the fire alarm. He marched over to the concierge desk and pressed the second button. All those present in the lobby had to cover their ears at the wail that came from hidden speakers. No one in their right mind could describe the excruciating audio merely a 'light pinging sound'. Stanley pressed the button again in an attempt to turn it off, but it kept wailing.

"Can you turn it off?" Barney the Banker asked in a yell that could barely be heard.

"I'm trying," Stanley yelled back, mashing the second button.

Like the instant the wailing came, the wailing stopped. Their ears didn't stop ringing for minutes. A panel on the concierge desk slid open and a lectern microphone rose up. Just as Stanley was about to speak into the microphone, a samba-jazz piece of music began to play quietly over the speakers, giving Stanley's announcement an inappropriately calm edge after the bone-chilling alarm.

"Could… could all resident in Tayel Tower please assemble in the lobby for an important meeting," Stanley said. Without any prompting, the microphone receded back into the desk and the music stopped. Stanley, Mandy and Barney stood still to recover from the dramatic ordeal. The elevator door opened, and out emerged Vermont the Violinist.

"What's going on?" Vermont asked. "Are you getting everyone together to search for King George the Two-Hundredth and Twenty-Ninth?"

"Yes, that's exactly what we're doing," Stanley said sarcastically. The elevator doors opened again to bring Elaine the Event Planner and Deborah the Debt Collector to the lobby. The stairwell door opened to reveal Paul the Policeman followed by Mooney the Millionaire. Minute by minute the residents of Tayel Tower materialized in the lobby, some highly concerned about the alarm, others more worried that their lies of going on holidays were being found out in the most public of ways. In the end, there were about 70 out of 102 residents standing in the lobby before Stanley. He couldn't believe it.

"What's going on?" Rosemary the Retired asked.

"We've all gathered to search for my grasshopper," Vermont the Violinist announced.

"No," Stanley said. "Actually, you are all here because you lied about going on holidays. Why did everyone pretend to leave? Just so that you could get me to do all of your tasks?"

"I had to cancel my plans," a voice from the back of the crowd called.

"It was a very last-minute decision to stay home," another voice called.

"I lost my tickets in a game of poker," said another.

"Space travel is too expensive," Jarvis the Jobless explained. "And I'm pretty sure it's because the government doesn't believe space is real."

"It's a major hazard for everyone to say they have gone away but stayed behind," Stanley said. "What would have happened if there was a real fire?"

The residents all avoided eye contact as they were reprimanded.

"I'm genuinely asking because I have no idea," Stanley said. "Is someone here a fire marshal? Is there a sprinkler system?"

"A lot of us have oversized mugs that could be used for fighting a fire," Barney the Banker said proudly.

"There is no shame with not having anywhere to go for the holidays," Stanley said. "All of you clearly care too much about what your neighbours think. Instead of all hiding away inside of your apartments, why don't you get together with your friends here in Tayel Tower and spend your holidays together?"

"That's a wonderful idea," Russell the Realtor said with a clap of his hands. "What time should we come to your apartment, Stanley?"

"No, I don't mean me," Stanley said quickly without thinking. "I mean… I already have something planned tonight with Mandy. And I have a lot of chores I need to get through for those who really did go away."

"Sounds like you don't want to hang out with anyone else either!" Paxton the Pacifist exclaimed.

"I just said that I have plans to hang out with Mandy," Stanley said. "She is someone I want to hang out with. I'm not saying I don't want to hang out with any of you, but…"

Stanley could see he was digging himself a hole. With quick thinking, he found a ladder out. "By the way, it should be noted that Vermont the Violinist's grasshopper has gone missing."

"Yes! Yes, it has!" Vermont said excitedly.

"Who cares about a stupid insect?" Deborah the Debt Collector said.

"Who cares?" Vermont repeated. "This 'stupid insect' is by far one of the rarest grasshoppers on the planet. Irreplaceable!"

Mooney the Millionaire shook his head and started walking to the elevator. "Don't waste my time with this nonsense. If anyone needs me, I'll be asleep, dreaming about not having to deal with my neighbour's petty issues."

"I will give one million dollars to the person that finds King George the two-hundred and twenty-ninth," Vermont announced with gusto.

Mooney the Millionaire stopped in his tracks. Vermont the Violinist could have made the prize a single dollar and Mooney would have slowed his walk away, but a million dollars turned the millionaire around. "What did you say?"

"I said I will give one million dollars to whoever finds my grasshopper," Vermont said confidently. The residents present pretended like this was a normal announcement. They pretended they didn't want to blind their neighbours to increase their odds. They pretended not to already start looking closely at the floor, on the walls, or on the roof of the lobby.

"Well," Mooney croaked. "I'm still going to go up to my room." He broke into a sprint towards the stairwell, causing the crowd to take a similar approach, running as fast as their legs could take them to different corners of Tayel Tower. Mooney the Millionaire got to the stairwell first, slamming the door behind him. He leaned against it as his eyes scanned over every conceivable angle. He felt someone push against the door.

"Mooney?" Paige the Psychologist asked through the door. "Mooney, I need to go up to my room."

"Take the elevator!" Mooney called back.

"I can't. The elevator is full."

"Then you'll need to climb up the outside of the building!"

"Don't be silly, Mooney," Paige said. "Maybe we should make an appointment to talk about this addiction of money you seem to possess."

"I am not possessed!" Mooney called back.

Stanley and Mandy stood by the concierge desk watching the chaos unfold.

"Well there's no chance of the grasshopper being lost for long," Mandy said as she watched Jarvis the Jobless look inside every unlocked mailbox.

"Does Vermont the Violinist have a million dollars?" Stanley asked.

"Probably. He's a world-class musician. I've heard he has performed for royalty," Mandy said.

Tayel Tower's front door swung open and in rushed a TV journalist and a cameraman. The TV journalist ran over to Mandy and Stanley, microphone ready.

"It is true that a man has offered a million-dollar prize for the whereabouts of his missing grasshopper?" the journalist asked, sticking the microphone into Stanley's face.

"Wait, who are you?" Stanley asked.

"We're from Channel 542 and we have just been given this most extraordinary story," the journalist said, moving the microphone closer still to Stanley's mouth.

"Well, yes it's true," Stanley said. "But he announced it

mere minutes ago. How did you find out?"

"We have sources," the cameraman said, attempting to surreptitiously pay Jarvis the Jobless a handful of mustard and ketchup packets.

CHAPTER THREE
THE GAG ORDER

The International Hairy Llamas Appreciation Day holiday ended abruptly as the residents, not only of Tayel Tower but the whole city, returned to their homes early in the hope of coming across a small insect that went by the name King George the 229th.

"This is King George Two-Hundredth and Twenty-Eighth," Vermont the Violinist said to the crowd of gathered journalists. Vermont held up a large poster of the grasshopper he had printed out as journalists' cameras flashed in Tayel Tower's lobby. "King George Two-Hundred and Twenty-Ninth looks practically the same as his father."

"Why is this particular grasshopper so important to you?" a journalist asked.

"That's a great question," Vermont said. "Why is your life so important to you?"

The returned question was not at all what the journalist was looking for. "Well, I… love my family. I enjoy my job?"

Vermont nodded. "I, to the grasshopper, the same. But for many reasons more. Any other questions?"

A man stood up. "Yes. Samuel the Salesman, Tayel Tower resident. Are you satisfied with your current car insurance rates?"

"I don't own a car," Vermont said.

"Well then are you satisfied with your current means of getting around?" Samuel said with raised eyebrows. "I can get you a fantastic price—"

"This is a press conference for a grasshopper," Vermont the Violinist interrupted firmly.

The dozen or so journalists, finding there wasn't much else to know about a grasshopper and a violinist, left the lobby to return to their offices where they would write stories to attract enough attention to their websites so they could pay their electricity bills at the end of the month.

The mad search continued up and down Tayel Tower, both inside and out. To say that every inch of the tower had been searched was an over exaggeration. Many residents were unfamiliar to the art of productive seeking, and spent the next day looking between two or three locations where the grasshopper 'must be'. The rooftop garden would have received a real beating had Boris the Body Builder not set up defences at the rooftop door to prevent anyone else from getting up there. He claimed the bucket of bees poised precariously above the door was for the protection of the plants, but passers-by could see Boris through the window checking under each and every leaf in the garden.

"On the bright side," Stanley said to Mandy on Sunday morning as they leaned back on the lobby couches drinking two cups of tea. "On the bright side, anyone who's lost anything will have found it."

Mandy nodded. "I won't lie, I did have a quick look around my apartment last night and found an old pen I lost."

"Well there you go," Stanley said. "Vermont losing his grasshopper did result in something good."

Norman the Nurse timidly approached the couple. "Hey, Stanley. Hey Mandy. How are you two this morning?"

"Good thanks, Norman. And you?" Mandy asked sweetly.

"Fine, fine," Norman said, his eyes searching the area. "Would it be alright if you two could just pop up off the couch for a moment? I think I lost a coin or something. I'm very clumsy sometimes…"

Stanley exhaled a laugh through his nose. "This couch has been searched by at least a dozen people. There is nothing here."

Norman nodded. "Thank you for your cooperation, Stanley and Mandy."

Norman had hardly walked ten metres away when Paxton the Pacifist approached the couches. "Right, you two. Jump up. Those couches need searching."

Stanley and Mandy exchanged a glance and moved off the couches to allow Paxton to search between the cushions.

"Where can we go?" Mandy asked. "Everywhere is a search zone at the moment."

Stanley checked the time. "Come with me to Ludwig the Lawyer's apartment—"

The sound of chirping crickets filled the lobby at an unnatural volume. Stanley and Mandy covered their ears looking around for the source. Over at the concierge desk, Vincent the Villain was holding his phone to the microphone, looking around with a smile at everyone's discomfort.

Stanley handed Damien the Doorman's master key to Mandy the Midwife. "I'll meet you at Ludwig's apartment!" he yelled. "Can you feed his lizard please?!"

"What?!" Mandy cried back, trying to read his lips.

"Can you feed Ludwig's lizard?!"

"What do I read?!"

"No, feed! Ludwig's lizard, Shakespeare. Do you know Shakespeare?!"

Mandy tilted her head. "I'll try!"

Mandy set off to Ludwig the Lawyer's apartment.

Stanley strode over to the concierge desk.

"What are you doing?!" Stanley yelled to Vincent the Villain over the constant drone of chirping.

"What's that?" Vincent asked, leaning in. His beautiful hair flicking Stanley in the face.

"I said what are you doing?! Turn that off!"

"But I'm looking for the grasshopper!" Vincent said. "It will be attracted to the noise and will come to me!"

"But that's ludicrous!" Stanley said.

"So is everyone spending a whole weekend looking for a single grasshopper!" Vincent yelled back. Stanley reached under the desk and pressed the third button, turning off the speaker system.

"You're not doing that to be helpful," Stanley said, shaking his head in an attempt to stop the ringing in his ears.

"No, not really," Vincent said. "But you ringing a fire alarm for no reason yesterday wasn't very helpful either, was it?"

"Mine had a purpose."

"Mine could have had a purpose," Vincent the Villain said, beginning to walk away. "Like how they discovered cheese; you can only try."

Stanley took the elevator up to the tenth floor and found Ludwig's front door open. He could hear Mandy talking to someone inside. Considering Ludwig hadn't come home, even at the announcement of a million-dollar prize, Stanley wasn't sure who else was there. He entered the apartment and rounded the corner into the living room to find Mandy reading something aloud from her phone.

"A kind overflow of kindness: there are no faces
truer than those that are so washed. How much
better is it to weep at joy than to joy at weeping!"

"Some light reading?" Stanley asked.

"I don't know why Ludwig wants you to do this. I think he might be playing a joke on you," Mandy said.

"Doing what?"

"Reading Shakespeare to a lizard. It's just silly."

Stanley considered bursting out in laughter, but he couldn't do it to the poor girl who was doing her best.

"Feed the lizard, Shakespeare," he explained. "The lizard's name is Shakespeare."

Mandy slumped her shoulders, feeling very embarrassed.

"No, don't feel bad," Stanley said as he crossed to where the lizard's food was kept under his tank. "What play was that from?"

Mandy laughed at herself. "I have no idea. It was the first thing that came up when I searched for 'Shakespeare quotes'. Much Ado About Nothing, I think."

"I remember studying Shakespeare in high school," Stanley said, going about feeding the lizard from the bucket of crickets. "I can't say I ever enjoyed it."

"No, it's not my cup of tea either," Mandy said.

"People put him on this pedestal as the god of English writing. I don't mean to say I could do any better, but—"

"Stop!" Mandy cried. Stanley froze with his hand suspended over the lizard's tank. Shakespeare, the lizard, was looking up with an open mouth wondering why his food wasn't falling from heaven. Stanley looked at the grasshopper in his hand to see King George 229th. He almost dropped the creature in fright. You, the reader, might be wondering how Stanley suddenly procured the ability to recognise one Acrididae from another Acrididae, given that many grasshopper subspecies, and it takes a trained eye and often a 12-question interview to determine the differences between one grasshopper and another. Stanley could easily see that the grasshopper in his hand was King George 229th thanks to the tiny golden crown that Vermont the Violinist had fastened to the critter's head.

"It's King George!" Mandy cried in excitement.

"Shhh!" Stanley said, fearful there were other residents in the hallway.

"What's wrong?" Mandy asked.

"I was in the apartment when Vermont lost the grasshopper. He'll be suspicious that I took it," Stanley said. "If we go back and say we found it, he'll think I stole it and kept it for ransom! I don't know what the laws are regarding the kidnapping of insects, but I feel like Vermont wouldn't take very kindly to it."

"I see," Mandy said. "Well, that grasshopper is worth a million dollars. Anyone you give it to is going to become an instant millionaire."

"Why am I always the one that has to make decisions about ridiculously large sums of money?" Stanley asked in frustration. "You take the grasshopper. You say you found it. You were the one that technically found him. I was about to feed him to a lizard."

Mandy did consider it. She wasn't interested in wealth and riches, but a million dollars handed to you on a platter, or in this case a glass jar that Stanley borrowed from a kitchen cupboard, is hard for one to resist.

"Okay, I'll do it, but we're splitting the money," Mandy said, keeping the jar covered to prevent his royal highness the grasshopper from escaping. Her hands shook as she considered that she was about to own half a million dollars.

"You and the grasshopper are splitting the money?" Stanley asked.

****

"Excuse me, ladies and gentlemen. I'd like to announce that the search has concluded," Vincent the Villain said over the speaker system. "In celebration of this miraculous occasion, I would like to press the fire alarm button."

The wailing could be heard blocks away as everyone in the lobby, residents, journalists and other treasure seekers covered their ears in agony. Not even Vincent the Villain could help cover his ears, but he did so with a satisfied grin watching everyone yell at him to turn it off. He shrugged his shoulders and left the building. Someone nearby the desk stopped the alarm.

Vermont the Violinist held the glass jar Mandy had handed him up to his eye to look inside at the creature. "You found—"

The jazz music began to play over the speaker system. Barney the Banker rolled his eyes and walked over to the protruding microphone at the concierge desk. "There is no fire. If anyone presses these buttons again, I will personally see to it that you are—" The microphone receded into the desk before Barney could finish his threat.

"You found King George the Two-hundredth and Twenty-Ninth!" Vermont the Violinist said joyfully.

A television journalist approached Mandy the Midwife with such aggression that she wasn't sure if the journalist was going to ask a question or attack her.

"Where did you find this grasshopper?" the journalist asked with a big open-mouth smile.

"I was helping a neighbour of mine by feeding their Lizard, and I happened to see this grasshopper with a crown on its head just... hanging around the apartment," Mandy said, unsure if it was a believable story. Stanley stood off to the side, curious to see if anyone would start wondering if he was present when Mandy found the grasshopper.

"And now you're a millionaire!" the journalist continued.

"Hang on a moment!" someone cried from Tayel Tower's front door. Everyone turned to see Paxton the Pacifist, Edith the Etymologist and Mooney the Millionaire walking towards the crowd wearing matching green baseball caps that read 'GAG' in big white embroidered letters. Paxton and his friends moved in front of the cameras.

"We are the GAG foundation," Paxton the Pacifist

announced loudly. "GAG stands for 'Grasshoppers Are Great', and we stand for the rights of grasshoppers everywhere. We are only a new organisation, founded less than two hours ago, but we stand for the rights of grasshoppers everywhere!"

"Paxton, what in the world are you doing?" Vermont asked with a sigh.

"We are intervening here because we stand for the rights of grasshoppers everywhere!"

Stanley raised his hand. "Is it just grasshoppers you stand for or…"

"Just grasshoppers," Paxton said.

"And is it grasshoppers just here or there or…"

Paxton considered his group's current infrastructure. "At the moment, we'll just focus on standing for the rights of grasshoppers here, but soon we will be looking to expand operations to standing for the rights of grasshoppers everywhere!"

Stanley nodded his head.

"I treat my grasshoppers with the utmost respect," Vermont said. "If you really want to make an example of someone that disrespects grasshoppers, try Ludwig the Lawyer. He feeds them to his lizard, Shakespeare!"

"Don't you go quoting 15th-century literature to me!" Paxton the Pacifist cried. "That grasshopper in your hand, as I'm sure you're aware, is a very rare Petasida ephippigera grasshopper, native to Australia and illegal to own as a pet."

Paxton was expecting there to be gasps of surprise from the audience, but none came. Everyone simply looked to Vermont for his reply.

"What utter nonsense," Vermont said. "And if it is true that this grasshopper is rare, then it must be the rarest and most special grasshopper of them all, given its royal heritage."

"That may well be," Paxton said. "But that gives you no right to ownership of a said Petasida ephippigera."

"Since when do you care, or even know, so much about grasshoppers?" Vermont asked.

"I don't. I know very little," Paxton said. He pointed to the woman to his left. "But this here is our good neighbour Edith the Etymologist. She studies bugs day in a day out, and even sometimes at night! And this is Mooney the Millionaire, the patron of our organisation."

"My motives are not monetary," Mooney said.

"No one suggested they are," Stanley said.

"Well, you know. I have a reputation—"

"So, in the name of justice and ethics," Paxton said vociferously, "we demand that the grasshopper be handed over for safekeeping and care to us, the GAG foundation, and we will not speak of it again. That's a GAG order."

"I refuse to hand anything—"

"The grasshopper has escaped again," Stanley calmly pointed out. Vermont looked down at the empty jar. In the commotion, he had removed his hand from the opening. Now there was a collective gasp from the crowd.

Vermont dropped the jar in fright, causing it to shatter on the lobby floor. "No one move! You might step on the grasshopper!"

"Over by the elevator!" someone called. Sure enough, standing in front of the elevator was the grasshopper, seemingly waiting to go up.

"No-body-move," Vermont said slowly, inching across the lobby. The elevator dinged, startling Vermont.

The elevator doors opened, revealing a very unhappy small scaled and small-scaled creature.

"You have arrived at the ground floor!" Ernest the Elevator Operator announced over the loudspeaker.

Shakespeare the lizard slowly walked out of the elevator, towards the grasshopper. No one in the lobby dared to make a sudden move, some out of fear for the grasshopper, and others out of fascination at nature apparently about to play its course. The lizard spotted the grasshopper. The grasshopper spotted the lizard. Some of the audience could have sworn the grasshopper raised a leg as if to request the lizard bow before him in respect. The lizard, out of respect, ate the grasshopper quickly and without regret, leaving only the tiny crown behind.

Vermont let out a sound of surprise and agony that sounded like a ghost being surprised at his surprise birthday party. A photographer from the newspaper walked up to the lizard and snapped a photo before leaving. The crowd, seeing that the million dollars were no longer available for the taking, dispersed back to their homes to grumble over a waster holiday. Vermont the Violinist was left staring at the lizard, who stared back with what could only be described as a satisfied grin. Stanley stayed behind as well to make sure the lizard that had been tasked into his care didn't run too far.

Ludwig the Lawyer walked through the front door in a cheery disposition and waved to the petrified violinist. "Morning, Vermont!"

Ludwig noticed his lizard on the lobby floor. "Shakespeare! What are you doing down here?"

"He was going for a walk," Stanley said, standing by the concierge desk.

"Ah, excellent," Ludwig said with a smile. "Has he been fed?"

Stanley nodded. "A royal feast."

Wray Wrigley's

TAYEL TOWER

Book 8

THE UNFORESEEABLE FUTURE

CHAPTER ONE
A COUPLE OF COUPLES

Love. To try and describe love is like attempting to describe gravity. Both concepts could fill a library of books, but the author would still have to take a side job as a horticulturist or haughty culturalist to pay their bills while they wrote the volume. For the sake of brevity, I'll simply describe love as a heaviness you feel when you see that someone special and gravity as the heaviness you feel when you eat too much. In Tayel Tower, there were very few couples in love. Couples that did fall in love and got married usually moved out of the building quite quickly, as the apartments in Tayel Tower were only big enough for a single occupant. Doris the Dominating and Hugo the Humble, a married couple going on 30 years, managed to live quite comfortably together in apartment 410 thanks to their complimentary personalities.

It is with utmost confidence that I narrate that Mandy the Midwife and Stanley were in love. Although it was still a young relationship, they were mere gnats in the flytrap of love, it could be seen by all that Stanley and Mandy were a true couple, devoted to each other and rarely seen apart.

"I think it's so lovely having young love here in Tayel Tower," Leah the Librarian said as she watched the couple walk through to lobby, holdings hands, on return from their Saturday lunch date.

"I'm sceptical," Marty the Mailman murmured.

"Of what? Of love in general?" Leah asked.

"Love?" Marty replied, looking up from the newspaper he was perusing. "What of it? I was saying I'm sceptical that they'll get the garbage shoot fixed. Jarvis the Jobless did a pretty good job on it." The sound of a jackhammer could be heard in the distance.

"He was just trying to be helpful," Leah said. "I'm sure I would have made a similar mistake, thinking a fridge could fit—"

The other residents sitting on the lobby couches shook their heads. None of them believed anyone could be so silly as to try and squeeze a fridge down a garbage shoot. Jarvis the Jobless, in his pursuit of removing a couch he had also tried to shove down the garbage shoot earlier that day, had proved them wrong. Now there was a fridge and a couch jammed in the garbage shoot and a removalist crew working from the basement attempting to remove the furniture using a variety of very noisy tools.

"I think love's a bit overrated," Samuel the Salesman said while rearranging the contents of his slippers, by which I mean getting the tiny rocks out of his slippers which got in there when he had to walk outside to deposit his kitchen bin into the back-alley's dumpster because a fridge and couch blocked the garbage shoot.

"Just because you haven't found love doesn't mean it's overrated," Leah retorted.

"I'd bet any of you a thousand dollars that if some gorgeous girl moved in this afternoon who was more appealing to Stanley, he would be off," Samuel said.

"You can't say that!" Leah exclaimed, clutching his arm. "What a horrible thing to say!"

"Hey, I'm not having a go at Stanley's commitment," Samuel the Salesman said. "I'm sure that the same thing would happen for Mandy. If a nice-looking guy arrived that better suited Mandy, she would probably reconsider as well. Stanley and Mandy are not married, they're dating. There is nothing wrong at all with either of them finding someone better suited."

"Yes, but—" Leah began, her voice trailing off.

"Ah, Good afternoon Alice and Norman," Damien the Doorman said, opening the door for another young couple.

Leah re-grabbed Samuel the Salesman's arm in surprise.

"Can you please stop grabbing me?" he asked.

"Look!" Leah said, very unsubtly pointing at the couple. "Alice and Norman are holding hands!"

Samuel turned his head and saw that it was true. Alice the Actress and Norman the Nurse were holding hands, appearing that they also had a wonderful time at lunch together.

"Not another one," Samuel said, shaking his head.

"Not another what?" Norman the Nurse asked, seeing the group sitting on the couches staring at him and his girlfriend.

"You're a couple now?" Marty the Mailman asked.

"Well, yes," Alice said with a smile. "We've been seeing each other for a couple of weeks now, and we've decided to make it official. We are officially a couple."

"What is in the water here?" Samuel asked. "All these love birds. You and I better be careful, Leah, and make sure we don't see each other under any good lighting."

Leah the Librarian, at least 30 years Samuel's senior, rolled her eyes. "You are just so cynical, Samuel. You just wait. There will be some girl that walks through the front door that sweeps you off your feet." She turned to Alice and Norman. "I think it's so lovely and we all wish the best for both of you."

"Thanks," Norman said with a big grin.

Yes, it was apparent that there was something in the water, and it wasn't just the extra fluoride Domonique the Dentist was secretly adding to the building's water supply.

Mandy and Stanley went up via the stairwell to relax in Stanley's apartment. Mandy the Midwife settled on his couch reading a novel she had picked up at a local book fair, and Stanley did various chores around the house he had been putting off.

"I mean, come on. A couch and a refrigerator?" Stanley said, clearing up some dishes from the night before.

"Jarvis was just trying to be helpful," Mandy said.

"Does he have any family or close friends who could, say, move in with him?" Stanley asked. "Then again, someone must have helped him pick up a refrigerator and squeeze it into the garbage shoot in the first place."

"I don't know if he has family," Mandy said.

"I'll be back in a moment," Stanley said. "I need to take my kitchen bin down to the dumpster. If I don't return within 10 minutes, call search and rescue."

"Maybe on your way you could take those old shoes

sitting by the front door," Mandy teased.

For the months that they had been dating, Stanley had had an old pair of sneakers sitting by the front door that were destined for the bin. He had believed that placing the sneakers into the garbage shoot on the ninth floor could have caused a blockage, which was evidently a totally unfounded worry seeing that Jarvis had managed to squeeze both a couch and a refrigerator into the garbage shoot.

"But I'll miss those shoes," Stanley joked. "They've always been sitting there to see me off to work in the mornings, and they're the first things that greet me when I come home."

"I'm sure you'll find someone or something new to do that job," Mandy smiled.

Stanley picked up the sneakers. "Are you thinking of my slippers? They could work."

Stanley didn't notice, too distracted was he with his girlfriend's lovely laugh, but a small piece of paper fell out of the left sneaker and floated to the floor.

"What's that?" Mandy asked, still grinning. Stanley looked down at his feet and almost fell down in fright. You might ask how a man forgets about a winning lottery ticket worth $29 million dollars. You might ask how that winning lottery ticket ended up in an old pair of sneakers. The answer to the above questions is one of two options: amnesia, or a promise made to a psychic that one would keep a lottery ticket secret until one finds out what to do with it, and one tried one's best to forget about it because it was easier that way than worry that they were carrying around a tiny piece of paper worth more than the whole ten-story building in which they lived. In this case, Stanley did not have amnesia.

"It's the lottery ticket," Stanley whispered fearfully. He bent down and picked up the piece of paper, holding it away from his body as if it might detonate.

"The winning lottery ticket? You still have it?" Mandy asked, closing her novel. Stanley just nodded. His eyes read over the seven numbers; the seven numbers that had caused such a commotion not long after Stanley moved into Tayel Tower.

"Well, surely it's expired by now," Mandy said.

Stanley turned the ticket over and held it close to read the finely printed terms and conditions. After speed reading a couple of paragraphs, he shook his head. "Nope. It says tickets are valid for up to one hundred and eighty days after the draw."

"The draw was about six months ago," Mandy said. Stanley, so desperate to be rid of the burden, went to his laptop on the kitchen table and did a date calculation.

"Guess when one hundred and eighty days is up?" Stanley asked Mandy.

"Today?" Mandy guessed

"Not quite," Stanley said. "But in two days' time! On Monday this ticket will expire!"

"And you just happened to find it today?" Mandy said, taking my need away to narrate that coincidence.

"That is quite an odd coincidence," Stanley admitted. He put the ticket down onto the kitchen table.

"What was it that Perry the Psychic told you after he gave you the ticket?" Mandy asked.

"I don't remember exactly, but he said something about waiting to give it to a new couple, or some new couple would know what to do with it," Stanley said.

They were both wondering the same thing, but it was Mandy that voiced it aloud. "Are we the new couple?"

Stanley didn't know.

"I'm not sure that I want millions of dollars," Mandy said.

"Me neither," Stanley agreed quickly. "But let's hypothetically say that we are the new couple. What would we do with the money?"

"Well, donate it, of course," said Mandy.

"Of course. We'd donate it," Stanley agreed without meeting Mandy's gaze.

"You wouldn't donate it?" Mandy asked.

"No, of course I would—"

A knock at Stanley's apartment door caused them both to jump in fright. Stanley hid the ticket under a tea towel. He opened his front door to find Alice the Actress and Norman the Nurse standing very close to each other in the hallway.

"Have we caught you at a bad time?" Alice asked, seeing the somewhat concerned expression on Stanley's brow.

"No, not at all. What can I do for you two?" Stanley asked, taking in a deep breath and putting on a smile. He looked down and noticed Alice and Norman had their arms around each other. "Wait, are you two finally together?"

Alice and Norman could do very little to hide their joy.

Stanley stepped aside and beckoned the couple inside. "Mandy! How long did I say it would be for Alice and Norman to become an official couple?"

"You said three months. I said one month. Why?" Mandy called back.

"I was right for once!" Stanley said proudly.

Mandy looked down the hallway and greeted the couple with a big smile. "Congratulations, you two!"

They all exchanged hugs. Mandy the Midwife knew Norman the Nurse from the hospital, and Alice and Mandy got coffee together one a fortnight or so. Stanley only knew Norman and Alice from brief conversations in passing with the pair, but the topic of whether they would work well together had been a keen topic of interest to himself and Mandy.

"I'm sorry to ruin your victory, Stanley, but we've actually been dating for a couple of weeks now," Alice said. Stanley shook his head. "I should have known. There was only a five per cent chance I was right over Mandy. Anyone for tea or coffee?"

Stanley went to the kitchen and filled the kettle with water. "If this isn't us growing old, I don't know what is. The old couple and the new couple getting together for tea and…" his voice trailed off.

Norman looked over at Stanley who had frozen with a distant stare while the tap filled the kettle. "Are you alright there? You look a little pale."

"Yes, yes, I'm fine," Stanley lied. "Mandy, could you come here for a moment please?"

Mandy came over to the kitchen. She was already wondering if Stanley was thinking the same thing.

"They're the new couple," Stanley whispered.

"How do you know?" Mandy asked quietly.

"I don't know if they're the new couple, I'm just saying they are 'the new couple'. Do you think we're meant to give the money to them?" Stanley asked.

"Maybe. It fits the bill of what Perry the Psychic said," Mandy whispered. "If we give them the lottery ticket, apparently they'll know what to do with it."

"Don't you think it's quite an odd coincidence?" Stanley asked. "The moment I re-find the lottery ticket, they show up at the door."

Stanley, in his distraction, didn't notice that the kettle was more than overflowing under the tap. Spilling a little onto his jeans, he poured out the excess water into the sink and dried off the kettle with a tea-towel.

"We should go back," Mandy said. "They'll think we're talking about them."

"We are talking about them," Stanley said. "What if Norman and Alice overheard what Perry the Psychic said the night he left, and they've just gotten together to take the money? How well do you know these people?"

"Well, I know Norman quite well. We work in the same ward at the hospital. Alice is also a lovely girl. I don't think they are the conspiring type."

Stanley found a packet of coconut cookies in the pantry he had been gifted from a client and arranged them on a plate. He went back into the living room with Mandy and began offering the plate of biscuits to his guests. Norman took one and said thank you.

"Oh, no thanks," Alice the Actress smiled.

"Are you allergic?" Stanley asked, pulling the plate away from the actress.

"Oh no. I just don't like coconut, to be honest," she said.

"Good for you," Stanley said. "Me neither. I don't

know which Coconut farmer started insisting that coconut should be put in all products, but every product containing coconut has been ruined. Mandy loves coconut."

"Same with Norman," Alice laughed. "He will just eat spoonsful of shaved coconut for dessert."

Mandy quickly swallowed her mouthful of cookie. "I do that too!"

"How good is it!" Norman the Nurse said to Mandy. "I don't know if you've tried it, but if you mix a little water into desiccated coconut and heat it in the microwave, it makes a coconut porridge."

"Who told you about coconut porridge?" Mandy asked excitedly. "I thought I invented that!"

Stanley and Alice exchanged a look of amazement at their significant other's passionate displays towards coconuts.

"So you're an actress, Alice?" Stanley asked for a change of topic.

"That's right," Alice said.

"Have you been in any TV shows or movies recently?"

"I've been in a number of TV shows but only in small roles. I haven't had the chance to be in a starring role yet."

"But she will be soon," Norman said supportively, placing his arms around Alice and giving her shoulder a squeeze.

"Do you know a man named Thomas Polls?" Stanley asked.

"No, I don't," Alice said.

"I went to high school with Thomas Polls. He's a TV writer now. I think I saw he's working on that show called Barney's at the moment."

Alice's eyes lit up. "You know one of the writers of Barney's? That show is super popular! If I starred on Barney's, all sorts of doors could open for me."

"Well, I'm sure I could introduce you to him," Stanley said. "I'll pass on your headshot or however it works."

"That would be amazing!" Alice said. She got out her phone. "Let's exchange phone numbers so you can introduce me."

Stanley noticed the discomfort in both Mandy and Norman as he input his mobile number into her phone.

Stanley hastily changed the subject again. "So, who wanted tea and who wanted coffee?"

He got their orders and left to the kitchen to prepare the beverages. Back in the living room, there was an awkward silence.

"Are you still enjoying midwifery?" Alice asked Mandy.

"Yes, it's great," Mandy smiled. "Working in a hospital is hard, as I'm sure Norman has told you, but it can be really rewarding."

"I have so much respect for anyone that works in a hospital," Alice said. "I wouldn't be able to do it. I can't stand the sight of blood or sick people."

"Alice doesn't even like it when I talk about it," Norman said.

Mandy nodded. "Stanley's the exact same way. Just the mention of broken bones makes Stanley uncomfortable."

"I heard that!" Stanley called, pouring the teas. "I had a bad experience growing up."

"Did you break your arm?" Norman asked.

Stanley paused. "I sort of broke someone else's arm."

"Playing a sport?" Norman asked.

"You could say that," Stanley said vaguely.

"He and his sister were playing with a dollhouse," Mandy clarified, having only managed to pry the story out of her boyfriend only weeks earlier. "Stanley passionately wanted one of the dolls. Stanley? What was the dolls name?"

"I'm sorry, I can't hear you," Stanley called back.

"Apparently in the fight for the doll, Stanley accidentally broke his sister's arm."

"It was my turn to have Naomi on Saturdays, and she knew that," Stanley said as he carried in the mugs of tea and coffee and placed them on the coffee table.

"So how did you two meet?" Stanley asked Alice and Norman. It was the most subtle question he could think of for investigating whether their intentions had anything to do with the lottery ticket.

Alice and Norman smiled at each other. "Well, it's quite a funny story," Norman said. "We obviously saw each other around Tayel Tower since I moved in a year ago, but it was actually… do you two remember the night of the fiasco involving the lottery ticket found on the lobby floor?"

Mandy and Stanley simultaneously inhaled their teas, sending them into coughing fits.

"Strong tea," Stanley said after regaining control of his lungs. "Yes, we recall that night."

"Well we met on that night," Norman the Nurse continued, "After Perry the Psychic left to go on his holiday, I returned to my apartment and found a letter outside my room that was addressed to Alice, and Alice found a letter outside her apartment addressed to me. I live on the eighth floor and Alice lives on the sixth, so it's quite a mistake for someone to make. We met in the stairwell on our ways to redeliver the letters to each other. Seeing the misdelivered letters as a very odd coincidence, we opened the letters together and found them to contain nothing at all."

Stanley listened with deep curiosity at all these strange coincidences.

"We were just as confused as you are right now," Alice said. "Anyway, we got talking about all that had happened that day, then we realised we were standing in a cold stairwell. So, we went out for a coffee and dessert to continue the conversation and it all sort of went from there."

Stanley did not like any of these coincidences. He wanted answers. "Does anyone know exactly where Perry would have gone for his holiday?"

"I'm not sure," Norman said.

"I would certainly like to ask Perry a number of questions."

There was a knock at Stanley's front door. He immediately knew who it would be, and wasn't at all surprised when he found he had guessed correctly.

He got up from the couch and opened the front door to find a man in a floral shirt.

"Hello," Perry the Psychic said. "I understand you want to ask me a number of questions?"

CHAPTER TWO
A PSYCHAL

Stanley stepped out into the hallway and closed the front door behind him.

"I do have a number of questions!" he exclaimed in a loud whisper

"I know," Perry the Psychic said with a smile. "I'm psychic. How are you doing Stanley? It's been so long."

Stanley begrudgingly shook the elder gentleman's hand. Perry's outfit and relaxed demeanour meant he always looked like he was going to or coming from the beach.

"I don't mean to be rude," Stanley said. "But your games with the lottery tickets have made me reach the end of my patience. Who is the new couple that is supposed to use the lottery ticket? Is it Mandy and me or Alice and Norman? Or is it someone completely different?"

Perry nodded patiently as he listened to the desperation in Stanley's voice. "It's interesting," Perry replied. "At some point in the future, I'm going to ask you to tell me a recap of all that has happened at Tayel Tower while I was away, so the only way I'm able to see what happened in the past is by you telling me in the future."

"I'm not going to tell you anything until we sort out this lottery ticket," Stanley said.

"I feel like there was something I was supposed to do today," Perry said, looking at his watch. "Oh well. Have a good day, Stanley."

Perry began walking back to the elevator. Stanley was not going to let this go. "You really came all the way up to my apartment to just acknowledge that I have questions, but you're not willing to answer any of them? You know what, Perry?"

"Probably," Perry replied.

"I'm just going to go and hand in the ticket myself, and take the twenty-three million dollars all for myself," Stanley threatened.

"That is interesting," Perry said, studying Stanley's face. The psychic pressed the down button on the elevator.

"Well, am I?" Stanley asked, hoping to read his future on the psychic's face.

"I hope I don't know," Perry said vaguely.

"Alright then," Stanley said. "I guess I'll go take the ticket to the lottery office right now and leave as a millionaire."

The elevator doors opened, and Perry stepped on board. He gave a smile to Stanley as the doors closed, leaving the young man in a state of frustration and bewilderment.

Stanley returned to his apartment where the other three were making light conversation about solar panels.

"It would be very handy if Perry didn't do what he does," Stanley said, slumping back down on the couch next to Mandy.

"What are you talking about?" Alice asked.

"Perry the Psychic has come back to visit," Stanley explained. "He says he's here to fetch a CD, but I don't believe it for a second. Far too many coincidences."

"What coincidences?" Norman asked.

Stanley avoided eye contact. He didn't want to explain that he might be withholding $29 million he was told to give to them. Thankfully, he didn't have to. His apartment phone began ringing loudly on the kitchen wall. Anytime it rang was a surprise to Stanley. It hardly ever rang, except for all the times recorded in these tales, and when it did ring it was either Samuel the Salesman offering the next big breakthrough in medicinal science, or Damien the Doorman forgetting the correct phone numbers and calling every apartment until he found the person he was looking for.

"Hello?" Stanley answered the phone.

"Afternoon, Stanley. This is Paul," said Paul the Policeman. "How is your day going so far?"

"Quite strangely, if I'm being honest," Stanley said. "How about yours?"

"Oh, yeah, pretty good thanks. Can't complain. We got a free lunch at work," Paul said. "It was Chinese cuisine, so you know, can't complain about that. I really like those little spring rolls. Whoever came up with them did a good job in my book."

"That's great," Stanley said, wondering if the policeman called him just to make small talk about Asian cuisines. "If you'll excuse me, I have guests over, so I'll need to get back to—"

"Oh, before you go, Stanley," Paul said. "Can I just get you to come down to the second floor for a moment? There's been a bit of a... I can't remember the technical term, but there's been a bit of a… when did you last talk to Perry the Psychic?"

"About two minutes ago. Why?"

"Well, apparently," Paul sighed, "according to this ransom note stuck to Perry's front door, he's been kidnapped… mannapped? In any case, he's apparently been taken and held for a ransom of twenty-three million dollars—"

"What a coincidence," Stanley said, shaking his head.

"and the note mentions that you've got the funds to pay for it."

Stanley put the phone down. "That's not a coincidence."

****

A crowd had gathered outside Perry the Psychic's apartment; 207. Paul the Policeman had stuck some police 'caution' tape around the random note that was attached to the apartment front door. There were hushed murmurs from the crowd of residents as Stanley and Mandy arrived. The crowd parted to allow Stanley to see the note up close. The note was written in black marker upon a paper bag and fixed to the door with stick tape at the corners.

Stanley read the note aloud:

"Dear Sir/Madam or whomever it may concern, I am writing to inform you that we have taken Perry the Psychic, of Room 207, hostage as of 1 pm today (assuming today is the 10th of October). Do not worry, we are keeping him very comfortable. He will not be harmed. Or maybe he will! (Don't worry, he won't be). In exchange for his release, we kindly ask for $29 million dollars to be left, in cash, outside this apartment by midnight tonight. If $29 million in cash is too hard to come by at short notice, please note we will accept the equivalent in Gold, but it needs to be the good and real gold stuff. Please, no plated jewellery. Please. Plated jewellery takes a long time to process and when you're in this business, time is of the essence; I'm sure you'll empathise with me on that point. Anyway, it might be helpful to talk to Stanley in apartment 909. He should have enough funds to pay the ransom. Well, that should be all for now. Thank you for taking the time to read this note. All the best, X."

"Who wrote this note?" Stanley asked in disgust.

"A 'Mr or Mrs X'," Rosemary the Retired said. "I don't know any X's personally."

"I have an ex-wife," Barney the Banker offered, stepping forward from the crowd.

"Really?" Paul the Policeman asked. "Is there any likelihood that your ex-wife could be the 'X' that wrote this ransom note?"

"Well, she passed away twelve years ago," Barney the Banker said, "but besides that, my ex wasn't the kidnapping type. If it was an arsonist's ransom note, I might be suspicious. But a kidnapping ransom note? That doesn't really fit her personality."

"I don't think 'X' is anything more than a nom de plume," Stanley said.

"My mother was a nom de plume!" Tanish the Taxi Driver said.

Stanley ignored him. "Did anyone see anyone coming or going from the second floor that could be a suspect? Did anyone see anything suspicious at all?"

"If you don't mind, Stanley, but this is a criminal investigation," Paul said. "You'll need to leave the questioning up to me."

Stanley pointed to the note. "The note names me. This feels like extortion."

"Spot on it's exhausting," Paul the Policeman said. "But don't worry, Stanley. You won't have to pay a dollar to these criminals. We will find them wherever they are in the world and bring them to justice."

"Have you checked inside his apartment?" Stanley asked.

"Checked for what?"

"For the criminals? Or Perry?" Stanley suggested, wondering why no one had apparently thought of looking inside. Paul the Policeman, seeing merit in the idea, stepped forward and gave two knocks upon Perry's apartment door. The audience leaned forward in anticipation.

"Hello?!" Paul called. "It's Paul the Policeman. Is there anyone in there?"

For a moment there was nothing but heavy silence, but then they suddenly heard footsteps coming towards the front door. Everyone jumped back. Stanley threw himself against the wall of the hallway. Paul the Policeman pulled out his baton and pointed it at the door defensively. The door slowly opened. A head poked out of the gap.

"Hello?" Clare the Cleaner asked, looking around at all the terrified faces.

"Clare, what are you doing in there?" Paul the Policeman asked.

"Cleaning," Clare said with a frown.

"Are you just cleaning? Or do you have something to do with the kidnapping of Perry the Psychic?" Paul asked.

"The kidnapping of--?" Clare couldn't even complete

the sentence, such was her shock. Her shock turned to anger. "You think I kidnapped someone? How dare you, Paul. Well here's a news story for you; I'm cleaning this apartment because I'm a cleaner! Look, I don't have time to play the weird games you other residents play. I tolerate it because the pay here is semi-decent and the lodging is rent free. But just let me do my job in peace, and I'll let you do your kidnappings and painting competitions and donut meetings and whatever else you do around here without comment."

There was a wave of apologies from Paul and the other residents. Clare the Cleaner exited the apartment with her cleaning supplies and left via the elevator in a huff. The crowds, seeing as nothing exciting was going to happen anytime soon, slowly dispersed until only Stanley, Paul and Mandy were left at the crime scene.

"Do you really have twenty-nine million dollars to pay the ransom?" Paul the Policeman asked.

"Coincidentally; yes," Stanley admitted.

"I didn't know being a business consultant paid so much. Good for you!" Paul said. "Or are you doing some other work on the side? My sister sells water she claims is from under the ground. I don't believe her, but I know she makes a nice little fortune from her gullible customers."

"No side business," Stanley said. "I'll be honest with you, Paul. Everything today has been one coincidence after another to the point where if you told me Perry was holding himself ransom, I'd believe it."

"I don't think it's illegal to hold yourself hostage," Paul said. "Uncomfortable; sure. But not illegal."

"I think it's possible that Perry is just doing this so that he can keep the lottery money for himself," Stanley continued. "Let's not forget that Perry is a psychic. If he knew someone was coming after him, don't you think he'd tell someone? Or at least not be where he knew he would get kidnapped?"

"But if he knew he was going to be kidnapped but avoided being kidnapped, then he wouldn't have seen himself being kidnapped!" Paul exclaimed.

Stanley didn't even pretend to understand the possible paradoxical implications of being psychic.

"Can you track the handwriting?" Mandy offered, looking closely at the neat writing on the ransom note.

Paul shook his head. "No, not easily. It's a little-known fact that most criminals actually write ransom notes using their feet to avoid being tracked by their handwriting. This one appears to have impeccable control over their toes."

"What do the police normally do when there's a kidnapping and ransom note?" Mandy asked.

"Well, usually the robber will leave a contact number, email address, postal address or some other method so that we can negotiate. This ransom note just says we need to leave the money by the door."

The elevator doors opened down the hallway.

"Delivery for Stanley!" Marty the Mailman called. Before Stanley could protest that he never ordered a cake, he was handed quite a large, heavy cake in a transparent plastic box. The cake had white frosting, six blue candles and paragraphs of writing written on top in black icing.

"Vanilla Café sent it," Marty the Mailman said. "The baker bloke said the customer paid a thousand dollars for it to be made and sent to you as soon as possible."

Marty left again, leaving Paul, Mandy and Stanley with the mysterious cake and even less clue about what was going on.

"It's another message!" Paul stated the obvious. Stanley, rotating the cake to read the spiralling message, read it aloud:

"Dear Sirs and Madam, my deepest apologies for this follow-up notice, but I have made sure this message is vanilla to show my gratitude for you taking the time to read this note. I wish to alter the plan, ever so slightly (due to an unfortunate mistake on no one's part but my own). Originally, I requested that the money be left in front of the apartment door. I would like to change that request to: could you please place the $29 million inside a paper bag and place that same paper bag into the garbage shoot at exactly midnight. I will be in the basement to collect the money when it reaches the bottom. Please be advised that if anyone comes to the basement for any reason, Perry the Psychic unfortunately will be shipped off to a distant location and never heard from again; most likely he will be hired out to tell companies what their competitors' next actions will be or tell fishermen the weather so they know whether to pack a t-shirt or a raincoat. Once again, thank you kindly for taking the time to read this cake. Best regards, X."

Stanley looked at Paul and Mandy with renewed hope. "X doesn't know the garbage shoot is blocked! This cake was obviously ordered before Jarvis clogged it up this morning!"

"Don't you think it's suspicious that the method that the kidnapper requested happens to be the thing that's blocked up today? It's almost a—"

"Coincidence," Stanley said, finishing Paul the Policeman's sentence. "We need to talk to Jarvis the Jobless."

By now the sun was beginning to set behind the city. Long shadows were cast by anyone standing by a window which is where Paul, Stanley and Mandy found Jarvis the Jobless. Jarvis was a fine, intelligent fellow. You wouldn't know it from some of the activities he undertook, but Jarvis had a Doctor of Philosophy in material design. His final thesis was about the strength of paper used to print theses on.

"Jarvis. How are you tonight, Sir?" Paul the Policeman asked. Jarvis the Jobless stood staring out the giant hallway window of the first floor. He did not turn around.

"Jarvis?" Paul repeated. Still no response.

"Jarvis?" Mandy tried, touching the old man gently on the shoulder. Jarvis' left hand shot up causing Mandy to jump back.

"I'll be with you in one moment," Jarvis said, continuing to stare intensely out the window at the street below. After Mandy checked the man hadn't passed out standing up, the three waited patiently for a minute. Stanley craned his neck to try and follow what Jarvis the Jobless was looking at, but all he could see were a few people milling around on the sidewalks. Nothing truly remarkable.

Jarvis suddenly spoke. "Could one of you please find me some dynamite?"

"Somewhat?" Stanley asked in alarm.

"Any explosive substance will do."

"Wait, Jarvis," Paul said frantically. "We have had this conversation before about no explosives in the building."

The elevator at the other end of the hallway opened and outstepped Samuel the Salesman holding a cardboard box. "I found one!" he called, holding up the box.

Stanley and Mandy huddled closer together in fright. Paul the Policeman stuck out his hand. "Samuel, stop right there. What is in the box?"

Samuel the Salesman froze, fear washing over him. "It's a brick."

"A brick of what?" Paul asked.

"I don't know," Samuel stammered. "Clay, I think."

"Is it an explosive brick?" Stanley asked.

"An explosive brick?" Samuel asked. "I don't think so. Well, the sign at the store didn't say 'explosive', so if it was I'd call that false advertising."

Jarvis the Jobless, seemingly unaware of the tension felt by the others in the hallway, walked up to meet Samuel. "Ah, Samuel. I'm very grateful for your help. Here's a lollypop for your time."

Jarvis handed Samuel a green packaged candy.

"Thank you," Samuel said, "but the brick cost two dollars."

"Charge it to my account," Jarvis said. Samuel, seemingly satisfied with the answer, left via the elevator. With anticipation and glee, Jarvis the Jobless opened the cardboard box and pulled out a single red brick. He quickly disappeared into his apartment, Room 103, with the brick in hand. Stanley, Mandy and Paul followed him in. Jarvis' apartment, although set out identically to all the apartments in the building, somehow was unrecognisable as a place of living. To begin with, every wall was covered in highly intricate paintings varying in styles from cubism to impressionist. There was furniture, but each piece of furniture seemed to be in the wrong place. Where a couch should have been, there was a bed. Where one would find a kitchen table, there was a small coffee table. Where one might place a fish tank or a television set in the living room, there was a microwave. And in the kitchen where one might find an oven, there was a pottery turntable. Stanley glanced through the bedroom's open door to see a couch neatly made up as a bed, and an oven instead of a wardrobe.

"Have you been doing some rearranging?" Stanley asked.

"Rearranging?" Jarvis the Jobless asked. He tilted his head as he looked around the room. "Ah, you must be referring to my vase of flour. It did give it a 90 degree turn this morning. Thank you for noticing."

"His apartment has always been like this," Paul quietly explained to Stanley. Jarvis went into the centre of the living room and placed the brick in the middle of the floor. He stood back and looked proudly at the placement. "Excellent."

"What's excellent?" Stanley asked.

"I've got somewhere to place my cup of tea for when I sit on the bed and watch the microwave."

"Are there any good shows on the… microwave?" Stanley asked, wondering if the microwave somehow received television programs.

"Well, it all depends on what you put in the microwave," Jarvis said. "Most of the time it's a pretty regular cooking show, but some things create real excitement. Popcorn? Bolognaise? They create excitement. If I'm in the mood for a real thriller, I'll microwave some milk! It's a pain to clean but keeps me entertained for a minute and forty seconds."

"Jarvis," Mandy said softly. "Just so that we can make sure you're okay; you did ask for explosives before. Why do you need explosives? What are you planning on doing with them?"

"Oh, don't worry, nothing drastic," Jarvis said. "I just wanted to test out a theory. You see, I was talking to an old friend recently, and he had some interesting ideas. His less interesting idea was that a fridge is able to fit down a garbage shoot. I think we can accurately call that a bad idea. His other idea, which I find quite fascinating and worth exploring further, is that if you place a small number of explosives inside of a potato, then you could get instant mashed potato."

"Mashed potatoes?" Mandy asked.

"Yes. Manually making mashed potatoes requires time and effort. I'm convinced pre-made mashed potato that you can buy at the store is fifty per cent mashed, and only fifty per cent potato. Why go to that effort when you can take an explosive potato, pop it in the microwave for less than thirty seconds, and with a 'bang!' you have mashed potatoes. It does make sense."

No one else in the room agreed.

"Who gave you this idea?" Stanley asked.

"Um," Jarvis said, turning the brick coffee table upside down. "I think it was--"

There was an almighty blast outside. Not the blast of an explosion, but the blast of thirty trumpets in the street below. The sound caused everyone in a 50-metre radius to drop whatever they were carrying or jump in fright. The reaction was great for the Olivia the Olympian practising high jump in her second-floor apartment, but horrible for everyone attempting the world record for the longest time balancing a fishbowl on their head in the building opposite Tayel Tower.

"What in the world was that?" Paul the Policeman cried. Jarvis the Jobless walked excitedly over to his window. "It's starting!"

"What's starting?" Stanley asked, still unable to see what Jarvis was looking at out the window.

"It's the annual invisibility parade!" Jarvis said, waving his hand in the air.

CHAPTER THREE
WHAT WAS THIS ALL ABOUT AGAIN?

"That's starting now?" Paul the Policeman asked. He turned to Stanley and Mandy, both of whom had little idea what insanity was going on. "I'm sorry, I need to get down to the street to help with traffic control for the invisibility parade."

"What, is, going, on?" Stanley asked, enunciating each word slowly as his brain struggled to process what he was being told.

Mandy was lost for words.

"Here, did you two want an invisible flag to wave?" Jarvis the Jobless said, holding nothing in his hand for Stanley and Mandy to take. Despite Stanley's searching, he didn't see any sign of anyone, invisible or not, in the middle of the street where a parade would be. It was true that the street had been cleared and policemen stood as a barricade along the sidewalks, holding back real, visible people from entering an invisible parade. The crowds in the streets had their cameras out to film proceedings.

After that first trumpet blast, there hadn't been another musical noise for a good minute. Suddenly the thirty trumpets could be heard again. The crowd let up a cheer, and more musical instruments could be heard. It was the sound of a whole marching band. Stanley wondered if he had gone crazy. How could all these people notice an invisible parade but he and Mandy? He could certainly hear the parade. Everyone throughout the city could hear the jovial trumpets, trombones, bagpipes and drums. Stanley and Mandy exchanged fearful glances. Forgetting to question Jarvis the Jobless any further about the kidnapping, Stanley and Mandy ran down to the street via the stairwell. When they reached the sidewalk in front of Tayel Tower, quite a large audience had gathered attracted by the noise and the police presence. None of the audience was looking at anything in particular, because there was nothing to see. Most of the cameras were targeted either at the empty street or the other people in the crowd to capture a memory of this strange event.

Stanley and Mandy found Paul the Policeman standing happily on crowd control duty with his back to the parade.

"Paul!" Stanley called over the blaring music. "What in the world is going on?"

"Didn't you hear?" Paul called back. "It's the Invisibility Parade! The flyers have been up for weeks!"

"Flyers? I didn't see any flyers—" Stanley said.

"Well of course not," Paul replied. "It's for an invisibility parade so the flyers are invisible. A great marketing campaign, if you ask me."

"And you can see the people in this parade?"

"Of course not!" Paul called back. "Otherwise they shouldn't be in the parade!"

Stanley ran his hand through his hair. He didn't know

who was going mad; everyone else for thinking that there was an invisible parade going past Tayel Tower or himself for not noticing what everyone else did. The music suddenly stopped, giving way to the excited chattering amongst the parade audience.

"What's going on now?" Stanley asked.

"Stanley," Paul said, shaking his head. "You're just being silly now pretending I can see an invisible parade." The policeman looked over his shoulder at the empty street. "Although it is possible that the parade has stopped for some reason."

"Ladies and Gentlemen," a deep, booming voice echoed from a speaker system hung from the lamp posts. "We are sorry to announce, but the invisible parade has been cancelled. I repeat; the invisible parade has been cancelled. I have been informed that none of the performers have shown up. The marching band that you could hear was, in fact, invisible people not officially registered to perform. They have been asked to leave."

Elaine the Event Planner, apparently one of the parade organisers, began sobbing profusely. Stanley, curious to find out who commissioned this absurd affair, gently approached Elaine.

"Hi Elaine," Stanley said. Elaine sniffled behind a wooden clipboard she held in front of her face. She moved the clipboard away from her face which had an expression halfway between devastation and elation; the type of face a lost dog has when they hear they have a new owner, but that the new owner also loves cats.

"Hello, Stanley. What can I do for you?" Elaine asked, wiping the tears from her eyes.

Stanley didn't know what to ask without sounding rude or accusing the woman of being crazy for thinking she was organising an invisible parade.

"Why did the parade stop?" he asked.

Elaine waved her clipboard towards the brightly lit roads, where the crowds had all but dispersed. "Do you know how hard it is to organise an invisible parade?"

"I can imagine," Stanley said.

For the first time that Stanley had seen, Elaine lost her smile. "You can't imagine. When I was hired to do this thing, I thought 'well, a parade is a parade. I've organised parades before'. But then the performers didn't show up to rehearsals, despite the back and forth emails. The performers were horribly indecisive about what they wanted to wear. In the end, I told them to wear whatever they wanted as long as the colours didn't clash. And then what happens in the end? They don't even turn up to the parade! To top it all off, I haven't seen Perry the Psychic!"

"Perry the Psychic?!" Stanley exclaimed at this new co-incidence. "Why do you need to see Perry?"

"He commissioned this parade. He hired me to organise it," Elaine explained. "I don't know why you'd pay so much money to put a parade on, then not even turn up to see it!"

Stanley was well and truly lost. More lost than he had been for all the other coincidences that had happened those past couple of hours; coincidences connected so tightly they couldn't be anything but uncoincidental.

Stanley and Mandy re-entered Tayel Tower and flopped down on the lobby couches. The time was 11:30 pm. He had almost forgotten about the ransom for all the other crazy things that had happened.

"I don't know what to do," Stanley confessed.

"Maybe we shouldn't do anything," Mandy said. "Maybe we should leave it up to the Paul the Policeman to sort out."

It was like a flashback in an old movie or a new book. Mandy remembered standing in Perry the Psychic's apartment ready to say goodbye to him.

"What should we do with the last winning ticket?" Mandy asked.

Perry looked up at the roof for a moment. "Give it to the new couple. They'll know what to do with it."

"We have to give the ticket to Norman and Alice," Mandy said firmly to Stanley. "We don't know what to do with the ticket, which for all purposes is the ransom money. Perry said they'll know what to do with it. I don't know why he didn't foresee his own kidnapping but he obviously knew the best advice he could give us was to give it to the new couple."

Although it was painful to think about giving the millions of dollars to someone else, Stanley knew Mandy was right. "Let's ask Damien if he knows where they are."

They walked briskly across the lobby to the concierge desk. Damien the Doorman was talking to the two maintenance workers who had been tasked with removing the miscellaneous pieces of furniture from the garbage shoot.

"All fixed now," one of the men said. "You know, in all my years in maintenance, this is only the third time I've had to remove a refrigerator from a garbage shoot. They're not an easy thing to remove so may I suggest informing your residents they should only take fridges by the elevator or the stairs."

Damien the Doorman, writing this all down on a pad of paper, nodded his head. "Yes, absolutely. I'll be sure to inform all residents fridges are only to be used inside the stairwell or the elevator."

The maintenance man placed his invoice on the concierge desk and left without another word.

"Good evening, Damien," Stanley said.

"Ah, good evening Stanley and Mandy. What can I do for you?" Damien asked.

"We were wondering if you had seen Norman the Nurse or Alice the Actress?" Stanley asked quickly.

"Norman the Nurse? He's most likely in his apartment eight-oh-three," Damien said. "Now, since you're here, I might as well inform you, and it's possible you overheard, but the maintenance people have requested that all residents place their fridges into the stairwell or elevator. It concerns me that the elevator most likely isn't big enough for over a hundred refrigerators, so, for now, could you both please put your fridges in the stairwell. Thank you."

"I don't think that's what he was requesting—" Mandy said.

"We really don't have time," Stanley said, aware that it was quarter to midnight and the deadline for the ransom was approaching quickly.

They ran to the elevator and pressed the 'up' button. They waited anxiously for the elevator carriage to arrive. After a minute of no sound or movement from behind the silver doors, Stanley suggested the stairwell.

The Tayel Tower stairwell was a great way to keep fit. Stanley, a resident of the ninth floor, had to go up one hundred and eighty steps to get to the level of his bed. The months of making this journey allowed Stanley to actually keep up with Mandy in that night's stair climb. But even Mandy had to slow down at each floor's landing to dodge the fridges which were beginning to pile up.

"Surely this is a fire hazard!" Stanley cried, squeezing between Belinda the Beautician and Boris the Body Builder's fridges on the third floor. On the fourth floor, Russell the Realtor was trying to manoeuvre his fridge through the stairwell door.

"No, put it back!" Stanley called as they ran past.

"I was told it was vitally important!" Russell called back.

They made it to the sixth floor but couldn't go any further. There were seven fridgess completely blocking their path. He and Mandy had no choice but to exit the stairwell onto the sixth floor. Stanley tried the elevator again but there was no response. The time was11:55 pm. There was five minutes until the ransom request expired.

"How serious do you think the kidnappers are?" Stanley asked, leaning against the wall, catching his breath.

"I don't know," Mandy said, "but are we willing to risk something happening to Perry the Psychic just because we couldn't decide whether to give the money, which was never ours to begin with, to set Perry free?"

Stanley pulled the winning lottery ticket from his pocket. It was quite crumpled now. Stanley looked across the hallway to the garbage shoot; just a steel door in the wall far too small to fit a fridge or a couch, but big enough to throw a lottery ticket to the kidnapper, whoever they happened to be, waiting in the basement at the bottom of the building. Somewhere in the distance, a loud bell could be heard chiming.

"It's midnight," Stanley said calmly. In one hand he held the ticket. His other hand gripped the handle of the garbage shoot door. He was waiting for the ringing bell to stop before he threw the ticket down.

The ringing bell grew louder as the door to apartment 602 opened and Matthias the Musician poked his head out into the hallway playing his cowbell; the source of the ringing.

"Oh, sorry," Matthias said, noticing an audience. "I didn't know anyone was awake. Tonight is cowbell night."

The door to apartment 601 whipped open revealing a dishevelled, red-faced Charlotte the Chef. "You say every night is cowbell night! Every night can't be cowbell night!"

Both apartment doors slammed closed again.

"What are you going to do?" Mandy asked nervously, her arms folded. "I say let's throw the ticket down."

Stanley took a deep breath, opened the garbage shoot and threw the $29 million-dollar lottery ticket down into the darkness. The ticket floated down like a feather on a breeze. A very smelly breeze.

"Oh, hello, Stanley and Mandy," Perry the Psychic said, emerging from the stairwell.

"Perry!" Stanley exclaimed. "They set you free!"

"Are you alright?" Mandy the Midwife asked. Perry, for the first time Stanley had seen, looked at the two of them in shock. "Huh?"

"You were kidnapped, and we just paid the ransom!" Stanley explained, looking the man up and down for signs of harm. Perry the Psychic didn't appear to have even a scuff mark.

"That was today?" Perry asked.

"Yes, just this evening," Stanley said. "We've been running around the building all night dealing with, million-dollar lottery tickets, ransom cakes, brick coffee tables, invisible parades and fridges in the stairwell to try and find you!"

Perry looked overjoyed. "That was today! This is exciting!"

"You knew you were going to get kidnapped?" Mandy asked.

"I knew someone would pretend they would kidnap me," Perry laughed, "but I couldn't remember on which day they would do it, given the large number of absurd events that have unfolded in such a short amount of time. But it doesn't matter, because I'm sure you did as I asked, which was to give the lottery ticket to Norman the Nurse and Alice the Actress."

Neither Mandy or Stanley met Perry's gaze. Perry shrugged. "Well, it was worth a try."

"What were you trying?" Stanley asked, not at all following Perry's scheme.

"I was seeing if I could change the future," Perry explained. "I created so many distractions for myself today so that I couldn't possibly foresee and remember all that happened. I tried to make myself confused and forget the future. I was hoping that by confusing myself, it would enable the future to change from what I have foreseen."

"You planned… everything?" Stanley squeaked. "You were never kidnapped?"

"No, of course not. It's virtually impossible to kidnap a psychic. If I foresaw a kidnapping attempt, I'd just avoid the kidnappers."

"You thought you could change your future by not thinking about it?" Mandy asked.

"That was the plan," Perry said sadly, "but it clearly didn't work."

"Maybe if you stop thinking or worrying about the future, you can just make choices not based on what you've seen in the future?" Mandy suggested.

Perry the Psychic took a moment to think about what she had just said. "You're might be right, Mandy. My goodness, Mandy, you're right! I can change the future by not thinking about the future! I think that's a life lesson that more people should live by! I could destroy the universe by accidentally altering the future, but I'm going to try it! I'm going to make my own choices and not think about the future!"

Stanley's head began to throb with all this talk of the future. He had thought a lot about his own future recently and he wondered if what Perry has said applied to him.

He excused himself from Mandy and Perry and pulled out his phone. He texted Richard Richardson, his boss, who he knew regularly worked until the early hours of the morning, even on weekends.

"I don't want the pay rise and promotion. I'm gonna stay here in the city," Stanley wrote in the text. He pressed 'send' and put the phone back in his pocket. He looked at Mandy and felt like it was the best decision he had made in a long time.

"One thing I know I can't change, however, is the fate of that ticket you just threw down the garbage shoot," Perry said.

"That's alright, we'll just go a retrieve it from the basement," Stanley said.

Perry scratched his head. "Uh…"

They navigated through the fridge-filled stairwell to the basement. Just as Mandy put her hand on the door handle for the basement, they heard an almighty loud explosion on the other side. Stanley, Mandy and Perry rushed into the basement to see Jarvis the Jobless leaning over something beneath the garbage shoot.

Jarvis heard footsteps behind him and turned around holding a bowl.

"Oh, hello, all. Have you come to try some of my mashed potatoes?" Jarvis asked.

Stanley could see bits of ticket throughout what looked to be a bowl of creamy mashed potato. Jarvis took a spoonful and popped some of his experiment into his mouth, struggling to chew past the bits of paper.

"It's good, but a little rich for my tastes."

The End